# SOCIAL MISCONDUCT

## S. J. Maher

Published by Simon & Schuster

New York   London   Toronto   Sydney   New Delhi

SIMON &
SCHUSTER
**CANADA**

Simon & Schuster Canada
A Division of Simon & Schuster, Inc.
166 King Street East, Suite 300
Toronto, Ontario M5A 1J3

This book is a work of fiction. Any references to historical events, real people, or real places are used fictitiously. Other names, characters, places, and events are products of the author's imagination, and any resemblance to actual events or places or persons, living or dead, is entirely coincidental.

This Simon & Schuster Canada edition April 2019

SIMON & SCHUSTER CANADA and colophon are trademarks of Simon & Schuster, Inc.

For information about special discounts for bulk purchases, please contact Simon & Schuster Special Sales at 1-800-268-3216 or CustomerService@simonandschuster.ca.

*Interior design by Carly Loman*

Manufactured in the United States of America

10   9   8   7   6   5   4   3   2   1

Library and Archives Canada Cataloguing in Publication
Maher, Stephen, 1965–, author Social misconduct / S.J. Maher.
Issued in print and electronic formats. ISBN 978-1-982109-06-6 (softcover).—
ISBN 978-1-982109-07-3 (ebook)
I. Title.
PS8626.A41725S63 2019 C813'.6 C2018-905217-1 C2018-905218-X

ISBN 978-1-9821-0906-6
ISBN 978-1-9821-0907-3 (ebook)

*For Camille*

Walkercahier.pdf

## Résumé

Razors pain you;
Rivers are damp;
Acids stain you;
And drugs cause cramp.
Guns aren't lawful;
Nooses give;
Gas smells awful;
You might as well live.

—Dorothy Parker

# 1

I dropped my phone into the Hudson River yesterday.

I was standing at the back of the ferry, traveling to Jersey City from the floating, glass-walled terminal at the foot of One World Trade Center. I stood there, in the wind and sun, like a carefree tourist, gaping at the Freedom Tower, and put my hand over the rail and opened it and let my iPhone X fall into the churning water below.

I didn't look down to see it sink below the surface, in case they were watching me. I don't think they were, though, because they didn't need to watch me. Not while I had the phone. But I couldn't be sure, and I can't afford to take any chances.

That's my new motto. Take no chances.

I keep thinking about that stupid phone, sitting on the bottom of the river, because I keep thinking, *Hey! This is boring! I should check my phone. Oh, I can't. It's on the bottom of the river.* That happens less often today than it did yesterday. I hope that soon it will go away completely.

I hate writing by hand.

I bought this notebook just before I got on the ferry, for $24.95, at a shop near the terminal, one of those places that used to sell books and now sells calendars and candlesticks. I wanted to see if anyone was following me before I got on the ferry, so I popped into the shop, looked around, saw a stack of Moleskines, and bought one on impulse, with cash.

It feels strange to be writing with a pen again, and not just because my hand hurts from where the subway train hit it.

My handwriting looks like it belongs to an earlier version of my-self, a junior high school student doing a book report, or sharing her feelings about One Direction. My words don't look like my thoughts, which are in Times New Roman or Helvetica, depending on my mood, not this weird girlish script.

I'm glad I have the notebook, though, because I need a record of important events that I can recall clearly now but that I know will fade or become distorted over time. This is my AutoRecover, my backup.

Also, I need something to do.

All I do is wait and think, try to figure out what happened to me, stare at the steel door and hope it doesn't open, and absently reach for my phone every five minutes, then remember that it's at the bottom of the river.

# 2

The phone was sitting in the middle of Rebecca's blond wooden desk when I first saw it, in its glossy white cardboard box, like a present waiting to be opened.

Rebecca's stylishly furnished office was at the front of the building, a brick room with windows overlooking Sixteenth Street—a contrast to the crowded, windowless space in the back where the click-drivers worked. On the window behind the desk there were a bunch of yellow sticky notes. Rebecca and her friend in the office across Sixteenth Street put emoticons on their windows every day, a playful interoffice social semaphore. Today it was a :-0.

She waited until I sat down, then looked at the box and smiled. I could tell she was relishing the tiny drama of the moment.

"So, Candace, I have some good news for you," she said.

I tried to look like I was mildly pleased. Inside: mariachi music.

I'd been driving clicks for SoSol for eight months, sharing a table with a half-dozen other sullen young people. We competed to see who could come up with the worst clickbait ads, taking ironic pride in fat-shaming celebrities, making self-loathing wisecracks to hide our grim competitiveness.

Working for the New Media Lab would be different. SoSol (formerly Social Solutions) was launching a marketing branch, with real clients, not the kind that sell weight-loss pills and herbal erection boosters to idiots.

I'd had the feeling I was going to get the job. Beatrice, my best friend among the clickbait crew, had also applied. She was smart and sassy but ostentatiously disengaged from her work, well past the point of the dignity-maintaining detachment I sustained, saving her real energy for her art and Rudy, her partner.

But Beatrice wasn't in here with Rebecca. I was.

Rebecca closed her laptop and leaned back in her chair.

"I just got the email from Craig," she said. "And I'm pleased to tell you we want you to be part of the launch team."

She smiled at me expectantly.

What to say?

"Awesome! Thank you for the opportunity. I'm really excited."

Is that what she wanted? Did she need more enthusiasm? Should I suck up?

Rebecca is early twenties, African American, like, really African, Kenyan or something, and beautiful, with shiny ebony skin and stunning lips and cheekbones, always stylishly dressed, like a model moonlighting. She's hard to read.

"I hope you're ready to work hard because I pushed for you to be on the team," she said, and looked at me.

What did that mean? Did it mean Craig, her boss, wanted someone else?

I thought he liked me. He's in his forties, gay, stylish, energetic, kind of a remote figure to the clickbait crew, but in the interview we seemed to connect.

I found him more straightforward to deal with than Rebecca. He seemed to only want me to demonstrate that I accepted his leadership and thought he was awesome, which was easy enough to fake. Rebecca always seemed to want something I wasn't giving her, or to be disappointed that I hadn't said something or done something that I didn't know I should say or do.

"Thank you, Rebecca. I'm pumped."

She looked at me with a brittle smile, as if she wasn't sure she'd made the right call.

"It wasn't an easy decision. There were *so many* good candidates. I felt, though, that your work here was so good we should give you a shot. You showed real initiative and creativity with CelluVibe."

I nodded modestly.

CelluVibe is a handheld electric massager that deluded fat girls across America use to vibrate their dimpled skin in the mistaken belief that it will somehow remove their fat cells. An ad I designed—with red circles around the cottage cheese on Britney Spears's thighs—blew out all our metrics, making lots of money for SoSol, coarsening the culture, ripping off countless lovelorn chubbos, and making me the secretly self-hating star of the clickbait crew.

"I was really pleased at how that caught on."

"Virality," said Rebecca. "That's what you bring. And that's what we need."

*Ask about money. Ask about money.*

"I'm really going to throw myself into this, Rebecca. This is where I want my career to go, so I'm supermotivated, partly because I'd like to eventually make a little more money."

Rebecca's smile got thinner.

"Would there be a raise, um, attached to the promotion?"

"Not initially. No. It's a start-up, so we are going to prioritize cost-control until it produces revenue. But if it works the way we think it will, it would be kind of normal for your compensation to be addressed."

Okay. So no raise right away, which wouldn't help me pay down my credit card debt, or allow me to travel anyplace interesting before I was too old to enjoy myself.

I was going to ask her when we might revisit the question when Kevin appeared at the door. Kevin was the tech guy, and the only lumpy person at SoSol, a sad wannabe hipster. He had a sandy receding hairline, a stupid sandy mustache, baggy jeans, and a faded Rush T-shirt. There was a chain connecting his belt to his wallet.

"Kevin, there you are!" said Rebecca. "Can you help Candace set up her new phone?"

He walked to the desk, opened the box, booted up the phone, got me to sign in with my iCloud password, and hovered behind me until I noticed from the reflection in the phone that he was looking down my scoop-neck top. He was actually gaping.

I grasped my collar and cleared my throat, and Rebecca turned around, saw what was up, and gave him a dirty look. He started and turned away.

"Dude, I got this," I said.

He blushed and walked backward to the door, babbling.

"No problem it should be okay now let me know if you have any problems it's pretty easy."

I gave Rebecca a quizzical look after he left.

"He was," she said.

"I know, right?"

"Totally."

"Creeper."

We shared a moment of wordless disgusted sisterly commiseration.

"So we'll get you a desk in the New Media Lab space once we get it set up next week," she said. "For now, you can work from your spot in Content Marketing."

"You haven't told Beatrice or the other applicants yet?"

I was nervous about that.

"I'm working on an announcement," she said, gesturing to her laptop.

"I have an idea for that," I said.

# 3

I am doing yoga on my sleeping bag, in the downward dog position, when I hear a noise from the hallway.

It is the first noise I have heard from outside since I got to this little room, and I am sure they are coming for me. My heart starts pounding. I drop to the sleeping bag and turn around, being very quiet. I make my breathing shallow.

The sound is from the steel door at the end of the hallway: the squeak of the hinges, a slow pneumatic sigh from the thing at the top that makes the door close slowly, then the tread of someone walking toward me.

*It's a hallway*, I tell myself. *It's just someone walking down a hallway.* A lot of that happens in the Big Apple. But I am petrified that they have found me.

I have been stewing about the GPS tracking on my phone and fretting about my carelessness. By now they would have reviewed the record. I imagine it would be like one of those Uber maps, showing my route from the moment I left the subway station and walked around Chelsea, with a straight line out into the river that ends at the point where I dropped the phone.

I should have used tinfoil.

Unless they are stupid, they will eventually figure out that I was on the Paulus Hook ferry and start trying to guess where I went when I got off. And I know they aren't stupid.

I think about that as I hold my breath and listen to the footsteps approach my door. It sounds like a man's tread: heavy shoes, in a steady, purposeful rhythm.

*Here he comes*, I think. *And you have nobody to blame but your own stupid self.*

I am terrified that he, whoever he is, will open the door and find me, my sleeping bag, my granola bars, my jug of water, my bowl of pee, and my Moleskine notebook, and I'll be trapped.

I can't run. There's only one door. Can I hide? Where? Could I tuck myself behind the cardboard boxes? I could! Nobody would see me from the door if I lie down behind them.

But that's stupid. If someone opens the door, it's because he thinks I might be here. He won't just take a quick peek and leave. He'll mean business, and be prepared to take me away in handcuffs, unless he plans to shoot me on sight. If I hide, I'll delay the terrible moment by ten seconds, and also I'll look pathetic. No. Better to let him see me calmly waiting. I can have my dignity.

Or can I try to run? If I stand behind the door, can I wait until he enters the room and then slip out behind him?

It's worth trying.

I ease myself off the sleeping bag and drag it behind me. Otherwise he'll see it when he opens the door. I try to be quiet but the sleeping bag rubbing against the concrete floor makes a tiny sound and I'm frightened that he has heard it.

The footsteps have stopped. I ease myself behind the door and press myself against the wall. I hold my breath and close my eyes, trying to prepare myself.

From the hallway, I hear the jingle of keys.

Then I hear a door open and slam shut. He's in another storage unit. I allow myself to breathe again. It's just some idiot fetching his golf clubs or something. I listen as he rummages around.

I tense when the door opens and slams again and the footsteps go by, and I stay still for five minutes after the big door at the end of the hallway closes. Could he be waiting inside for me to betray my presence by making a noise? No. But I stay still all the same, my back flat against the wall.

I start to think about how silly it is to still be standing there, and how scared I am, and start to worry about my thinking. I can't let myself lose touch with reality. I will have to leave this place eventually, and I won't be able to manage it if I'm a head case.

I decide to continue my yoga routine, finish what I started. I need to feel my muscles tighten and relax, stop my frantic brain from fretting.

Then I pick up the Moleskine and here I am.

Hi!

My fingers hurt. I don't like writing by hand. I miss my phone. I miss my laptop. I miss the sun. I miss everything.

# 4

Rebecca agreed that it would be fun and appropriate to announce my appointment with a selfie.

I really wanted the right kind of image to announce my first Big Girl Job.

I had decided to give up on normcore, the better to blaze a path of social business success. I was wearing a charcoal skirt suit, a scoop-neck powder-blue Armani silk blouse, chunky black glasses, black pumps, and an L line necklace, because Brooklyn, bitches. I had pulled my tangly red hair into a bun, with a few locks hanging down, to soften the look.

Rebecca was wearing a figure-hugging gray pencil dress with a big gold necklace. She folded her arms across her chest. I stood next to her. We both looked up at the phone I held in my outstretched arm, smiling while I snapped bursts of shots.

We looked like a stock photo: Businesswomen in Hip Office.

Rebecca's phone rang.

"We done?" she asked and picked up the phone before I could reply.

I went to the bathroom to sit down to flip through the pictures. I sent the best one to my sister, Jess, and asked if it would do for a job announcement selfie. She responded by texting me back with thumbs-up emoji.

Big sister had had a real Big Girl Job for two years, as a lawyer at McNally-Blenkhorn, uptown, which is great, except that she works such long hours she often doesn't have time to pee, so she replies to my rambling, neurotic messages with emojis. Before I sent the announcement, though, I had to deal with Beatrice, who was sitting at her terminal, typing away, her arms bare except for her sailor's tattoo, a topless girl in a bandanna with a huge bottle of rum.

She looked up with a smile.

"Sup, bae?" she said. "Did you get it?"

I made a complicated nodding frowny face at her. She was my only real friend there. I was afraid she would hate me.

But she got up and hugged me. "You got it. Yeah!" She pulled me into her warm body and held me tight, squeezing even. "We gonna celebrate. I'm happy for you," she whispered. "Really."

"I was afraid you would be sad you didn't get it."

"Zero fucks," she said, and I believed her. That's sort of her motto. What a relief. I needed her to be my friend.

She plunked herself down.

"Did I show you my newest picture?"

Beatrice had been taking screenshots from porn videos, printing them on fabric and then needlepointing them. She had lined up gallery space in Williamsburg and was rushing home every night to stitch.

She pulled her needlepoint frame out of her purse to show me a half-stitched image of a woman with feathered hair fellating a man. The colors had that faded VHS look.

After I cooed admiringly, I finally got to turn to my laptop to roll out the job announcement. I took the best selfie, cropped it and adjusted the color, then sent it out to Twitter, Facebook, Instagram, and Snapchat.

Pumped to start at SoSol's New Media Lab! Thanks to Rebecca Manawa for the great welcome!

I wanted the world—boom—to see me looking good in my new job, and I didn't want the world to know that I was petrified to be revealed as an imposter, so I had already created a strategy for this moment, a social storyboard.

I had imagined my college, coffee shop, and bookstore friends learning that that weird bookworm girl who wasn't very good at making lattes or working a checkout scanner had a fancy new job.

I had also imagined JFXBF finding out that I'd landed a real job in social while he was still pulling pints in Williamsburg and JFXBFNGF made eyes at him from her ugly barstool.

I linked to a blog post I had ready comparing the social media revolution to the impact of the Gutenberg Bible, eight hundred words of semismart stuff I'd pillaged from a paper I wrote in my last semester at NYU, updated with hot links and illustrated with gifs from TV shows.

I sat back for a few minutes to see who liked and favorited my post and watched the click counter on my blog sluggishly turn over.

Then I put my sock puppets to work, using them to send congratulatory messages to myself.

Amazing!
They're lucky to have you!
You go, girl!

The fake messages mixed with the real messages from real friends and soon my social feed was a churning celebration of my awesomeness, which was what I needed to happen.

From time to time I checked JFXBF's Instagram and Facebook. I half thought he might cryptically subtweet me, as I kept cryptically subtweeting him, but he maintained radio silence. His last post was still an out-of-focus five-day-old picture of a pint of passionfruit stout, which sounded like the most piss-tasting thing you could think of.

Anyway, fuck him.

# 5

I am so over this storage room.

I'm not sure how much longer I can bear it. I don't even know how long I've been here because I can't see the sun. It's a windowless cinder block box with a gray steel door in one end and a bare light bulb overhead. I don't have my phone or computer or a watch, so I've lost track of time. I'm pretty sure today is Tuesday, since it was Monday when I arrived, and that was yesterday, but I am kind of fuzzy on the last few days.

I don't really remember getting here, but apparently I was dragging a plastic bag full of pathetic convenience store supplies—a gallon jug of water, a dozen granola bars, and two apples—because I found that next to me when I woke up.

I seem to have also dug through my sister's old camping stuff, because my face was buried in her musty old sleeping bag. And I think I must have taken some Ambiens, because the pill bottle was next to my hand.

It was terrible to come to my senses, to remember why I was here. I wished I could go back to sleep. But I couldn't, because I had to pee.

There's no bathroom. I found an old orange plastic bowl in a box of my sister's discarded kitchen stuff and decided that would have to be my toilet. I tore the top off a box to use as a lid to cover it when I was done. Ugh.

Then I did an inventory of my sister's stuff.

Aside from her old tent and some bags of unfashionable clothes,

I found boxes of old documents and books, both kinds of skis, some lame appliances: a juicer, a waffle iron, an old white microwave, and a broken step machine.

I hunted around for an outlet, then plugged in the microwave and set the clock, so I could keep track of time. I guessed that I had slept for twelve hours, and that it was about 10:00 p.m. Monday when the Ambien kicked in, so I had set the microwave for 10:00 a.m. I could be way off, but it was better than nothing. It's now 8:21 p.m. on Tuesday, according to Candace Standard Time.

I will eventually have to get out of here, if only to get more supplies, and I can check the time then.

For now, I need to stay hidden. I figure if they lose track of me for a few days, it will be easier for me to slip quietly out of town, and onto whatever comes next.

At least that's what I think in my better moments. In my weaker moments—and I have a lot of them—I wonder if I should let them catch me. I could talk to a lawyer. Maybe there's a way out of my situation that I can't see. Likely not, but maybe. Whatever it is would probably be bad, though. And right now I am free, kind of, so no.

I've also been thinking about a third option. If I don't want to let them catch me, and I don't want to go on the run, I could, you know, not do either.

I feel that like an undertow in my mind, pulling me down. Would it be so bad if I stopped existing? It could be better for a lot of people, including me. I am in a terrible position and it's hard to imagine all the things that will have to happen before I can relax and just live my life. So it might be better, really, for Candace to, um, exit.

The only problem? I've got just three Ambiens left, which wouldn't do the trick.

I want to write down the Dorothy Parker poem I like, but I only remember the last stanza.

> *Guns aren't lawful;*
> *Nooses give;*

*Gas smells awful;*
*You might as well live.*

I promise myself I'll look it up and write the whole thing in the front of this notebook the next time I can google.

# 6

Rebecca interrupted my social festival of congratulations to ask me to go for lunch with her and Craig.

In the elevator, she asked me how Beatrice took the news.

"Zero fucks," I said. "Exact quote."

"Interesting. I thought she wanted the job."

"I don't know if she's cut out for social. She's so into her art."

We walked over to the five-way intersection at Fourteenth and Hudson, to Dos Caminos, a Mexican place with a terrace. It was full of social media and fashion swells eating tacos and drinking margaritas in the sun. Stylish clothes. Tinkling fake laughter. It was the world of successful Chelsea people, and I was joining it. I felt nervous and happy. Rebecca led me to a table where Craig was sitting with one of the best-looking men I've ever seen.

Craig was dressed in skinny jeans, a stylish tie, and a blazer, with Ray-Bans on his forehead, managing to look immaculately groomed in a way that only gay men and some straight Frenchmen manage. His companion was tall and slim, with tousled chestnut hair, and so good-looking that I wanted to stop and stare at him. He was wearing khakis and a blue button-down shirt.

"So, Candace, congrats!" said Craig. "Welcome aboard!"

"Thanks! I'm excited, guys."

They had beers in front of them. Craig already seemed a bit buzzed.

"You earned it. Nobody in Content Marketing drove more clicks. And that's the spirit we need at the New Media Lab. It's a start-up, and we have to think that way. We eat what we kill. No kill? No eat. It's all about conversions."

The waitress arrived, but Craig kept talking.

"We have clients lined up for you both, so you can get going, like, this afternoon. Start data fracking, kicking ass, taking names."

He did a drumroll on the table with his fingers, then noticed the waitress.

"We ordered," he said. "You guys know what you want?"

Rebecca asked for chiles rellenos and a glass of Chardonnay.

I ordered a Perrier and the chopped salad, without the goat cheese.

Handsome Stranger, who had been sitting quietly, stuck out his hand.

"I'm Wayne, by the way. I think we're going to be working together."

I got a good look at his eyes for the first time. They were grayish blue, with long, almost girlish lashes. He had a beautiful nose, long and straight, and perfect lips. I didn't want to look away but I couldn't hold eye contact with him. Luckily, Craig was still blathering on.

"I want you two to think of yourselves as community managers, influencers, curating content, putting SoSol into the bleeding edge of social marketing. This is a major pivot. You need to think big. Look at where we are."

He gave us a second to think about that.

"This is Silicon Alley. The opportunities for synergies are all around us. We can be the red-hot wire connecting Madison Avenue to the HTR. But I need big-time buy-in from you two. I've picked you because I think you both are already awesomely virality-aware. Now you need to turn that up to eleven. You need to *be* social, think social. I want you newsjacking, connecting with fanbassadors, gamifying the brand experience for clients."

"So, in practical terms, do you think that means Twitter, Facebook, Instagram?" asked Wayne.

"Good question, Wayne! We need to be omnichannel, channel-agnostic. The channels are increasingly irrelevant. We need to be

Web three-point-oh. Fish where the fish are. I want you to live in the analytics, be where you can be the most impactful."

"You're getting me pumped up," said Wayne. He didn't look pumped up. "Can you tell us about the clients?"

"I think you're going to like this," said Craig. "For you, I've got Cheese of the Month Club, an innovative upstate start-up that sends artisanal cheeses through the mail."

Wayne and I wore identical fake smiles.

"And Candace is going to be driving clicks to Bowhunting.com. We were really lucky to get them. Big market presence."

I'm vegan, which Craig should have known, if he'd bothered to find out anything about me, by, like, looking at any of my social media accounts before he decided to hire me for a social media marketing job.

I was trying to think of how I could tell him that I couldn't possibly ever direct a single click to Bowhunting.com when Wayne spoke up.

"Would it be okay if we switched?"

Craig looked irritated.

"I guess so. Why?"

"I think Candace might be a vegan."

He looked at me and I nodded. Did he figure that out from my lunch order? Likely. Who but a vegan would order the salad with no cheese?

"I would have a hard time having anything to do with a hunting website," I said. "I mean, cheese is kind of problematic, actually, because of the way they take calfs . . ."

Craig looked surprised, irritated, then bored.

"Never mind. The cheese site is great."

He nodded, ready to move on.

Then my new phone rang, which shocked me, since it was the first time and it was the steel drum ring, which I hate, and I reached for it suddenly and knocked Wayne's full draft over, dumping all of it into his lap.

Fuck!

"Oh my goodness! I am so sorry."

I jumped up. The crotch of his pants was totally soaked. He pushed his chair back and stood up, laughing. Without thinking, I reached over with a napkin to pat the front of his pants dry.

He grabbed my wrist to stop me, smiled, apologized, took the napkin from me. I sat back down and buried my face in my hands.

# 7

It's hard to make a decent noose out of torn-up T-shirt strips.

I'm feeling pretty low. Forlorn. I can't stop thinking about all the terrible things that have happened, and I can't think of anything good that might ever happen to me. *Hopeless.* That's the word. I don't know where hope fits into the category of human needs, but I know that I have none, and it makes me . . .

Well.

Also, I am out of Ambien. Last night, after all my writing and organizing, I decided to have a little Ambien vacation and enjoy a spacey few minutes of numbness before blanking out. It is great, amazing, until I wake up and realize that there will be no more Ambien. I take that hard.

One minute I'm lying facedown in my sleeping bag, pondering my grim position and the grimmer Ambien-free future. The next minute I'm suddenly purposeful—Miss Busy rummaging through the boxes of old clothes, cheerfully looking for something I can use to make a noose.

I don't remember, or don't want to remember, how I got from one state to the next.

But I do realize I have decided that the world would be better off without Candace. Everything will be easy! Everybody wins! There comes a point where anguish is unendurable. I reach it. Sue me.

I find a shitty old canary-yellow T-shirt that's easier to tear than the other shitty old T-shirts. It says DANBURY HALF MARATHON on it. I sit cross-legged on the sleeping bag and have a demented craft session, tearing it into strips until there is no T-shirt left and then braiding them into a bunch of really shitty little ropes. I knot them together and I have a four-foot rope that, surprisingly, feels kind of strong.

I think I can tie one end to the steel cage around the light fixture, stand up on the microwave, and then kick it away.

Then it occurs to me that I don't know how to make a noose.

The point of hanging, I believe, is to break your neck. It's the knot that does it, and your body's sudden weight.

Otherwise, you're just strangling yourself, which I don't think works, because if you change your mind, you can just undo the rope.

Wouldn't you change your mind when your brain starts to get starved of oxygen?

So, how to make a noose? I would google it, but I can't, so I have to improvise. I loop the rope around, fuss with it, but after a few minutes I realize that I'll never figure it out.

Okay.

Maybe a loop will do it. I tie the knot, test it on my forearm. It seems strong.

Then I haul the microwave over, climb on top, stand on my tippy-toes, and tie one end to the steel cage. The other end, the end with the loop, I put around my neck.

I realize then that I need to move the microwave. I need it not to be right under me because I could step back onto it. I should have it a couple feet away, so that when I step off it, I will be hanging directly below the light, with nothing under my feet but air. That ought to do it.

I can't help but find it strange that I do all this in a state of cheerful busyness. I'm not thinking about anything beyond accomplishing each little task.

Miss Busy, who has always been there for me when I need her, is back running the show. She's the one who gets up on the microwave, puts the noose around my neck, and takes a step forward. It's kind of scary, though, because she isn't checking in with me. She knows how to fix the situation, always has, and I guess I am okay with that, at least until I feel the rope bite and suddenly she is no longer in charge. I am, and I don't want to choke to death.

For a moment, probably about a second, actually, I kick and grab at the rope around my neck. I wedge my finger under it, but it's too tight and getting tighter. Oh God. No. I can't breathe. I feel my face turning red. My neck is constricted. My eyes feel bulgy. I gasp for air. My tongue sticks out. This is bad. THIS IS BAD.

Then there's a jerk, and one of my knots lets go, the rope parts, and I fall to the floor.

After I catch my breath, I remove the noose, throw it in the corner, and, eventually, pick up my notebook to write.

I miss Ambien.

# 8

After the beer spill, Wayne was really gracious and polite, and he suddenly went from very attractive coworker to guy I have a crush on.

*No*, I kept telling the crush. *Stop that.*

We left Craig and Rebecca at the restaurant to conspire and walked back to the office together. I wished the walk was longer.

I thanked Wayne for switching projects with me.

"No problem," he said. "Do you like the way I cleverly manipulated the situation to get Bowhunting.com all to myself?"

"You can have it."

"Big client. Outfoxed you there, Walker. Also, I don't have to try to sell cheese by mail."

He winked at me. I tried not to look at his long lashes.

"Are you kidding?" I said. "The world is waiting, patiently next to its mailbox, for a new way to get Gruyère delivered."

The truth is, I was feeling worse and worse about the job. During lunch, Craig let us know that Alvin Beaconsfield, the venture capitalist backing us, had approved the budget for two staff for the summer only. That's why he kept going on about eating what we kill. There was no budget for data or support, no plan, just contracts with two companies that would pay SoSol a percentage of any sales. And, he let us know, that there would likely only be one position available in the fall. He didn't spell it out, but it was clear enough. He'd set everything up as a competition. The first prize was a job. The second prize was no job.

I'd never really wanted to do this kind of work. At school, I'd hoped to publish a series of books about ethical veganism. I imagined myself finding the writers, designing and editing the books, and distributing them to widespread acclaim, seeing them nestled on bookshelves across America, next to *Eating Animals* and *Thug Kitchen*. Gwyneth Paltrow would love them. But in my first year at New York University, which I mostly spent smoking weed with JFXBF, the financial crisis hit.

I eventually realized that my prospects of landing a decent-paying publishing job were roughly zero. I became deathly afraid of ending up like one of the terminally underemployed Occupy Wall Street losers I saw in Zuccotti Park, substituting pointless activism for a career.

I wasn't particularly good at college, but I discovered I had a touch for social media. I was quick and clever, had a personality I didn't mind projecting, and I knew how to drive clicks. It was one area of the economy that was growing, so I threw myself into it in my last year at school, volunteering to promote campus events and organizations, learning the greasy little tricks that allow you to herd people like sheep, building my following, developing a sassy online persona.

I did all that because I wanted to be employed, so I had done my best to nod enthusiastically during Craig's pep talk, and, at the end, when he'd mentioned a party that night that Alvin was throwing in a Brooklyn club, I perked up.

"He wants to meet you two," he said.

"It should be fun," I lied. "I can't wait."

# 9

Digging through Jess's camping gear, I find her old canteen, which I haven't seen since I was ten and Jess was twelve.

When we were little, we used to go on family camping trips. Mom and Dad would load up the Subaru station wagon and we'd drive for hours, with Jess and me whining and picking at each other in the backseat; then we'd all sleep in a big square tent in some park for a week. Mom would cook on a propane stove, Dad would sit in a camp chair and drink cans of Bud, and Jess and I would run around in the woods and play games she made up. She would be the brave princess and I'd be her sidekick, or I would be the kidnapped princess and she'd be my rescuer, fighting dragons or orcs or witches until she found me, and I had to thank her for saving me from being eaten or boiled alive or whatever.

Jess would always have her old-fashioned canteen, with its fuzzy wool cover and leather carrying strap, and would dole out water to me in her bossy way.

The last time I remember seeing it was on our last camping trip, just before Jess's social life got to the point that she didn't want to go away in the summer anymore.

We drove up to Nova Scotia, the longest drive yet. By then, we'd stopped playing make-believe and would just explore, but Jess still bossed me around and she still carried the canteen.

On that trip, we were staying at a campground by the sea. On our second day there, Jess and I wandered away from the tent and took a trail through the woods that ended at a sandstone cliff overlooking a little island topped with pine trees. Jess decided we should explore it.

We scrambled down the cliff, got our flip-flops and feet up to our ankles coated in sticky red mud, and managed to climb up to the top of the island, where we sat in the sun on the springy ground, looking out at the vast mudflats and the brown water. There were seagulls wheeling around in the sky, cawing, and we sat there trying to figure out what they were doing. Eventually I realized that they were picking up clams, flying into the air, and dropping them on rocks below so the shells would break and they could eat the meat inside. Jess didn't believe me at first, but finally had to agree that was what was happening. Some of the gulls would hang around and try to steal the clams when they landed rather than finding their own, so there was a lot of frantic wing flapping and screaming.

When we got bored with the gull show and went to go back, we stood, openmouthed. White rips and eddies of churning water filled the little cove between us and the cliff on the other side. The tide had come in, cutting us off from the mainland. It looked dangerous. Mom and Dad wouldn't want us to go in.

I was scared and wanted to wait on the island to be rescued, but Jess said we had to cross right away or we'd be stuck there until the tide went out again. She took my hand, yanked me with her, and waded into the water.

"Come on, Minnow! Let's go!"

She had to pull me hard to get me to go farther once I saw I was going to get my white shorts wet. After a few steps it was up to our waists. I pleaded with her to turn back but she kept pulling me behind her, until the water was over our heads and she had to take her hand away to dog-paddle. I cried but I followed her out to where the current caught us and swept us toward the shore. I started to go under, but she grabbed me and held my wrist so hard that later I had a bruise on it, and dragged me to shore. Then we trudged, wet and shivering, back to the campground, where we ran to Mom's and Daddy's arms. They hugged us frantically and yelled at us and got us dried off and dressed in fresh clothes.

I haven't thought about that day for years, and I sit for a while on Jess's sleeping bag, holding the canteen with my eyes closed, reliving it. It hits me hard, thinking of her little hand on mine, pulling me from danger.

I think that was the end of a happy period, before I realized some things about life, things I had a hard time absorbing. I try not to think about any of the bad things.

Anyway, nobody will miss any of the stuff in here, but sooner or later someone—the super, I would guess—will want to clear everything out. Whenever that happens, it would not be good for them to find a dirty, freaked-out girl living in a concrete room that is six paces wide by twelve paces long.

I know the dimensions because today I started an exercise regime: a half hour of pacing the length of it.

I decided on that this morning. It is superpathetic, but I'm pretty sure you shouldn't spend all day with your face in a musty sleeping bag, staring at the wrong time on a microwave clock.

I guess that's not all I do. I also write in my notebook, eat granola bars, drink water, and occasionally pee in the bowl. It's weeks until I next have my period, which is good, because I don't have any tampons, but I'm afraid that sometime soon I'll have to move my bowels, and I really don't want to think about how it will be in here after that happens. I'm already wondering if the pee in the bowl is permeating everything, making me smell like a bag lady.

This is not a good life for Candace.

# 10

When I got back to the office, I introduced Wayne to Beatrice and the rest of the clickbait squad. We found him a workstation, recently vacated by Chas, a heavily pierced and habitually hungover club kid who'd stopped showing up that week.

"Do you mind if we leave Chas's stuff here in case he comes back?" Beatrice asked Wayne.

Chas's stuff was a Tupperware container and a Mr. T bobblehead.

Wayne, who didn't seem to have any of his own stuff, didn't mind. He got his laptop set up.

Beatrice watched him and then gave me a knowing smile.

"I need a health break," she said.

I followed her downstairs, took one of her cigarettes, and we smoked and watched the Chelsea pedestrians walk down Sixteenth Street.

"New boy is totes hawt," she said.

"Stop!" I said. "I know he's cute. I'm trying not to have a crush on him. Did you, um, notice the big stain on the front of his pants?"

"What? No!"

"I got flustered at lunch and dumped a pint in his lap."

"You did not!" She laughed.

I nodded and smoked.

"Totally did. A full pint. Right in the junk."

Beatrice squealed and did a little dance.

"I was humiliated," I said. "I even tried to dry off the front of his khakis. He had to stop me."

It felt good to laugh with Beatrice. I was still worried she was hurt that I got the job.

"So are you pumped about your promotion?"

"No. I mean, I guess. I want to try something new. I'll probably suck at it."

I shrugged. No big deal.

"I don't have much else in my life right now," I said. "You have your art. And you have Rudy."

Rudy is a trans man who works as a chef in a Brooklyn restaurant that specializes in cooking with game. I like them—that's the pronoun I was supposed to use for him, I mean them—but I couldn't make myself go to their restaurant, where, I imagined, a bunch of bearded hipsters would go on about how much they love venison marrow, the thought of which made me want to be ill.

"It's awesome for you," said Beatrice. "I could see you being a big-shot social media superstar. If it works."

"I know. It likely won't work."

"Cheese by mail. Honey, I'd like some Roquefort. Can you order some so that we can get it delivered next week?"

I laughed.

"Kevin thinks it's going to flop," said Beatrice. "He thinks Craig and Rebecca don't really know what they're doing beyond pumping clickbait for weight-loss pills."

"Likely true. Whatevs. I can always go back to fat-shaming Britney."

"Follow your passion!"

We shared a bitter laugh and went back upstairs.

# 11

I use the last of the water to clean myself up a bit, do my makeup, and exit the storage room, trying to remember to look as though I was just someone coming back from a perfectly normal trip to a storage place.

I walk down the hallway, take the concrete stairs up to a side exit of the condo building, and use a rock to wedge the door open a few inches so that I can return that way without going through the lobby, where there are cameras.

It is morning, as I thought it would be. I'm relieved to see the sun low in the east.

I walk down the alley and out onto the sidewalk, where a fair number of people are going about their business.

I'm wearing Jess's old jean jacket, hoping it will help me blend in with Jersey proles, with a bandanna around my head made from an old black T-shirt. I have to do something about my hair.

It feels great to be outside again, but I can't stand and stretch and soak in the sun. That's not what people do when they come out of condo storage closet hallways. I even brought an empty cardboard box with me, to look the part.

I want to walk down to the river but I have to go the other way. It's strange to not be able to use a map on my phone, but after walking a few blocks away from the river, I find Newport Centre, a big mall, right where I thought it would be.

My first stop is a sports cap store, where I buy a New Jersey Devils hat, on sale for $9.99. I'm relieved that the young guy behind the counter doesn't ask me anything about the Devils, because all I know is that they're a hockey team and I like the little red Devil logo.

I'm really hungry, so I go up the escalator to the food court and have a foot-long veggie sub, which I really enjoy, although I'm nervous, so I sit hunched, trying to keep my head down, like some homeless person, which I guess I am.

Then I go to the CVS, where I buy a bottle of Clairol chestnut hair dye for $14.99.

The middle-aged Hispanic lady behind the counter smiles at me.

"I hope you not going to dye that pretty hair," she says.

I blush and feel panicky. She looks at me, I imagine, suspiciously.

I smile. "It's for my sister."

Who asks their sister to get them hair dye? Dumb. Dumb. Dumb. She looks at me even more strangely. Has she seen my picture? I have to assume that she has. In fact, I have to assume that she is calling the police as I walk out of the store.

Take no chances.

At the exit, I see the cover of the *New York Post* out of the corner of my eye. There I am, on the front page! It's a crop from the selfie I tweeted the day I got the promotion. The headline says "Cops Hunt Hipster Killer."

OMFG. My stomach jumps and I almost vomit. I start to sweat. I have to stop myself from breaking into a run. I glance back at the cashier, who is staring at me.

I force myself to walk slowly out into the mall, then find the nearest exit, which leads to a concrete stairwell to the parking garage. I run down the stairs, then wander around looking for a way out. I end up walking out through the exit for cars, climbing up the steep ramp to the street.

I head down toward the water, ready to take off if I see cops. As I walk I think about ways I could run to get away. If the police come around that corner now, I'll run back into the parking garage. If they come up behind me, I'll run for the park across the street. I'm hyper-alert, glancing around, heart pounding.

I see no police. Okay. Focus on the situation. I need to find a place to dye my hair. I walk to the river, to a marina. When I was young, my dad had a boat, so I know there are always showers at marinas.

I stroll into the building and go downstairs, where I know the bathrooms and laundry will be, at the back, for the boaters. The bathroom door has a key code. I wait in the laundry room until I hear somebody coming down the stairs. Thankfully, it's a woman. I follow her into the ladies' room.

I hide in a toilet stall until she leaves. Then I have a shower, which feels great after my days in a storage locker. Then I dump the dye in my hair. I don't have a towel, which is awkward. I have to hang around in the shower stall until the dye turns my hair a mousy brown—the box says twenty minutes. I force myself to stand in there for about that long, shivering, planning my return to the storage closet.

I get dressed and dry my hair under the hand dryer. Then I put on my normal makeup, which is subtle. I need more if I want to look like a Jersey mall rat, so I slather it on. I put on the hockey cap and examine my look. Not bad. I mean, it's awful but it's the look I'm going for. I stand there, looking at new Candace, getting used to her face. I wish I had some gum to chew. That would finish the look. Maybe a cigarette.

At a 7-Eleven, I buy a small bottle of water, a frozen pad Thai dinner, and a few more granola bars. I take note of the time—11:07 a.m.—on the cash register, so that I can set the clock on the microwave back at the storage locker. I count the seconds as I walk back. One Mississippi. Two Mississippis. Three Mississippis.

Thankfully, the door to the storage locker hallway is still wedged open, so I manage to get back into my little concrete cave without going through the lobby.

Three hundred and sixty-eight Mississippis. I reset the clock on the microwave from 12:28 p.m. to 11:13 a.m. It's pathetic to think how happy it makes me to bring Candace Standard Time into alignment with the rest of the world, but that's my life now.

# 12

When I got back to my desk after smoking with Beatrice, I called Irene Winslow, the genius behind Cheese of the Month.

I introduced myself, talking quickly and cheerfully. I was a keener.

"Hi!" she said. "Where are you?"

"Like, physically? Sixteenth Street. New York City."

"New York City! Wow. Big time. You going to sell some cheese for me?"

Irene told me she had started the business as a hobby because she was frustrated by her inability to get her hands on the kind of cheese she wanted in her home of Clayton, New York, way upstate.

"Up here it's just cheddar cheddar cheddar."

"No way," I said, not bothering to tell her that I hated her and myself for promoting a product that harms animals.

To keep cows producing milk requires them to be inseminated repeatedly—raped, really—or their udders dry up. Then their calfs are taken from them at an early age while the mother can do nothing to stop it. I've seen heartbreaking videos of the mothers wailing. Most of the calfs end up being fattened in veal pens, living their short lives in their own filth, never knowing their mother's love, or the pleasure of the sun, before they're murdered and butchered and sent to Italian restaurants so that disgusting people can eat veal.

So I hate cheese, and I hate the way people think it's weird not to eat it, like I'm a freak because I don't want to participate in the (government-subsidized) industrial-scale slaughter of baby animals. But I can't say any of that to Irene.

"You would not believe how bad the selection is in the big grocery stores," she said. "It's just sad. And when they do have something interesting, it's always overpriced and half the time it's stale."

Irene had one of those twangy upstate accents, and she was a talker. She told me she'd slowly built up a list of a couple hundred customers, as a hobby, but after retiring from teaching chemistry, she wanted to expand, start making bank.

"I hope you can crank up some sales, because nobody wants to live on a New York state teacher's pension, honey."

"I am sure we can," I said. "We have lots of ideas. I can't wait to get started."

"One thing I was nervous about. I want it to be clear that what Craig told me is right. There's no way you end up sending me a bill for your time, right?"

"That's my understanding. We only get paid for conversions."

"For your information, I'm taping this. I told Craig the same thing. I want to protect myself. This recording is to make sure that I don't get ripped off."

"Gosh, I'm just the clickbait girl. I'm not the right one to ask about contracts."

She babbled on, telling me how Craig had emailed her and pitched her on letting SoSol market her cheese. The best thing was that it wasn't going to cost her anything. She just had to share the revenue from expanded sales with us.

Rebecca and Kevin were walking toward me. I waved them over.

"Rebecca, I'm just talking to Irene, from Cheese of the Month," I said. "She wants to be sure she won't get billed if there are no sales, right?"

"That's entirely correct, Candace. Let me talk to her."

I gave Rebecca the phone and she soothed Irene.

Kevin smiled at me.

"Hey, Candace," he said. "New phone okay?"

"Yeah. Super." I wanted to hear how Rebecca dealt with a prickly client, but I had to deal with Kevin blathering on while I smiled and nodded.

He kept me occupied until Rebecca gave me back the phone, rolling her eyes to show how she felt about Irene.

"Hi, Irene?" I said. "It's Candace again. Did Rebecca explain everything?"

"You could say that," she said. "Or you could say that I explained there's no way I'm going to get stuck with a bill."

"Great! I'm really happy you guys sorted that out!"

What a cranky lady. I told her she had nothing to worry about and she was welcome to tape our call. Finally I could demonstrate my enthusiasm for cheese marketing.

The exchange gave me new doubts about my exciting new job. Craig spammed her, she said okay, and now I was supposed to magically increase her sales.

"I'm sure we're going to help you sell a lot of cheese," I said, although I didn't know how.

"Great. I need the money. Thanks to the president, the economy is doing better, but taxes are still too high."

Ugh. A Trump fan.

"You can say that again," I said, hoping that would help me get off the phone.

Wrong.

She couldn't believe the government waste, all the welfare mothers taking tax money while pensioners had to struggle to make ends meet. I impatiently drummed my fingers and listened to her go on. How entitled did she feel, to start babbling at me about her know-nothing political views while I was in no position to contradict her?

"I agree completely," I said. "It makes me sick to see what's happening in this country."

Let's wrap this up.

"Yeah? I thought you'd all be a bunch of liberals down there in Manhattan."

So she knew she was likely forcing someone who disagreed with her to listen to her nonsense. What a hateful old bag.

"There are a lot of people who don't understand," I said, lowering my voice. "I have to be careful what I say, because I don't want people to think I'm right wing or whatever, but not everyone here voted for Hillary."

She liked that and laughed, and I was eventually able to steer her back to business and get her off the phone.

I spent the rest of the day working on cheese-loving online personae.

I have dozens of fake Facebook and Twitter sock puppets—I think of them as characters—who are all friends with each other and as many other interesting people as I have found time to friend.

Most of my sock puppets are attractive young women, since I find it's—doy!—easy to get guys to be your friend if you're an attractive young woman.

I get the pictures from real Facebook profiles of strangers.

I decided that the chief cheese lover would be Linda Wainwright, my most popular online alter ego, a blond-haired beach girl whose profile picture I snagged from a South African's Facebook page.

It's a stunner. She's on a beach, grinning like crazy, half out of her wet suit, water glistening on her bikini-clad body as the sun goes down behind her, her short blond hair all tangled. She looks wholesome, athletic, and fun.

Linda lives in Toronto, is moderately liberal in her politics, likes outdoor activities, yoga, Arcade Fire, Beyoncé, and Patsy Cline. She loved *Breaking Bad* but also enjoys *The Bachelorette*, although she's a bit embarrassed about it. She's sad when celebrities die, or when terrorists attack Paris.

Where my posts are often ironic or dark, Linda is straightforward and happy. She posts cheerful, optimistic memes.

Over two years of intermittent sock-puppeting, I'd built quite a social network for Linda. She had 724 Facebook friends and double the numbers of followers on Twitter and Instagram. She was my best sock puppet, a fun person, and, coincidentally, a big booster of yours truly.

Just that morning she'd posted a cheerful, encouraging message on my Facebook page after I announced my new job: Congrats! You're so smart!

Lucas White, Linda's friend, a hot black guy with a nice smile and spiky dreads, posted on Facebook to congratulate me and ask if I still had time to work on our documentary. Of course, Lucas!

Ling Mai, a pretty, pierced Asian girl who was friends with Linda and Lucas, sent me messages on several platforms congratulating me.

*Well, Linda, Lucas, and Ling Mai,* I thought, *you are about to reveal to your online friends a hitherto carefully concealed love of cheese.*

I spent hours having them join cheese fancier groups, even filched a few old posts from real cheese lovers, and had them post them on their blogs. Soon Linda and her friends would be well-loved guideposts to the cheese world. Then they would discover Cheese of the Month and would not be able to contain their enthusiasm.

It wasn't a great plan, but it was all I had. Wayne was adorable, but our relationship would work better if he worked someplace else anyway.

I could support him emotionally when he got outsourced, help him find more satisfying, rewarding work. It was the kind of funny story we could tell people years later sitting on the porch of our summer place in Martha's Vineyard.

# 13

I decide to do a complete inventory of the storage locker, to see if there might be anything that will help me make my escape.

I drag everything out of Jess's old bags of clothes and find a few useful items. Unfortunately, there's no underwear, which is what I need the most, but there are some old T-shirts I can take.

There's nothing useful in the kitchen stuff—why did she ever come to own an egg separator? In the camping stuff, though, there's a nice little black canvas daypack, which will be my getaway bag.

I start going through the boxes of documents. There are a lot of old essays and notebooks from law school, some old rental agreements and bills. I'm surprised to find a bunch of stuff that has to do with me.

When I was in my first year at college, I fell in love with Gary, a young English professor, while sitting in a Shakespeare class that I had dreaded taking. He was brilliant, or seemed so to me, and he did lovely recitations, making the text come alive, which made me get Shakespeare for the first time.

Near the end of first semester, I went to see him during office hours and asked his advice about how I could study Shakespeare more intensively. He knew I had a crush on him. He encouraged me, lent me a book—*Will in the World* by Stephen Greenblatt. I emailed him a few days later, told him I loved it. He suggested that I return it to his apartment.

Quivering with nerves and desire, I turned up, clutching the book, and he invited me in, gave me a glass of wine, compared me to a summer's day, and we made the beast with two backs.

We had a brief, intense affair, which ended suddenly two days later when he left me in his apartment briefly to go out for wine. I used his laptop to go online and a Facebook message notification popped up on the screen. It was from his wife, a Harvard professor, whom I hadn't known existed.

I slapped him when he returned, stormed off and got drunk and cried on the shoulder of JFXBF, who was also in the Shakespeare class. He comforted me and soon he was my bf.

Gary didn't take it well and sent me harassing emails, wanting to see me. I told him no, then ignored him, then he sent an email where he basically threatened to flunk me if I wouldn't see him.

I didn't know what to do, so I asked Jess for help. She was in her first year of law school, so she relished the opportunity to play law talker.

Big sister dealt with it. Gary disappeared and stopped emailing me, and a new professor was teaching his class. I got an A, which I deserved. JFXBF got a C.

I never knew how she did it. Sitting on the sleeping bag, I learn how.

She had printed out all the emails she sent Gary, copied to the head of the English department, and all the emails they'd sent her.

He had repeatedly emailed her, basically pleading to keep his job, begging for the chance to apologize. He denied ever threatening to flunk me and said the emails that he sent were only an effort to meet with me to make sure I was okay, to sort out the end of our relationship and make sure that we could continue in our roles as professor and student. He quoted from his emails at length, trying to show that they weren't threatening.

She ignored all that and insisted that the school had to make a change so that I could receive the same chance as any student to get a fair grade, and, fairly quickly, he was gone.

I sit on the sleeping bag for an hour, reading and rereading the old email chain.

I find it depressing, both because Gary, my former boogeyman, comes across as so pathetic, and because Jess can't help me now.

# 14

Wayne was waiting outside Output, a big Brooklyn nightclub, when I got there for Alvin's party.

He was facing the other way, looking elegant, leaning on a bus stop pole, reading his phone.

He hadn't noticed me, so I stood there for a moment, behind one of those little caged sidewalk maples, and looked him over. He was still in khakis, but was now wearing a blue polo. He must have gone home to change.

I smoothed out my suit and tried to think about what I should say to him. I was still thinking when he spoke without turning.

"Are you spying on me, Candy?"

I started, felt myself blushing, and then realized that he had used his phone's camera—selfie style—to look behind him.

I tried to be nonchalant.

"Oh. Hi, Wayne. Spying? Not at all. Just waiting for Rebecca. I hadn't noticed you."

He turned to me and smiled.

"Do you mind if I call you Candy?"

I had to stop myself from fiddling with my hair and tried to look away from his smile, but instead ended up looking at the front of his pants.

"The beer is gone."

"Not really. It's still there. These are different pants. I went home to change."

"God, I felt like an idiot. I'll have to find a way to make it up to you."

I realized as I said that that I was still gazing at the front of his pants and seemed to be suggesting an indecent quid pro quo. I blushed again and quickly looked up at his eyes, which was another mistake.

"Maybe I can help you find bowhunting hot spots or something," I said.

Thankfully, Rebecca arrived then, ending Blush Fest 2018. She looked great in a low-cut lime-green cocktail dress. She dealt with the bouncers so that we strolled right in.

It was a normal Brooklyn club, with a crowd of twentysomethings drinking cocktails and trying to look hip. A lot of the guys had beards and there were a lot of retro clothes, but some of the people had also spent money on nice nightclub outfits. Some of the girls were dancing to the throbbing trap music. A crowd was lined up at the bar.

Rebecca led us upstairs to a rooftop patio, where a blond girl in a black minidress was standing guard at the entrance. She and Rebecca kissed cheeks and we proceeded to the bar, where a handsome, tousle-haired young man was making cocktails.

"Have you ever had a Paper Plane?" he asked us. "Drink of the night!"

"I'll have one of those," said Rebecca. She looked at us. "Three of those. They're delicious."

I took a nervous sip. She was right.

The night felt alive with possibilities. This was the not the kind of party I usually attended. The people were more glamorous, richer, more blasé. Before I could really take it all in, Rebecca was off again. We followed her across the patio and up to a smaller terrace, with a view of the glittering lights of Midtown in the distance.

A florid-faced man in expensive-looking slacks and a shiny polo shirt was holding forth there, surrounded by a seemingly admiring group of young people.

"Rebecca," he called out, pulling away from his entourage. "Hey, sweetie."

They did the two-cheek kiss and Rebecca introduced us.

Alvin Beaconsfield was tall, taller even than Wayne, and powerful looking, with big arms and shoulders and thick legs, although he had a good-sized potbelly.

His hands were big. His red face was big. The hair on the back of his head was wiry, standing on end. In the front, he was balding, save for a defiant half-moon-shaped tuft on his forehead.

"So you're the social media wizards, are you?" he said. "Damn. Damn! Gonna make some money off you!" He was smiling and waving an empty cocktail glass.

He turned to Rebecca.

"Honey," he said, passing her his glass, "go tell Dave to make me another one of these things, a double this time, and bring back the same for Candace and Wayne here, too."

He was awful.

"I am glad you guys signed on. I had a look at your résumés. Impressed."

He turned to Wayne.

"Tell me. Why did you come to us? With a computer science degree from MIT, this seems an odd choice."

Wayne smiled and tossed a lock of hair off his brow.

"I know a lot about computers," he said. "But not much about business. If you study killer apps—the billion-dollar apps—you learn that most of the time the secret behind them is social. I want to learn that."

God, he was confident.

"Also, it's right around the corner from my apartment. I can wake up at eight forty-five and be at my desk by nine."

"Ha!" said Alvin. "Ha! Ha! Good stuff."

He turned to me.

"And how about you, hot stuff? You have a degree in English lit, seem to have the social touch. Why aren't you working for a publisher or university?"

I wanted to say: *Because I couldn't get a job at a publishing house or university, as you must know, you disgusting man.* Instead, I gave him my sassy smile.

"I think social media, and not print, is the dominant medium of our era, and it's changing so quickly. I want to ride the wave. I think of it like surfing."

He smiled and clapped his big, meaty hands together.

"Good stuff. A couple of little go-getters. Good good good. I told Craig to hire go-getters and he did. And he's told you there's no job in the fall if you don't make conversions?"

I nodded.

"He mentioned something about that," said Wayne, as if it didn't really concern him.

"Good," said Alvin. "Great. Fuck yeah. Get you two hotshots hustling, show us what you can do."

He laughed and we laughed with him.

"Sounds like a good deal," said Wayne.

There was something about that that Alvin didn't like. He beckoned us toward him, glanced around to make sure nobody else could hear us, and fixed each of us with a separate short look to make sure he had our attention. He was drunk.

"The deal," he said. "You want to know what the deal is? I made money when I sold WhizIt. That's the situation."

WhizIt, I had learned from Google, was a social address collection and sorting company. Beaconsfield and the other NYU computer nerds who started it sold it for hundreds of millions.

"I could sit around and do nothing, have blow job contests for the rest of my life." He clapped his hand over his mouth.

"Oops. Sorry, Candy. I should have said fellatio contests. You know, round robins. In Maui. Cocktails. Fast boats. Cocaine. Fake titties."

He pursed his lips and shook his face, blowing air through his lips to give the impression, I realized with horror, of a man rubbing his face between fake breasts.

"I would be bored," he said, suddenly, and frowned. "I would get so bored. So I amuse myself. I buy media, restaurants, bars, start-ups. I buy them to have fun and end up making money. I throw parties."

He gestured at the patio, then leaned in and whispered in my ear.

"To be honest, I get a lot of interesting pussy this way."

I pulled away and gave him a thin smile, but it was forced and he knew it and he met my eye and held it. I wanted to slap him or throw my drink in his face. I actually thought about doing it but realized: oh, it's empty.

Wayne laughed, uneasily.

"Here comes Becca with the drinks, Wayne," Alvin said, looking up. "Tell me, how'd you like to get your wiener into that? Huh? "

A pained bark of a laugh came from Wayne.

"I know you would, unless you're a fag. You a fag, Wayne?"

Wayne laughed, nervously. "No," he said.

"I didn't think so. Craig would have told me."

I was furious. He couldn't talk like that. I opened my mouth to tell Alvin that what he had just said was offensive, inappropriate, and illegal. Then I felt Wayne's hand on my arm, just above my elbow, squeezing gently, twice.

I interpreted the squeeze to mean: *It's not worth it. Ignore it.* And also, *I like you.* I held my tongue.

Then Rebecca was there delivering the drinks and Alvin was winking and leaving us.

Rebecca smiled at us.

"Too much," I said. "I can't even."

"Do we have to, in the normal course of our jobs, have anything to do with Alvin?" Wayne asked.

Rebecca's smile froze.

"Did Alvin say something inappropriate?" she asked. "He does that."

"You could say that," I said. "Worse than that. Illegal."

She held up her hand.

"I don't want to know," she said. "I don't really feel like looking for another job this week."

She turned to Wayne.

"You might not ever meet him again," she said. "Craig and I deal with him but you likely don't have to."

She could see we were unimpressed.

"He enjoys shocking people. That's his idea of fun. But he also likes to give opportunities to talented people. Like you two. How are your projects going?"

"Just getting started," said Wayne. "Learning about bowhunting."

"Same with me," I said. "Except, you know, cheese."

"Bowhunting," said Rebecca. "Right. I wanted to talk to you about that. Have you ever tried it?"

Wayne laughed.

"I grew up on the Upper West Side," he said. "So, no."

"I have," said Rebecca. "I actually brought down an elk once. The head is still on the wall of my dad's garage. One of my proudest moments."

"Where did you grow up?" Wayne asked.

"Northern Michigan," she said. "My dad is a big hunter. I grew up eating more game than beef."

"I'm a vegan," I said. Neither of them looked at me.

"Wow," said Wayne, leaning toward her. "I need to pick your brain. I don't know anything about bowhunting."

"I think hunting is wrong," I said.

They ignored me.

"In fact, I think cheese is wrong," I said.

"It's really hard," said Rebecca. "You have to scrub yourself clean, so that you have no scent, and stay absolutely still, so animals will approach you. I wasn't good at that part. Staying motionless, waiting for Bambi to come along."

She mimed standing straight and pulling back a bow, with her legs spread and her chest pushed out, which made her boobs stick out of her low-cut dress.

Wayne was, I thought, watching her with unbecoming interest, which made me suddenly cross.

"Why don't I get us some more drinks?" I said.

Neither of them noticed when I left.

# 15

I realize that I'm not thinking about giving myself up or ending my life anymore.

After successfully leaving my lair, dyeing my hair, replenishing my supplies, and avoiding detection, I feel sort of cheerful and myself for the first time since things went sideways. I'm still psychotically depressed about recent events, when I think about them, but I'm not thinking about them. I'm thinking about the future.

As I do my morning pacing, I make up my mind. Time to go. I stop pacing because I suddenly see I should save my strength. Time to get out of town.

I think the lady at the mall may have seen my picture on the front page of the *New York Post*, but she was likely too dumb to make the connection. And they don't carry that paper everywhere. And that was yesterday's paper. There will be some other nonsense on the front page today.

It's a big country. They can't all have heard about the hunt for the Hipster Killer.

I don't have enough money for an airplane ticket. In fact, after buying hair dye, a sub, and some granola bars, I have $84, which I don't even want to spend on bus fare. And for all I know, they're watching the bus stations.

I'm worried about cameras and computer programs that can pick someone out of a crowd. I don't know much about facial recognition software, but I figure I should stay away from the obvious places.

I need to find a way out of town and I can't be too picky about it. It's time to improvise. I'm thinking about what I know about the neighborhood, when I realize what I should do.

Last year, the only time I paid Jess a visit to see her boring but nice waterfront condo, I reacted with a poorly disguised mixture of envy and disgust so she took me to a nearby dive bar called Lucky 7, where she thought I'd be more comfortable. I was. It was exactly like the place where JFXBF worked in Brooklyn: loud punk music, black walls plastered with stickers and graffiti, terrible bathrooms, really cheap drinks. I wouldn't know anybody there. I can have beers and see if a way out of town presents itself.

First, I need to dress for nightlife. I rummage through Jess's discards for something that looks a little bit rock and roll and try on some outfits. I finally settle on an old pink tank top, which is way more revealing than the clothes I normally wear. Oh well. It doesn't look too slutty under the jean jacket.

Then I pack up my little bag and make my final exit from my concrete bunker. I take my pee bowl outside and dump it, so that nobody could know someone has been living there.

I wander until I find a Dunkin' Donuts, where I sit down to write and enjoy a coffee and (vegan) hash brown, which leaves me with $82.

Then I go to the bathroom to do my makeup and poof my hair, trying to look like a Jersey mall rat out on the town.

# 16

My cheeks burned and my legs were wobbly as I left Wayne and Rebecca. I felt hurt by their inattention and worried about the exchange with the awful Alvin. I wanted to get away but didn't feel that I could, so I went to the bathroom, splashed water on my face, and decided to take a pill. I had no Xanax, so decided to make do with an Ambien. Just popping it gave me the reassuring feeling that soon I'd feel a little numb.

I took a deep breath and headed back to the bar.

Dave was mixing cocktails, chilling glasses with dry ice and shaking his cocktail shaker in a showy way, instead of just pouring drinks. Everyone was thirsty, staring at him, thinking, *Hurry the fuck up.*

I felt anxious standing there by myself while everyone else was mingling, so I lowered my head to my phone to pretend I was busy with something. I popped open Bumble and left-swiped randomly through the stream of dudes, not seeing anyone who caught my eye.

Then, whoops, there was Kevin's weird face in a bathroom selfie.

Kevin, 28.
IT professional.
City College.
Info: Chicago guy enjoying the heck out of NYC.
Interests: Classic rock, South Indian food, outdoor activities, finding the truth.

Although we worked in the same office, I didn't know much about him. He and Beatrice were friends, but I never hung out with them. I flicked through his pics. In the first he was at the Manhattan entrance to the Williamsburg Bridge, striding toward the camera, wearing skinny jeans and a thrift store cardigan with a deer on it. There was a pic of him drinking beer on the patio of a Brooklyn dive with some friends, a shot of him on a nature trail, a picture of him at a museum, and a selfie of him standing, looking serious, outside a school.

Someone jostled me from behind and I looked up.

"Oh my gosh," I said, startled. "Kevin!"

He turned to me, apparently not noticing that I was standing next to him, and gave me a half smile.

"Oh, hi, Candace. How's the phone?"

I laughed.

"Great. You will not believe this but I was just using it to look through Bumble and guess whose profile I found?"

His half smile froze.

"No idea," he said. "Who?"

He looked away as if to compose himself and then looked me in the eye. It was unnatural, robotic.

"Yours!" I said and held it up to show him.

He looked rattled.

"That's not really a thing," he said. "I mean, I don't use it. A friend told me I should set it up, so I did, and I tried it out but I decided it's not for me. I need to delete it."

What to say? I don't care, weirdo.

"It's a silly way for me to waste time, like when I'm waiting forever for a drink," I said. "I only ever swipe left."

"Right. Of course. So did you meet Alvin? That's why you're here, right?"

"I did. He kind of freaked me out."

He arched an eyebrow.

"What did he say?"

I realized I didn't want to tell him. I didn't want to talk to him at all.

"Nothing really. He was kind of . . . raunchy. Not what I'm used to. I'm from Connecticut."

"He's an interesting man. Did you know he actually knows the president?"

"Trump?"

He looked at me like I was stupid.

"That's his name."

"I did not know that."

"There he is!" said Kevin, looking across the bar to where Alvin was waving his arms and talking to a drunk-looking, overly pierced young woman.

He turned to survey the room while she laughed at whatever he said. He spotted Kevin and me and waved. Kevin waved back.

I was afraid he'd come over. I didn't want to talk to him.

"Time for me to get another drink," I said. "See you later."

I left without waiting for him to say good-bye and pressed myself closer to the bar. Looking over my shoulder I could see Alvin approaching Kevin. He looked around the bar. I didn't want him to see me, so I ducked behind a guy in front of me.

He looked over his shoulder at me.

"Hoiding farm alpha, are ye?" he said.

He had fine, spiky black hair, pale, stubbled skin, and bright blue eyes. He was wearing a crisp open-collared shirt and a slim-cut blue suit and had a chic-looking laptop bag over his shoulder.

I blinked at him and stammered.

"Pardon?"

"Hiding from Alvin, are you?"

"Oh," I said. Right. Burry Irish accent. "Yes. Just a bit."

I felt myself blush.

"Right. All right. I'll hide ya, Red."

He stepped between me and Alvin.

"I think he's looking for ya," he said, out of the side of his mouth.

"Don't kid. That's mean."

"Seriously. He's looking for someone. Might not be you, I suppose. Why would he be looking for you? He fancy you?"

I tried to make myself smaller. We were now standing with our backs to each other, talking over our shoulders at each other.

"No. Well, I don't know. He just hired me. He gave me a funny look and told me he likes investing because of the 'interesting pussy.'"

I made quote marks in the air.

He laughed and turned around and I blushed again.

"Coast's clear," he said. "He went out on the balcony with a balding hipster."

I sighed with relief and I think I smiled at him.

He gave me a funny little smile back.

"I have two questions for you," he said.

"Go ahead," I said, trying to maintain my poise.

"Number one: Did you just make quote-mark signs with your fingers?"

I laughed.

"Yes. How could you tell?"

"I heard it in your voice. Number two: Are you Candace Walker?"

How did he know that?

"I am. And you are?"

"Declan Walsh," he said.

His hand was cool and firm and strong.

"Have we met?"

"Only on Twitter. I'm @ShouldBObvious."

"Wow. Nice to meet you! Wow."

I was actually excited. We were Twitter friends, having traded wisecracks about knucklehead social media self-promoters.

"I recognize you from your legendary selfies."

I was flustered and flattered.

I really liked @ShouldBObvious on Twitter. He was funny and smart. But I'd had no idea who he was in real life.

"I didn't recognize you because you never post selfies, which is lame AF."

"Not many people know that I'm @ShouldBObvious," he said. "Like, five people. It's sort of a secret identity."

"It was. Now I know."

"I should have sworn you to secrecy."

I took out my phone, as if to check it, then snapped a quick picture of him.

"Hey," he said. "No fair."

He was frowning with surprise.

I showed him the picture, turning so that we were rubbing shoulders, which felt a bit cheeky.

"I'm looking forward to sharing this with the world via social media," I said.

"You could blackmail me with that. I'd best be on my best behavior."

"You'd best."

We were finally at the bar. We got four Paper Planes.

"I don't have to reveal your big secret," I said. "We can negotiate."

We strolled toward the upper terrace.

"What do you want in return?" he asked.

I peeked around the corner and spied Alvin talking to Rebecca and Wayne.

"You can start by delivering these drinks to the lovely girl and the gentleman talking to Alvin."

"You mean the beautiful Rebecca?"

"Yes."

"I shall deliver these to them in exchange for a ninety-six-hour embargo on my secret identity."

He took the drinks and strode off onto the balcony.

# 17

It feels so good to drink a beer again.

I'm at the end of the bar at Lucky 7, across from the jukebox, next to a mirrored pillar, with my black backpack at my feet, my jean jacket over the back of my stool, and most of a $5 pint of beer in front of me next to my Moleskine.

That means that with tip I'm down to $75, but I don't care. I need to have a beer or six.

And I need to make friends. That will likely get easier when the place gets a little fuller and everybody, including me, gets a little drunker. For now, I'll keep writing.

I am able to check myself out in the mirrored pillar, and I have to say I'm looking fairly cute, if your taste runs to Jersey mall rats.

My brown hair is styled, my makeup freshened. And the tank is the right size for my sister, but too small for me, so my cute little blue bra straps peek out.

I look like someone else, which is what I want, although I don't really like the look of the person in the mirror. Still, I have to admit, she looks loose and friendly, which is the idea.

The bartender, who has big muscles covered with tribal tats, seems to think so. He keeps smiling at me. I fight my instinct to ice him, as I normally would, remember that I'm here to make friends, and force myself to smile back.

"You look better with a smile," he says, like he doesn't have the faintest clue how totally rapey that is.

I don't get it. Half of my social media feed is made up of women explaining how that kind of comment is belittling and sexist, to the point that I'm sick of reading the same messages, but then you go into a dive bar and some meathead tells you to smile, like it's his prerogative to advise you on your appearance, that he assumes your role in life is to please him.

I hate him but I force myself to turn it up a little. I need the bartender to like me.

"What you writin'?" he asks.

"My life story."

"Is it interesting?"

"Not yet."

I close my journal and smile more at him.

I need to make friends.

Our terrible flirtation is interrupted by the arrival of a boy carrying a guitar case. He's one of those guys who doesn't seem that cute when you first look at him but gets cuter on closer inspection. Big brown eyes. A little stubble. Long, messy hair.

He is, of course, in the band that will play here tonight, and he needs to know where they can park their van. Tattooed bartender goes to find out, which leaves cute boy standing there next to me.

Well, hello.

I take a sip of my beer and don't look at him.

He pulls out his phone and flicks through it, bored. He puts it back in his pocket.

"Hey," he says. "Do you mind if I ask you a question?"

"Depends what it is."

"How come you aren't looking at your phone? You're just sitting at the bar, not reading your phone. Nobody does that anymore."

I smile at him.

"I've decided to take a break from my phone, just to see if I can live without it."

I lean over and take a sip of foam from my fresh second beer.

"Wow," he says. "Awesome. I've thought about doing that. How's it going?"

"Awful."

He introduces himself. Pat is an adorable puppy of a boy, with a shy little private smile.

"I kind of hate my phone," he says as he waits for the bartender. "I hate the way I can't stop myself from looking at it whenever I'm not doing anything else."

"That's what I'm trying to get away from. I want to work on my attention span."

He nods enthusiastically, like he knows precisely what I mean but didn't know it until the moment I said it.

"Exactly. It's like the world's stupidest addiction," he says. "Like, I could be addicted to cocaine or Oxy or something fun, but instead it's my stupid Android."

I laugh.

"I hate it. Happens all the time. I'm practicing my guitar, reading a book, pleasuring myself, whatever, and I suddenly think: I should check my phone. Then I'm reading some stupid thing on Twitter or looking at a cat video."

I find myself giggling, not fake-trying-to-make-friends giggling, but actually giggling.

"That's what I miss," I say. "Blanking out."

"How long's it been?"

"Only four days. I got into a fight with Verizon, which they won, and I thought: time for a little break."

"You going to get another one?"

"Maybe after I finish my thesis."

I had worked out my story as I drank my beer.

I am Lisa, a master's student in English literature at Cornell. I came down for the weekend with my friend, Samantha, to stay with her at her boyfriend's place in Hoboken. But we got drunk in the Village last night and she fell and broke her ankle, and I don't have my license, and now I'm stuck here and need to get back upstate. But I have no phone, which sucks, because I can't get in touch with anybody.

Pat buys my bullshit story.

"Really? Wow. Tough weekend."

Then Sexist Tatman is back, with parking information, and Pat is gone.

"Did you finish your life story?" says the bartender.

"Working on it," I say.

My hand is cramped and ink-stained but I want to finish writing the part about the party.

# 18

I was chatting with a cute rando when Declan came back from delivering the drinks. I let him wait for just a minute before kissing off the other guy and turning to him.

"Mission accomplished?"

He nodded.

He led me away to two open stools at the edge of the lower patio. We sat and looked at the flat Brooklyn rooftops and a lot full of trucks surrounded by a high steel fence.

"So how do you know Alvin?" I asked.

"I own one of those trucks down there. They're full of antique Irish guns. I'm here for an exhibition at the Flatbush Museum of Arms. He's on the board."

"Really? Wow."

"No. Not really. I work for iMetrics."

"Jerk," I said and punched him on the arm. "I believed you!"

He laughed.

"So that explains why you're so smart about social media stuff," I said. "I mean, kind of smart. Not totally stupid."

Oh sheesh.

iMetrics is a behind-the-scenes social media powerhouse. Their stock has twice doubled in the past couple years after they convinced Facebook to let them help with their data sorting.

The value of most social media enterprises is the information they collect on customers. Every email you send, every Facebook post you make is a tiny bit of information that, properly sorted, is worth money.

iMetrics was better at fracking data than anyone, pushing it past the point of creepiness. They were the first, for example, to tell tampon retailers to time their social media ads to the time of the month when their customers would be thinking about buying tampons, which they could do by cross-referencing drugstore loyalty program data with Facebook profiles. And they did it all without attracting unwelcome attention, because they were, so far as anyone knew, doing things ethically and legally, employing as many lawyers as programmers. If anyone might know how to make Cheese of the Month work, it would be Declan.

"If you give me some advice about my first social media client," I said, "I might be prepared to extend the embargo on your secret identity still further."

"Maybe. What kind of timeline are we talking about here? I may need to get plastic surgery in Venezuela."

"How about thirty days?"

"Ninety. And that's firm. I need time for the scars to heal. Let me get more drinks. Guard my laptop."

My third Paper Plane was empty but they didn't seem to be affecting me.

"Sure."

When he went to the bar, I sat down, pulled out my phone, and went to iMetrics's website. There he was, on the Who We Are page: Declan Walsh, Vice President for North America.

Rich, young, handsome social media genius with a cute accent. Out of my league. Best squeeze him for info while maintaining what dignity I could.

When he came back with drinks, I explained the Cheese of the Month project. We were seated side by side, looking out over the city.

"Hm," he said, when I was done. "Have you got any data?"

I shook my head.

"No addresses? Subscription list from Cheese Lovers Monthly?"

"Nope."

"Budget?"

"Zero."

"Well," he said, frowning. "It's a very twentieth-century idea, cheese by mail. I don't see the demand. The grocery chains are good at figuring out what customers want. I know, because I sell them data. And even if you were to find the demographic that for some reason loves cheese but lives far from a decent cheese shop—French professors in small college towns, say—I find it hard to imagine they'll be a growth market."

"I don't need a long-term plan. I need to produce a little bump, get some pecorino out the door, so they'll give me something else to do."

He made his hands into a steeple and pursed his lips.

"You need data."

"What kind of data?"

He smiled, raised an eyebrow, and took a sip of his drink.

"The kind of data you can't get without money," he said and leaned back on his stool. "Ideally, you want to know who loves cheese and lives far from cheese shops. You want the kind of data Facebook and Google have."

"Or iMetrics," I said, taking a big sip of my cocktail. I made my innocent face.

He smiled and narrowed his eyes.

"Or iMetrics. But they don't give that kind of data away. It's money. Nobody gives away proprietary information because some hot redhead at a party asks for it, even if she's superfuckable."

Grrr. I can't believe he said that.

"Well, thanks for saying that I'm 'fuckable,'" I said, making air quotes. "But for the record, I haven't asked you for anything, except advice. What I am not asking you for, just so we are clear, is proprietary information."

I stood up but my exit wasn't quite as dignified as I'd hoped, since in my rush, I bumped into some guy as I stomped off.

It was Kevin.

"Oh gosh. Sorry, Kevin."

"No problem."

He gave me a weird, too-bright smile.

Declan was calling to me.

"Hey! Candace!"

Kevin saw him and stepped toward him.

"Oh hey. Declan. Alvin said I should introduce myself."

I made my getaway. Time to go. I headed to the upper terrace to say good night. On the way, I ran into Wayne.

"There you are," he said. "We were wondering whether that Irishman had abducted you."

He was holding three drinks.

"Here," he said, handing me one. "Come chat with Rebecca and Alvin."

"Okay," I said, even though I was starting to wonder if I'd had too many.

I followed him to the upper terrace, where Rebecca and Alvin were leaning against the railing. I had just forgotten about Alvin and was suddenly looking at his big red face again. Rebecca was holding his arm in a friendly way.

"Hi!" she said. "Were you conspiring with Declan? I bet that was fun."

"It was," I said, smiling brightly.

"Watch him," said Alvin. "He probably gets a lot of pussy with that brogue of his. But he hasn't got as much money as he says he does."

Rebecca laughed and gave Alvin a look of mock horror.

I didn't laugh.

"Alvin," I said. "It was a pleasure to meet you but I think I should be going. This is a getting little too X-rated for a nice girl from New Haven."

Rebecca and Wayne laughed nervously, but Alvin's smile was suddenly gone.

"Too X-rated?" he said. "What? They don't have pussy in New Haven?"

Pig.

"Thanks for everything," I said.

I gave Wayne a playful punch on the shoulder. Rebecca walked with me as far as the bar.

"That was awkward," she said.

I suddenly felt sick to my stomach. If it wasn't for the Ambien, I likely would have vomited. "I hope I haven't messed up my new job on the first day."

Rebecca smiled and shook her head.

"I should have warned you before we came," she said. "He's provocative. That's how he tests people. He thinks you see someone's real character more quickly if you make them uncomfortable."

"I hope I didn't flunk the test."

"I vouched for you."

"Thank you, Rebecca. You're like my guardian angel."

We were at the top of the stairs.

I put my empty glass down on a table and turned to go just as a couple came in. I stepped back, out of the way, and bumped someone behind me.

I turned and saw Declan standing there, frowning, holding two drinks, with a big fresh orange stain on his white shirt.

"Oh no," I said. "I'm so sorry."

"You're having a bad day for spills," said Rebecca, laughing.

"No problem," said Declan. "I thought I'd bring you a drink as a peace offering."

"I think I've had enough drinks," I said, feeling woozy. "I'm sorry I spilled your drink. Oh gosh."

"No problem," he said. "Let me walk you out."

I said good night to Rebecca, got some napkins from the bar, and gave them to Declan. He mopped at his shirt and followed me as I headed for the stairs.

"I wanted to apologize," he said. "I can't believe that I said you were, um, fuckable. This is why I don't usually go to parties. I'm a disaster. It's invariable and tedious."

I smiled at him.

"You know you could go to parties and just not say things like that, right?"

He looked pained but he was nodding.

"This is a work event, and that makes my comment doubly inappropriate. I hope you see I was being flip, not, ah, I don't know."

"Abusive?"

"Right."

"Thank you," I said. "Apology accepted."

I started down the stairs. He followed me.

"You still want some advice?" he said. "Real advice? I think I might be able to help you. I hadn't thought about it enough when I spoke."

"Don't worry," I said. "Your secret identity is safe with me. Good night! It was a pleasure to meet you. Sorry about spilling the drink."

I elbowed my way through the crowd to the exit. It was noisy and crowded.

He was still following me.

"Really," he said. "I want to help. It's an interesting challenge."

We stood on the sidewalk. He fiddled with his phone and handed it to me.

"Put your contacts in here," he said.

Hm. Okay. I typed in my Gmail address and cell phone number.

"That's kind of you," I said. "But I don't think I'll blow your @ShouldBObvious cover."

"Let me hail you a cab," he said, and he stepped out into the street, stuck his fingers in his mouth, and whistled, impressively. A taxi pulled up immediately from the corner cab stand.

He opened the door for me.

"Thank you." I reached out to shake his hand. "It really was very nice to meet you. I'm sorry about my temper tantrum and spilling your drink."

He stepped toward me and took me gently by the arm.

"I enjoyed all of it. Even the temper tantrum. Especially the temper tantrum. Reminded me not to be so full of myself."

He was standing very close to me. I looked up at him and felt woozy, in a good way. He took my hands in his, holding them lightly.

"I'll send you some notes. Or maybe we can get together for a wee chat."

I nodded up at him. He was so handsome.

"I'd like that."

I decided to give him a peck on the cheek. He turned his head, though, and I ended up kissing him on the lips. It was surprising and nice and lasted longer than either of us, I think, expected it to. I fought the urge to throw my arms around his neck, to pull him into the cab with me.

"Oh my," I said.

"Arg," he said and moved to kiss me again. I held him off.

"I've had too much to drink. I need to go home."

I looked over his shoulder to get away from his seductive, blue-eyed gaze.

Rebecca and Wayne were stepping out of the club together.

"Fuck," I said.

I pulled away from Declan and looked away. Did they see us kiss? Fuck. I dropped into the taxi and Declan followed me.

"Two stops, driver," he said.

"I'm going to First and Bedford," I said.

He put his arm around me.

"I'm in Park Slope. Why don't you pop up for a wee nightcap?"

I smiled at him.

"Not a chance."

# 19

I have now had three beers, which means I'm down to about $60, not that I care too much. I'm starting to feel pretty buzzed. And I'm glad to have finished recounting the story of the party.

The Lucky 7 is filling up. There are lots of tattoos and piercings and hipster beards.

I'm idly watching Pat and his bandmates—An Infinite Number of Monkeys—set up in a corner at the end of the bar.

All of a sudden a muscly, low-browed guy in a Rutgers University lacrosse jersey is next to me.

"Hey, can you help me and friends?" he says.

Well, hello, Douchebro.

He gestures at two other guys sitting at a high-top table by the door. "We're having an argument and we need a female opinion."

His name is James. He has a Jersey accent, a confident smile, and smells of horrible aftershave.

"I might be able to," I say. "I guess if I give you an opinion it would be a female opinion."

He tries to figure out if that's funny, gives up, and goes on with his spiel.

"So, our buddy Dave was supposed to come out with us tonight but he had a big fight with his girlfriend and bailed on us."

"Bummer."

"I know, right? Anyway, he just moved in with this girl, Julie. They're both third-year Rutgers, like us."

I make myself smile. I hate guys like James, but I came here to make friends.

"Everything was going great until she unpacks one of his boxes, finds a bunch of pictures of his ex. She blew a gasket."

The last bit sounded super New Jersey, like his real voice coming out by mistake. Blewagaskit.

"Wow."

"Yeah. So they're having a big fight and he blew off a night with the bros. She says—get this—he has to burn all the pictures or she's moving out."

I try to figure out how I am supposed to react. I think I'm supposed to find it fascinating instead of transparent and stupid.

"That's crazy!" I say. "So what's he going to do?"

"That's what we're trying to figure out, dude! That's what we're arguing about. I think she's loco. My bud Kevin thinks she's right. Jeff isn't sure. That's why we want to know what you think."

On the one hand, I suspect this is a made-up story to give him an excuse to talk to me. On the other hand, I need a way out of town. Was this guy headed up to Rutgers? Also, I have an opinion.

"You know what?" I say, giving him my best mischievous smile. "I think she sounds like a crazy girl. And I should know. I might be a crazy girl myself."

Douchebro loves this. He is my new best friend. The fact that I don't like him at all makes the whole getting-to-be-friends experience less appealing than I would like, and he keeps touching me, which I fucking hate, putting his hand on my arm, my knee, or my waist as we talk. He often stares at my breasts. I think, *Do women usually put up with this shit from you?*

But he tells me he's driving to Binghamton University in the morning, so that he can attend "an awesome kegger" his friend is having.

Oh my God! I go to Cornell! And BTW, it's near Binghamton.

I tell him my tale of woe about my friend Samantha's broken ankle and he says I can get a ride up with him and his bros tomorrow if I want. I should come to the kegger. It will be an epic party!

I suddenly like him a lot better, which means I have to listen to him tell stories about how great he is.

I find people like him impossibly irritating. I have to make it into a game to keep myself from laughing at his ludicrous self-praise.

"I was actually offered lacrosse scholarships at five schools, but Rutgers offered me the best deal," he says. "They were basically throwing money at me."

"You must be an awesome player."

Big smile. A point for me.

"I'm pretty good. If I didn't get hurt last year, we would have made the nationals. Coach begged me to play even though my knee was fucked up. He would have fucking blown me. Dude. He was desperate."

Ha ha! You're such an asshole.

"Get out." How could he think I would find this interesting?

"Wilson would shit if he knew that I fucked both of his daughters, in the same weekend, while he was off with the team, getting his ass kicked by Penn State."

"No way. Both of them?"

"Dude, yes way. One on Friday. The other on Saturday."

Dude. You're doing it wrong. You're not supposed to brag that you fucked sisters. That shows contempt for women, which we don't like.

"You're bad news!"

"Ha ha. Not really. I'm really loyal to my friends."

"Are you?" Batting my eyes. Looking at him admiringly.

"Oh yeah."

Suddenly all serious.

"I really look out for them."

Wheels turning in his little brain. Think of an example!

"My buddy Jeff, the one with the pimples, I'm always trying to get him laid. I'm an excellent wingman. And dude needs the help. He's a great guy, but he's got bad acne, and a small unit, but I do everything I can to get his dinky stinky."

Dinky stinky.

Piece of shit. Piece of shit. Piece of shit.

# 20

I was a little hungover and a little nervous to go to work the morning after Alvin's party. I felt uncomfortable about my showdown with Alvin and embarrassed that Rebecca and Wayne may have seen Declan and me kissing.

Rebecca was supernice, though, greeting me with a smile. She didn't mention the kiss, said that she hoped I'd had a good party, said Alvin is a handful and not to give that business another thought. If I ever feel weird about anything, let her know.

Wayne was acting strange.

"Hey, party girl," he said, too loud, with a too-big smile. "How you feeling?"

He definitely saw me kiss Declan.

"Not bad," I said, cheerily. "How are you?"

"Awesome!"

I tried not to think about him and got down to business. I started to turn more of my social media sock puppets into cheese enthusiasts, exchanging cheese messages with Linda and sharing links, generating followers, building cheesementum.

I was going to switch gears, start doing some research, but first I checked my phone.

I had a new text message from a number I didn't recognize.

How's your head?

Not bad. Who's asking?

You spilled a drink on me.

Oh hi! :-) Want the truth?

Truth.

Head is bad, but working hard and stoically at cheese-
related social mediafying. Did the stain come out?

Threw the shirt in a bucket of water, rubbed
it with salt. Will drop it at the cleaners.

Send me the bill.

Or give it to you.

Okay. :-) When?

I should have been coy, but I wanted to see him again.

Not sure. May have to go out of town on business
this week. But I have something for you.

???

Super secret.

Tell.

Promise not to tell where it came from?

Cross my heart.

K. xoxo

Then he texted me a download link. I clicked on it, and it opened in my phone's web browser. There was a file called ch33z3lov3rz.zip.

I downloaded it. My phone jammed and I had to wait impatiently while it rebooted, then had to reenter my password before it would restart.

The file was a database, with a long list of Facebook addresses, more than three hundred thousand of them.

Facebook assigns each user a unique signature. There are thousands of John Smiths. They all want to have their user name as John Smith, so Facebook assigns each of them a name, beginning with John Smith, followed by a string of numbers.

If you have someone's Facebook address, you can send them mail, sign them up to groups, and use utilities to search their profiles to fish for contact info, group membership, and lots of other information.

Declan had sent me a csv file with thousands of Facebook addresses. So many names! If they were cheese lovers, then I could get all the clicks.

Ka-ching!

I picked a name at random—CarlSagoya863654—and poked at his profile. He was a chef at a small restaurant in Olympia, Oregon, and a bit of a cheese nut. So was SarahMcMaster802388, of Portland, Maine, and ElinorVaux50938, of Lincoln, Nebraska.

All I had to do now was find a subtle way to spam them all. There were so many names I could try some experiments. I could send a thousand cheese nuts a message and invite a thousand others to join a group, then see which tactic was more successful. Then I'd refine the pitch and try variations on thousands of more cheese nuts and find the approach that would maximize the sale of disgusting dairy products.

I had to text Declan back.

OMFG. I can't believe you sent me that file. TY TY TY :-D.

He replied immediately.

What file?

You know what file.

I don't know what you're talking about.

Yes you do. Oh wait. No you don't. Sorry. Wrong number.

That's right.

I want to buy you dinner to thank you.

For what?

I want to hear about your antique Irish guns.

Okay then. I may have to travel today.
Will let you know when I'm free.

I owe you one.

A big one. And I intend to collect.

:-)

I met with Craig after lunch, told him I had figured out an approach for Cheese of the Month that I was sure would work. I needed him to set me up to track the clicks and conversions.

He asked me for my plan, but I was coy. He agreed to let me loose for a few days.

I was at my desk, happily running search queries through the list when Kevin showed up.

"I hear you're ready to make some sales," he said. "Let's get you started."

He watched while I filled out the forms to set up a conversion-tracking account, typed in some authorization codes, and soon we were waiting for the program to respond, which took a while. A wheel went around on my laptop screen.

*You like standing over my shoulder, don't you?* I thought.

"Did you have fun last night?" I asked.

"Fun? I guess. I was only there to talk to Alvin about a project."

"Cool. Something interesting?"

"You could say that, Walker," he said. "Walker. What kind of name is that?"

"Standard-issue American surname, I guess. From English, for one who walks."

He laughed.

"You have a sense of humor. Where you from in Connecticut?"

"New Haven. Well, the suburbs."

"I went to Newtown this spring," he said. "Sort of a research trip."

"That's where I'm actually from. I just say I'm from New Haven because people know it. And it's where we did our shopping and stuff."

"And it's more cosmopolitan. Like you."

The wheel finally stopped turning. I was set up.

"Thanks, Kevin!"

"That's what they pay me for, Walker."

I got up to go to the bathroom, so that he would finally have to leave.


By the end of the day, I'd sent out three cheese pitches to three different groups of five thousand cheese lovers and was ready to track the results.

It was exciting to watch the clicks add up, and I whooped and bounced up and down in my chair when I got my first conversion.

Wayne, who was the only person in the office by then, looked up from his desk.

"Sell some cheese?"

"I did!" I said and got up and did a little cheese victory dance. "My first conversion."

"Congratulations!" he said. "I have yet to drive any traffic to Bowhunting.com. If I buy you a drink, will you tell me your secrets?"

"I would love that, but I'm supposed to go to an event with a friend tonight."

I looked at my phone to check the time.

"Shit, I'm already late. Rain check?"

"Sure!" he said, with a bright smile, but he looked disappointed.

# 21

After An Infinite Number of Monkeys finish setting up their gear, Pat finally comes back to the bar to get a beer.

*Save me from Douchebro. Save me from Douchebro.*

"So," he says. "Are you really looking for a ride to Cornell tomorrow?"

"I am. I guess. I mean, I don't really want to take the bus. I hate the bus."

"We have a gig in Scranton tomorrow night."

"Wow," I say. "Do you have room in the van for me?"

"I don't know," he says. "Have you ever worked as a roadie?"

I shake my head.

"I don't see myself carrying amps and stuff."

"No?"

Fuck it.

"I see myself as more of a groupie than a roadie."

Me: Straight face.

Him: Double take.

Ha!

Me: "Just fucking with you."

Him, leering cartoonishly at my cleavage: "Too bad. I keep hoping we'll get groupies."

"Hm," I say. "Maybe you're not good enough."

They aren't, I soon learn.

They are thrashy but muddy sounding, with a lousy singer, doing a bunch of originals that all sounded like variations on the same lame Wolf Parade song.

I watch them, start on Beer 5, and daydream about breaking up the band and helping Pat start a new, better band, which would deepen his feelings for his awesome, supportive girlfriend, the successful social media entrepreneur.

I don't notice that someone is repeatedly calling my fake name until Douchebro puts his hand on my arm.

"Lisa," he is saying. "Didn't you hear me?"

"Sorry! The music is too loud."

"I know! And not very good."

"Terrible," I say, and we laugh together.

"So are you serious about wanting a ride upstate?" he says. "Because I'm going in the morning."

"Oh my God, that would be great. I just can't face the bus."

"I'll take you if you want. Where you staying?"

"I'm supposed to go back to my friend's place in Hoboken."

"Cool. Want a shot?"

"Sure! I mean, no. What kind?"

# 22

I was late to meet my friend, Francis, at the Guggenheim, so I texted him as I rushed to the 4 train. I couldn't resist checking my cheese stats and was thrilled to see I had four conversions since leaving the office.

Oh happy day!

I stewed through the subway ride without internet. I checked my phone as I went up the subway steps—five more conversions. Yes!

I couldn't find Francis when I got into the big open space at the Guggenheim, and found myself wandering among the prosperous-looking Upper East Side animal lovers. Everyone seemed to know one another but me. There were a lot of happy squeals of surprise, cheek-kissing, sotto voce gossip. I felt underdressed and anxious. I decided to discreetly pop an Ambien and look for a drink.

Then I spotted Francis. He was chatting with a slim, good-looking Asian guy, both of them drinking champagne and laughing. They wore tight Humane Society T-shirts. Both of them looked like they spent a lot of time at the gym.

"There you are!" said Francis.

We kissed and he scooped a flute of champagne from a passing server.

"I want you to meet Jason," he said. "Jason, this is Candace, my unreliable but gorgeous and hilarious friend. Jason volunteers for the Humane Society, at their East Village shelter. He was just trying to convince me to adopt a kitty."

Francis and I have been friends since we met at a film class at NYU. Neither of us discovered a talent for filmmaking, but we discovered a shared love of animals, black-and-white melodramas, and flirting with cute guys.

"Oh, Francis. I don't think you should get a kitty. You can barely look after yourself."

"Shush," he said and put his finger to my lips. "Don't tell Jason anything bad about me."

"I have a feeling you'll both want kitties after I show them to you," said Jason. "You could always foster one for a week or two, see how it goes. But don't blame me if you fall in love."

"Shut up!" I said. "You have kitties here?"

Jason nodded.

"Fair warning, though. They're really really cute. You're going to want one. They're upstairs. We like to show the donors what we do, hit them in the heartstrings. Want to see?"

"Take me to them now!" I said.

First, I made them pose for a picture with me, clinking glasses, and tweeted, instagrammed, and snapchatted it to promote the event. Then we went up the circular ramp to the second floor, where volunteers and supporters were fussing around a hamper of kittens.

We wedged our way into the group and Jason pulled a tiny little calico from the hamper.

"This is Rose," he said. "But you can change her name when you adopt her!"

Rose was so cute! She was calm in Jason's arms, looking around, licking her little nose. She meowed once, and Jason started to pet her behind her ears and she licked at his hand and started purring.

"Hello, nice lady," I said.

I closed my eyes and told myself that I was in no position to look after a cat.

We passed Rose back and forth and took turns snapping pics of each other holding her. I put her on the ground and dangled my earbuds for her to bat around, and another kitten, Smokey, wanted to get in on the fun. I got some great pictures of the two of them frolicking.

Eventually, I left Jason and Francis to play daddy and daddy with the kittens and went to find the bathroom.

While I peed, I checked my phone. I had sold five more Cheese of the Month Club subscriptions. Ka-ching!

And I had a new text from Declan!

Are you ready to do me a favor now?

Sure.

You won't want to do it but you kind of have to.

What is it?

If you don't do what I ask, you'll be sorry.

???

When you're finished peeing, don't pull your panties back up.
Put them in your purse. I want you to walk around without them.

I dropped the phone. How did he know I was peeing?

I picked the phone back up and wiped it with some toilet paper. Ew. Bathroom floor.

There was a fresh message.

Do what I say.

You're being creepy. Like, really creepy. Stop it.

Don't pull your panties up. I want you to
walk around with no panties. Do it.

I don't think this is funny. I don't like this.

I closed the chat window.

I sat there and tried to figure it out. He had to be at the Guggenheim. He must have seen me go into the bathroom. Maybe he came to the event after I tweeted about it. He must be the creepiest creep in the history of creeps. It was hard to reconcile the sweet Irish boy I had kissed the night before with the freak on my phone. Wow. Just wow.

I decided to text Francis.

Francis, don't hate me but I need you to do me a favor.

What is it, darling?

I just got a supercreepy text message from someone I think is at this event.

I remembered that I had a picture of Declan. I texted it to Francis.

He's cute.

I think he's a weirdo. Do you mind watching for him near the bathrooms? I'm afraid he might be spying on me.

Affirmative. Deploying.

I finished up in the bathroom, washed my hands and fixed my makeup, and checked my phone.

Francis reported back.

007 here. No sign of creepy hot guy.

Are you out there?

Agent Jason and I are surveilling the door.

Be right out.

They were waiting for me, leaning against a railing. There was no sign of Declan.

"FML," I said. "That was weird AF."

I showed them the chat and started telling them about meeting Declan the night before. Someone came out of the men's room just as I started and the sound of the door made me jump.

"I think I need to get out of here," I said. "I'm totally freaked out."

"Of course," said Francis. "I've had enough kittens anyway."

"Thank you, sweetie. I don't want to leave here alone."

Jason had to stay to look after the kitties. We went back for one last look.

Rose and Smokey were curled up together in the hamper, their heads on each other's paws. I had to take one more picture. It was really cute.

I tweeted it with the text: These little cuties need someone to look after them!

Then my phone died. That was weird, since the battery should have had some life left, but it shut down and wouldn't reboot.

# 23

When An Infinite Number of Monkeys finish their first set, Pat comes back to the bar. Douchebro is with his friends.

I like Pat a lot better, especially after he stops making terrible music, and I start flirting fairly outrageously, asking him about his life as a rock star and letting him know that I like him, talking fast, touching him, trying to make him like me.

I'm getting a little drunk, and starting to get carried away. When he leaves to go to the bathroom, I give my head a shake. I have to keep my eyes on the prize: a ride out of town.

Then, suddenly, James is also at the bar. When Pat comes back, I'm forced to introduce them to each other. They shake hands, then things get awkward.

"Hey, bro," says James. "Cool music. Awesome hobby. I bet chicks like it."

Pat smiles.

"I like it," he says. "I don't know how awesome it sounded tonight, though. Sounded kind of muddy. You play?"

"No," James says. "I play lacrosse."

He taps the logo on his shirt and flexes his big chest muscles.

God. He's awful.

"Cool," says Pat. "That's the one like field hockey, right?"

Douchebro scowls, then laughs and puts his hand on my shoulder, trying to demonstrate ownership.

I give him a weak smile and turn and make an isn't-this-awkward face at Pat.

"That's the one," says James. "It's not for everyone. It's a bit rough. How you doing, bro? You look tired."

Pat smiles again.

"I am tired. But it's time for me to play again. See you around."

He winks at me and says, "See you later," then heads for the stage.

James takes this as his cue to take Pat's spot and starts to really lay it on. He touches me a lot and keeps giving me these little spiels, telling stories designed to show what a good guy he is. It is increasingly awful, but I play along, and he buys more shots. Every now and then I look up and watch Pat play.

James starts to talk about his place, which is nearby, and suggests I could crash on his couch so that we could get an early start in the morning.

"I don't know," I say. "My friend might worry. I have no phone."

"I can text her," he says, taking out his phone. "What's her number?"

"Eight. Two. I can't remember. Shit. Eight. Two. Four. I have to pee. Can you watch my stuff for me?"

# 24

Francis and I had a drink at a little French place a few blocks west of the Guggenheim, and I told him the whole story of Declan, the cheese list, and the creepy texts. He theorized with me about it, trying unsuccessfully to figure out how Declan could have known I was in the bathroom. Then he walked me to my subway platform and waved good-bye as I started the long ride back to my messy little apartment in Williamsburg.

When I got home, I plugged in my phone and it immediately booted up. The battery indicator showed that it was a quarter charged, which I couldn't figure out.

I had a fresh text message from Declan.

I warned you.

WTF?

I also had a bunch of emails from Twitter, telling me that my cute kitty pic had been retweeted by a ton of randos.

I clicked on Twitter to look and opened the most recent retweet, which was prefaced with "I volunteer!"

When the picture opened, I felt like I had been punched in the stomach.

Somehow, I hadn't tweeted the cute kitty pic, but a topless selfie.

Oh no. Oh no. Oh no.

I jumped to my feet and shook the phone.

No. No. No.

I could not have tweeted the world a topless pic! I did, though. There it was.

I'd taken the picture last Christmas, when JFXBF was with his parents in Indianapolis and texting me about how much he missed me. I was missing him, and feeling sexy, so I took a nudie shot of myself in the bathroom mirror and sent it to him. I was smiling seductively, trying to look pouty, with my boobs stuck out.

OMFG.

I dropped to my knees and started to sob. I had to repeatedly wipe the tears out of my eyes to page through the tweets.

Someone called @amateurhawties, who had 180,000 followers, had retweeted my picture.

I had a bunch of direct messages from friends letting me know that I'd tweeted a topless picture of myself, and a bunch of lewd tweets directed at me, mostly offering to look after my cuties.

There were 138 retweets, some terribly crude, some without comment, a few that were sarcastic or insulting, mocking the size of my breasts. What was wrong with people?

It was like a nightmare, except that I was awake, hunched over my phone, sweating and pinching my lips and cursing.

I closed my eyes and tried to clear my head.

I needed to get rid of the tweet, explain that it was sent in error, and reconcile myself to the fact that no matter what I did, my topless selfie would be out there forever.

I'd have to put in some serious time on search engine optimization, so that this pic wouldn't be the first thing you'd get if you googled me. Jess would maybe help me. Oh God. How could I have been so stupid?

I deleted the tweet and sent a new one: Photo in last tweet sent by mistake! Apologies! :-( These are the cuties I meant to send. I uploaded the cat picture and checked the tweet immediately to make sure I'd sent the right one.

Then I replied to all the emails and DMs expressing concern, explaining that I'd sent the topless selfie by mistake. Then I checked Twitter again. Some jerk called @BlackPillForever had tweeted a screencap of my topless shot, making fun of me for deleting it.

Attention whore gets second thoughts!

He also tweeted a link to my Facebook profile and LinkedIn profile.

I checked his profile. His avatar was an old black-and-white picture of Zorro, with his mask and black hat. His biography said "Supreme gentleman with no Stacy."

I paged through his tweets, which were full of vicious attacks on female celebrities and weird acronyms and slang that I didn't know or want to know.

I blocked him, blocked @amateurhawties, blocked all the weirdos who'd retweeted the pic with rude comments, and started to think about how I could get past this.

I realized I'd better send an email explaining the situation to Craig and Rebecca.

I was starting the painful task when I got a new text message.

It was from Declan.

Nice little titties. Small put perky.

I had decided not to reply to his texts anymore. I stared at it, trying to understand how the nice Irish boy had turned so creepy, when another text popped up.

I told you you'd be sorry.

I blocked the number and knuckled down to hours of social media damage control.

# 25

At the end of the night at the Lucky 7, Douchebro and I are at the bar, him buying Jägerbombs, bragging to me, his hand on my ass. The band is done. The place is emptying out.

Pat comes by to wave good-bye, and I see that he's leaving with his arm around a girl. She's a stringy-haired pale girl with a tatted muffin top.

*Why did you flirt with me, you jerk? Hope you're happy.*

I turn away for a minute to watch them leave—without a backward glance—but I keep an eye on Douchebro in the mirrored pillar next to me.

The minute I turn, I see him drop something in my shot. He's trying to roofie me!

His plan is obvious. I'd get all groggy and wake up the next morning on his couch with no memory of being used as a sex toy all night.

What a pig. What a fucking pig.

I turn and smile at him.

"Hey, sexy," I say.

He smiles down at me and squeezes my ass.

I put my hand on his bicep and squeeze it.

"You must work out a lot."

"Not that much, really. I've always been strong."

He thinks I'm buying his shit.

"You probably have girls throwing themselves at you all the time, don't you? Big man on campus."

He shakes his head. "Not really." But smiling so I'd know that women were, in fact, constantly throwing themselves at him.

"Liar," I say. And I drop my hand from his bicep to his chest.

"No, really. They're not."

I have to stop myself from laughing. I believe him. Women are definitely not throwing themselves at this guy.

"I know that's a lie," I say. "Well, I'm not going to be another one of them. I'm not easy."

"I know. I can tell a classy girl when I meet one."

I suddenly launch myself drunkenly at him, planting a kiss on his disgusting protruding lips.

I put my right hand on his belt buckle. With my left hand, I grope for the two Jägerbombs on the bar.

I brush the front of his pants with the back of my hand. Ugh!

Desperate times. Desperate measures.

I keep my tongue in his mouth while I slide his Jägerbomb closer to me. I slide mine toward him. I can feel his penis harden against my hand. It is so gross. I will need Purell after this.

"Fuck," he says, when I pull away. "You better be careful. You're going to get me all excited."

"I'm sorry. I promise I'll be good. I'm a good girl, really. Time for me to go to my friend's house. Yup. Got to call a cab."

"Wait. We've got to do these last Jägers first."

I look down, as if surprised to see them in front of us on the bar.

"Oh my God! Shots!"

"Shots shots shots shots!" he chants.

We toast and drink. He is trying to hide his smile.

# 26

I was in the office an hour early, waiting for Kevin, jittery from about a bucket of coffee, snappy, exhausted, and hyperalert.

I'd slept for about an hour, although I spent hours in bed, with my eyes closed, trying to sleep. I eventually took two Ambiens but even then I couldn't stop thinking about how that photo would follow me for the rest of my life.

No matter what I did, anybody I ever met could check out a picture of my breasts. Also, by reacting the way I did, and blaming myself, they'd believe I'd tweeted the picture myself as a way of getting attention. Many anonymous assholes had already concluded that's what I'd done. And lots of people, including my bosses, my family, guys I'd want to go out with, might think that was true.

My brain entered an awful feedback loop, thinking about my situation and dwelling on how awful it was.

I wrote and deleted a half-dozen clarifying tweets, and I emailed Francis for help. He advised me to do nothing right away.

When I finally managed to do a little clear thinking, I realized that someone must have hacked my phone. It had to be Declan. When I opened that file he sent me, I had to enter my password. He must have hacked me then.

I decided to email Kevin.

**To:** Kevin Reisenger
**From:** Candace Walker

**Date:** June 20, 2018, 12:38 a.m.
**Subject:** So, I have a little problem.

Someone seems to have hacked my phone and tweeted a private picture from my account. Can you meet me early tomorrow to unhack my phone?

He replied almost immediately.

**To:** Candace Walker
**From:** Kevin Reisenger
**Date:** June 20, 2018, 12:44 a.m.
**Subject:** So, I have a little problem.

That's terrible, Walker. Do you have any idea who did this? How do you know you were hacked?
    I can meet you at 8 a.m. so we get your phone cleared for the start of the workday.

I realized on the way to the subway that I wasn't sure how to handle the whole thing. I needed Jess's advice. I texted her as I waited for the L train.

> Sis, I have a little problem I'd like to talk to you about. Someone hacked my phone and tweeted a topless pic. If you have a minute this morning, I'd like to talk to you about next steps.

I managed to get a seat and settled in to fret. I spent the trip being bumped by a squat Hispanic woman standing in front of me. Her gray potbelly, peeking out from under her cheap polyester tank top, was right in my face. I felt irritated by her and looked up at her haggard, acne-scarred face. She looked back at me and I quickly turned my eyes back to my knees. Her face was so forlorn, so sad, as if she had never known love in her life, not from her parents or a lover or a friend.

Involuntarily, I started to imagine her life as an unwanted child in Mexico or Puerto Rico or some other poor hot place, living with a father who didn't love her. I didn't like thinking about that, and I didn't want to look into those sad black eyes again.

When we got to Union Square, we returned to cell service, and I had a text from Jess.

Call me.

I called her from the platform.

"Hey," she said, quietly and flatly.

"So, it seems bad," I said.

"I found the tweet. How did it happen?"

"I'm not sure. I think I got phished. I was at an event with Francis last night. I got some weird, harassing messages from this guy, Declan. I wouldn't do what he asked. Then my phone went dead. When I got home, I rebooted the phone and the tweet was up."

"Then you tweeted that it was a mistake. Was it a mistake? Did you do it or were you hacked?"

"I was hacked."

"How sure are you?"

"I don't know. Pretty sure."

"Pretty sure. Well, the answer's in the phone. You need to get it to your IT department, tell them it was hacked, get them to check it out."

"I know. I have an appointment at eight with the IT guy."

"Tell him you were hacked. Don't tell him you're not sure."

"Okay."

"I have to be in a meeting that started five minutes ago. Are you okay?"

"Yes. Stressed."

"Keep it bottled up. Let it out later. Be professional. K?"

"K."

"Gotta go. Talk later. You got this."

———

I was at my desk, typing up some thoughts to give Craig on the whole mess when Kevin arrived, carrying a big coffee and looking dumb in baggy jeans and an OBEY T-shirt.

"Hey, Walker," he said. "How's it going?"

"Terrible. Someone stole a . . . private . . . picture of me and put it on the internet. Really bad."

He kind of froze in his tracks.

"Right. That is bad."

"My phone was hacked. Someone sent me harassing texts, then my phone went dead. When it came back to life, he had tweeted out a topless pic of me."

He headed for his little windowless office, which was full of shelves loaded with computer parts and spools of wire. I followed him, speaking at an overcaffeinated pace, telling him that I hoped he could find out who had hacked me.

"On Twitter you said that you sent the pic by mistake."

"I didn't. I was freaking out when I sent that. I was hacked."

"How sure are you?" he said, easing into his office chair.

"Really sure," I said. "I tweeted the kitty pic. I wouldn't tweet that other pic. Never. No way. Why?"

"It was on your phone? That topless pic?"

"I guess. Does that matter? I mean, I suppose it was in the cloud. It's still private. People aren't supposed to steal your private pictures, right?"

"I can't tell anything until I look at your phone." He held up his hand to get me to stop talking, then extended it.

I gave him the phone and continued to explain what I thought might have happened.

He plugged it into his Mac and then waited. Nothing happened.

He fussed with it.

"Was it powered on a minute ago?" he asked.

"Yes, it was at, like, 80 percent."

"It doesn't seem to be now. We might have to wait for it to power up."

It eventually rebooted and then it had a funny screen with the Apple logo and timer bar.

He looked up at me.

"Did you mean to wipe your phone?" he asked.

"What?"

"This phone is being wiped. As we speak. It's just finishing. Did you wipe it?"

"What? No. No! I don't know how to do that. I just handed it to you. It was . . . normal, like, a minute ago."

He looked down at it and up at me.

"Well, it's not normal now. It's been bricked. Either you did it, or someone hacked it, and they did it."

"They can do that?"

"If the phone was compromised, yes. They could do it remotely at any time. Maybe they decided to wipe the phone before I could plug it in and download data that would have showed their footprints."

"But how would they know you were going to do that?"

He looked away, sighed, and looked back at me.

"If they turned on the mic, they could have heard us talking."

I stared blankly at him.

"They can do that?"

"They can do that."

I sat down on the desk.

*Maybe that's how Declan knew I was peeing,* I thought. *He could hear it. Creepy!*

"Someone can use my phone like a bug?"

"Yeah. Depending on who it is, and what they can do, they might even be able to do it when the phone's powered down."

"What?"

"It depends on the capability of whoever hacked your phone. It would take me about ten minutes to set up your phone so I could hear everything when it's on. The NSA or Mossad could do it so they could hear what you're doing when the phone's powered off."

"I don't like that."

"The point is, I don't really know what they could do. For all I know, they could turn it into a bat and have it fly back to their office at night."

"What?"

"I mean I don't know what they can do. They can do lots of things."

"More than listen to me?"

"They can listen to you, know your location at all times, know when you go to sleep, when you wake up, see all your texts and, uh, pictures. Did you have other private pictures on your phone?"

Shit. Likely. I hadn't thought of that. I wasn't going to tell Creeper Kevin that.

"They would have everything that was on my phone?"

"Sure. If it's compromised, it's compromised. Same goes for any accounts you used on your phone. Twitter. Facebook. Instagram. Snapchat. Gmail. It's best to assume it's all compromised."

"Fuck. I'd better change all my passwords."

"Let me see if I can find anything on this. Do you know what a Faraday cage is?"

I did not.

"It's used to shield a phone from electromagnetic waves, including radio waves. Ideally, if your phone gets hacked, you put it in a Faraday cage, get it to a shielded room, hook it to a computer, and you can see what the hackers were up to. They can't wipe it then."

"Do you have one?" I asked him.

"No. I'd use tinfoil, like the cops do. When they arrest gangsters, they wrap their phones in tinfoil, so they can't be remotely wiped. You got to use a lot, wrap it good."

"Thanks," I said. "I'll keep that in mind."

# 27

Jess got roofied by some scumbag in her sophomore year—no assault, thank goodness, because her friends realized that she was acting weird and hustled her home, but she had a total blackout, which was scary. So for a while I was obsessed with roofies and read a bunch of horror stories online.

It takes about twenty minutes for the drug to kick in, after which the drugged party gets groggy and suggestible. I want that to happen to Douchebro, but not while he is behind the wheel.

My plan is to make him wait in the bar for a bit, but as soon as we down the last Jägerbomb, he is raring to go.

"So were you serious about the couch?" I ask him, touching his arm. "I really would love a drive tomorrow, and I'd rather not go back to Hoboken tonight."

"Totally," he says. "No prob. It's a comfortable couch. We can have a nightcap, then I'll tuck you in."

"Are you sure?" I ask. "I'm pretty tired. I mean, I don't want you to get the wrong idea. I may seem like a crazy girl, but I'm actually pretty conservative about some things."

Translation: You're not getting laid.

"Oh yeah!" he says. "No problem. I'm tired myself."

Ha. He thinks I'll be drugged and compliant within half an hour. I hate him.

It feels strange to present as relaxed and drunk, when I am actually furiously angry.

"Should we do one more shot?" I ask. "No. Wait. You have to drive, don't you? Are you all right to drive?"

He is keen to get me out of there.

"I'm fine. I've only had a few. No problem. But I shouldn't have any more. You ready to leave?"

"Yes," I say. "But first I have to pee."

I kill five minutes sitting in a stall. I'll just have to keep him occupied in the parking lot for five minutes before the roofie kicks in.

When I get back to the bar, he smiles at me, looking drunk but not drugged.

"There you are," he says and kisses me. Fuck.

I hope this works. I really do not enjoy touching this guy.

He pulls me close and puts his tongue in my mouth. I squirm but let him kiss me. Gross. Then the bartender breaks it up. I'm sure he's disappointed to see me in the arms of Douchebro rather than him.

"Guys," he says. "We're closing. You don't have to go home, but you can't stay here."

There is a crush of drunken hipsters at the door.

Oh shit. One of the people trying to get out is Irena, an irritating Russian Jersey girl I knew from a class at NYU.

The second I catch sight of her, our eyes lock and she smiles in recognition.

"Candace!" she says. "Hey!"

"No, I'm Lisa."

She frowns in drunken confusion.

"Candace?"

"I don't know you."

I grab James's hand and pull him back into the bar. There's another exit, and I tug him toward it. I don't think he heard my exchange with Irena.

"Come on," I say. "This is bullshit. Let's go this way."

He follows me.

# 28

I found Rebecca and Craig in his office. They were sitting around the coffee table where they had interviewed me for the job.

I stuck my head in the door and smiled.

"Guys, sorry to interrupt, but I have an, um, issue I'd like to fill you in on."

"Sure," said Rebecca. "What's up?"

I sat on one of the chairs and put my Mac on the coffee table.

I had made a quick PowerPoint presentation, explaining that I'd been hacked, and was taking steps to mitigate the situation.

The last screen had a picture of me shrugging and the text: Likely negative impact on SoSol = zero.

What could they say? I had it under control.

I quickly pivoted to my cheese success, flipping through slides showing the numbers. I had forty-eight conversions and revealed my plan to top one thousand in the next few days.

I showed how I had used different strategies with different groups and tracked the response rate. I followed up with how I intended to refine the pitch with two more test groups before blasting it wide and sitting back to enjoy the cheese harvest.

"Wow," said Craig. "If you're right, this is going to earn us some money. Good for you!"

I grinned. "Yay me!"

Rebecca asked, "So how did you find these cheese lovers?"

I had thought about lying, telling them that I'd harvested addresses, but I was afraid they'd ask me to replicate the technique, and I couldn't.

"I managed to get my hands on a list of cheese lovers. From a friend."

I could see Rebecca was composing a follow-up question, but Craig clapped his hands together.

"You used your initiative," he said.

I decided to feed him some of his own bullshit.

"I'm matching customers with a service they didn't even know they wanted. This is the kind of thing social does way better than traditional advertising."

"The potential is huge," he said.

"I find it really exciting. I can't wait to take what I've learned from this and apply it to something more interesting."

"Hm," he said. "I might have something in mind for you."

He glanced at Rebecca, who looked displeased.

"We haven't got it sorted out yet," she said.

"No. But I want to give Candace something to think about."

Rebecca turned to me.

"You'll have to promise to keep quiet about this until Alvin gets the contract signed," she said.

I nodded enthusiastically. "I promise."

Craig smiled.

"We're very close to a deal with WordUp," he said. "It's modeled on our arrangements with Cheese of the Month and Bowhunting.com. We only get paid for the conversions we bring them. The idea is that they're outsourcing their social media marketing, so they can focus on the customer experience."

"Wow," I said. "Just wow."

WordUp was a new advertising-driven online publishing portal aimed at mobile phone users. The idea was to feed texts to commuters who want to read—mostly genre fiction—on the bus or subway. Legacy publishing was trying to sell them books. WordUp was giving them stories, all for free, betting that they could make enough money through clickthroughs to make it pay.

I had applied for a job there and got nothing but an automatically generated email thanking me for my interest. I so wanted to be part of it.

"I think you should get first crack at WordUp," said Craig. "You'll have to be more careful to get approval for branding and messages, since we can expect WordUp to track what we're doing more closely than the cheese people, but I like your approach."

"I really really would love to work on WordUp. It's such a paradigm shifter, potentially. And I get it. I love books. My degree is in literature."

"We need to talk with Alvin," said Rebecca.

"Right," said Craig. "I just want to let you know what we're working on, get you thinking about. Don't talk to anyone else about it."

"And keep focused on Cheese of the Month for now," said Rebecca. "Let's see how those conversion numbers go."

I promised I wouldn't breathe a word to a soul and expressed enthusiasm for continued cheese work.

Back at my desk, I entered social media damage control mode for a while. I blocked some people discussing my topless selfie on Twitter and sent out a few social media tweets, to remind people that I was not an amateur hawtie.

I googled myself and discovered that my topless selfie was enjoying a second life on a Reddit forum, where a lively conversation was taking place about me. Some anonymous posters were convinced that I had posted it on purpose. Some of them thought it was especially pathetic, considering that my breasts were so small. In spite of myself, I found that hurtful.

Most pathetic were confused guys defending me by saying I should feel free to share a picture of my breasts. The worst was an argument between a guy who said I deserved to get raped and another guy who said I wasn't hot enough to rape.

It made me so furious. Who were all these horrible men?

I thought about replying, writing an acid open letter mocking them, or maybe engaging with one of them, humiliating him on Twitter, and then screencapping it, putting it online, hoping it went viral, but I decided not to. Whatever credit I earned in the social media world would inevitably lead to even more people googling my topless self. Did it matter? Everyone I knew would see the stupid picture at some point.

I researched Reddit's policies around inadvertently released selfies and sent them an email asking them to remove the picture and the discussion forum, which I copied to Jess.

I wanted to start working on a campaign for WordUp, but first I needed to move some cheese. I wrote two slightly different spam pitches for two groups of five thousand cheese lovers, sent them, and then checked my sock puppets.

Linda had been pumping Cheese of the Month with scheduled tweets and Facebook messages.

Irene Winslow, the Cheese of the Month proprietor, had sent her a cheerful message on Facebook thanking her for her support!

Linda sent her back a chatty message, telling her that she was friends with me and that I was working hard to make the project work.

"It's really helping," Irene replied immediately. "I can't believe how well it's going this week!"

# 29

James is parked on a dark, empty side street, which is good. I hustle him along, my arm in his, telling him how nice he is to let me sleep on his couch but warning him that he shouldn't expect anything, trying to act like a drunk college girl. I'm looking over my shoulder for that fuckface Irena, who had to be sure that it was me she saw and is likely now talking to the police.

James keeps trying to stop to grope me, but I keep him moving, thinking, *Please, roofie, do your stuff! Please drug this muscle-bound bro.*

When we get to his car, a tacky yellow Mustang, he's still talking pretty clearly, still sounding drunk but not drugged.

"There's my girl," he says. He pats the car trunk affectionately and presses the unlock button on his keychain.

"Awesome," I say. "Your car is so cool!"

I need a few more minutes. I can't let him drive. He'll pass out and kill us both.

"God," I say. "I'm feeling kind of . . ."

I stop on the sidewalk and put my hand on my head.

"You're just tired," he says. "Hop in."

"I don't know. I think I might need to . . ."

I turn to a wall and lean against it, smooshing my face against the bricks.

"So tired," I say.

"You're fine," he says and puts his hand on my back.

Oh fuck.

"You're going to be fine."

He rubs my shoulders. I can feel how powerful his hands are. They're disgusting.

I freeze. He'll leave me alone if I freeze.

"I wanted you from the first moment I saw you," he says, and his kneading slows and becomes rhythmic. It's his idea of foreplay.

I am inert as he rubs me. He presses his big, muscle-bound leg between mine and starts to lightly scratch my back.

I think about running. I think about screaming. I don't do anything.

Suddenly I can feel him erect, pressing against my behind.

"No," I say. "Don't. Wait."

"Don't worry. It's all fine. I'm going to take care of you."

Then his mouth is on my neck, and I am trapped by 250 pounds of steroid-pumped Jersey bro. He sucks at me.

I struggle to control my rising sense of panic. He wraps his arms around me and grabs my breasts roughly. Wow. He's going for it. My heart thumps. I am going to have to run for it. Except he's an athlete and can catch me in about ten seconds.

Maybe I should make myself vomit, or pee myself, or poop myself, desperate anti-rape techniques I learned about at college.

"I'm going to thuck you so hard," he says and slides his hand inside my bra.

I feel like a trapped thing. Wait. Did he say *thuck*?

I wriggle, try to push myself off the wall but he's too heavy.

"What are you going to do to me?" I ask him.

"I'm going to take you home and thuck the thucking shit off you."

His voice is slurred. It's working. Oh please, let it work.

I manage to turn around to face him. His arms drop to his side. He stares at me with a dazed smile.

"Yeah?" I say. "You going to thuck me good?"

I put my hands on his shoulders and give him a kiss on the lips.

"Yeth," he says. "Thuck. You."

He's suddenly like a broken automaton with a huge erection.

"Yeah," I say. "We're going to do it! You ready?"

He nods stupidly. I pull the keys from his pocket, then walk him around to the passenger door. He's collapsing as I get the door open and I have to wrestle him into the seat and lift his enormous right leg into the car and slam the door.

Then I'm behind the wheel. I start the car.

Oh, this is good!

# 30

After my meeting with Craig and Rebecca, I went back to see Kevin. He had reinstalled the software on my phone.

"Did you find anything?" I asked.

"Sorry. It was wiped clean."

"Isn't that weird?"

"Kind of. I mean, not something we have ever had to deal with here. It's odd, for sure."

"How can I prevent it from happening again?"

He told me again to reset all my passwords, which I did for the next hour, setting up my phone again, which was tedious.

Every now and then, I'd peek at my mentions, which continued to be a nightmare of anonymous men's rights activists and perverts and weirdos. Some of them had seized on feminist blog posts I wrote in college, decided that I was a "social justice warrior," obviously a desperate, attention-seeking slut, and made memes of my pic, tweeting with abbreviation hashtags I didn't understand or want to understand.

Block. Block. Block.

I also had a lot of supportive messages from friends and strangers, which I spent some time liking. I wasn't ready to respond to what had happened to me. But I did send some messages from sock puppets, trying to guide the conversation—simple messages of encouragement—being careful not to use the puppets I was using to sell cheese.

Beatrice arrived and put her hand on my shoulder.

"Hey, honey," she said. "How are you? Want a smokey treat?"

I really did.

"So?" she said in the elevator. "How you doing?"

"Better than I was this morning. Did you see the tweet?"

"I did."

"Kind of a disaster."

She gave me a smoke.

"They're just boobs, you know?" she said. "You know how many girls have had this happen to them? Life goes on. Any idea how it happened?"

I told her my tale of woe as we puffed on her menthols. It felt nice to have a cigarette and great to unload. I swore her to secrecy and told her about my suspicions about Declan and the file I'd opened.

"Holy fuck. You got phished."

"I know. It's so strange. He seemed like such a nice guy. And super-successful. Why would he want to do something like this to me?"

"Are you sure it was him? Could it be your ex?"

"I don't see that. He doesn't have the skills or the, um, ambition. And he's got an ugly new girlfriend. Why would he want to fuck with me?"

"But he has the picture, right? Because you sent it to him? And he might have your social passwords?"

I hadn't thought of that. It was true. JFXBF and I used to use each other's laptops and phones all the time. If he wanted to, he could have recorded all my passwords. But he couldn't even keep track of his own passwords. It didn't make sense.

But it did get me thinking about JFXBFNGF, who did social for a bunch of Brooklyn pubs. Could she be trying to destroy me? Great. Another suspect to fret about.

My legs felt weak and I felt nauseated.

Beatrice asked if I was okay.

"I'll be fine," I said.

But inside, I was thinking, *Time for an Ambien.*

# 31

James's apartment is in a drab concrete building in a depressing area on the edge of Jersey City and Newark. The elevator smells like old pee and Lysol.

I prop James against the wall and press the button and get him, eventually, into his apartment. I steer him to his bed, plop him face-down, and liberate his wallet.

He has $77. That means that I have $122. Not good. I dig into the front of his pants and pull out a wad of ones and fives. $134. Still not good.

There is also a pill bottle in his pants, with five little white pills in it. Roofies.

I leave him in dreamland and wander around his apartment, looking for stuff to steal.

There isn't much, unless you like sports posters, girlie mags, or empty pizza boxes. It is a sty, which makes sense. He is a pig.

I go into the bathroom, have a quick shower, and then rummage through his medicine chest, but it doesn't have anything good, unless you like body spray.

In the fridge, I find a couple of green apples. I eat one and put the other one in my bag for later. There's a decent chef's knife in a drawer, which I take.

In the living room there's a lousy laptop, which Douchebro is too stupid to protect with a password.

I open an incognito browser window and google news about the Hipster Killer. I'm shocked at how many stories there are. I read them all, which leaves me a nervous wreck. I've been painted as a monster and have no idea if I could ever convince anyone of the truth. I'm overwhelmed by the horror of my situation, by the false picture of me given out by the media and police.

I sit quietly, breathing slowly. I can't solve this all right now. I have to focus on one thing at a time and forget about clearing my name until I'm in a safe space.

One thing at a time. Take no chances.

I don't dare log into my email or social accounts, since they might be able to track me that way, but I decide to check into Facebook as Linda Wainwright.

I log in, no problem, and then Linda sends a quick Facebook note to Irene Winslow, proprietor of Cheese of the Month.

> Hey Irene,
>
> I don't know if you've seen the news but it looks like Candace is in some kind of trouble.
> She seemed so nice but the things they're saying about her are so terrible!
> It must be really upsetting for you after all the work she did promoting your business.
> I don't know what to think.
> Anyway, I hope you're doing okay in spite of it all. Let me know if I can help. I really admire you and your business and I hope this doesn't wreck it all.
>
> Your friend,
> Linda

Then I close the laptop and go stand in the bedroom doorway, looking at Douchebro, who is comatose, lying facedown on his messy bed. I need your PIN, buddy.

This is a job for Miss Busy.

# 32

After my smoke with Beatrice, I went to Washington Square Park to eat a tofu burrito from by CHLOE.

As I started on the burrito, I got a text message from a number I didn't recognize.

I hear you're going to work on the WordUp campaign.

Who is this?

Want a list?

I don't know who this is.

Say yes. Of course you want a list.

I shivered, freaked out. Was this Declan? Did I want to know or did I want another list?

I found myself typing.

Yes. I want a list.

Course you do.

Then there was a link to a file. I clicked it: goodr3ads3mailz.zip.

It was like I was watching someone else. I was desperate to make a success of WordUp but I did not want to get phished again. I pinched my bottom lip and tried to figure out what I was doing and why. It was too late for that, though. I had already downloaded the list.

I decided not to open it on my phone. I emailed it to myself.

I texted the number.

What is this?

Entire Goodreads membership list.

All of it?

All of it. You're welcome.

Who is this?

This time when I ask you to do
something for me you'd better do it.

Suddenly I felt queasy. I put down my burrito and stood up. I looked around the park, wondering if somebody could be watching me.

My phone pinged. There was a fresh text.

Are you going to do what you're told this time, Sugar Tits?
Think about how you can show me you've learned your lesson.

I tried to think of something to text back and then decided to block the number. I shouldn't have engaged, but it was too late now. Time to close the door on this.

I needed to call Declan, tell him that I couldn't handle his weird games. I started running through what I would say in my head.

*I enjoyed meeting you the other night, but I find the texts offensive and upsetting and I think it would be better if we didn't communicate further. I've repeatedly expressed that through our electronic communication.*

Or would it be better just to say hi, tell him I wanted to talk to him about his texts, and see what he said? He might apologize right away.

I got back to my desk, but before calling, I decided to have a look at the list he'd sent. I opened it on my Mac. It was a cvs file with 75 million email addresses. If it was the list of all Goodreads members, I had the key to turn WordUp into a huge overnight success.

I needed to test the addresses. I created a Gmail account called Goodreadsrewards and wrote up a quick promotional email, offering free e-books. I included a link to a dummy click-counter site and sent the email to five hundred addresses. The counter started to go off immediately. It worked. They were Goodreads members. I hoped they'd get over their disappointment about the lack of free books.

I decided to call Declan in the hallway, from my cell phone, so that nobody could eavesdrop.

I googled his office number, entered it into my phone, and got his receptionist, Amanda.

"I'm afraid Mr. Walsh is not available at the moment; can I take a message?"

"Yes, please. Ask him to call Candace Walker."

Next, I tried the number he texted me from.

It didn't even ring, but connected immediately with what sounded like a maniacal man. He laughed for a few seconds, then took a deep breath, and laughed even harder. It was a nasty laugh, a cackling. I could tell after a minute that it was a recording, like a laugh track from a horror movie. Then the phone gave the "call failed" beep.

I got chills. Who would set up something like that for their cell phone message?

I decided to call Declan's office again.

"Amanda, sorry to be a pest," I said, "but I wonder if you could add that it's important that Mr. Walsh get back to me as soon as he can."

She agreed to pass on the message.

When I got back to my desk, Wayne was there for the first time that day.

"Hi," he said. "I'm really sorry about your, you know, pic."

"Ugh," I said. "Thank you."

I felt horrible to think of him looking at the picture. And it pissed me off to think that he, and other so-called decent guys, would look at it, invading my privacy.

I didn't know how to express any of that to him. I sat there, trying to think of what to say, and gave up. Back to work.

I checked the cheese conversions. Ninety-two! I analyzed them by pitch. There was little difference between the two most recent come-ons. Likely not statistically significant. I was probably good to go with a blast to the whole list.

I whooped and did one of my little cheese conversion dances.

Wayne looked over at me.

"More cheese success?"

"Ninety-two conversions, and I'm just getting started. Ready to send out the big blast. I think I'll have a thousand tomorrow."

Beatrice looked over and smiled, but she looked irritated.

I felt embarrassed to have celebrated while she was likely smarting at being overlooked for the job I was now enjoying. I worried that I seemed obnoxious.

"How's Bowhunting.com going?" I asked.

"Oh, crappy," he said. "It's not going to work. The search engine optimization is already nearly ideal. I think if you're into bowhunting, and you're online, you already know about Bowhunting.com."

"I think you need a new client."

"I know. I'm supposed to meet with Alvin tonight to talk about the next project. Rebecca's going to ask you to come as well."

# 33

When I leave Douchebro's sty, I have his bank card and PIN, $134 in cash, a chef's knife, a green apple, five roofies, and a disgusting yellow Mustang with a quarter tank of gas.

I drive north, looking for a quiet bank machine. I find one, in a closed minimall, park in the next minimall parking lot, tuck my hair up under my Devils hat, keeping my head low, so the security camera won't get a good shot of me.

Score. The PIN works. But he only has $64 in his bank account. Loser.

Oh, well. I now have $198 in my escape fund, and also a car.

I figure I should cover some ground before dawn, because I don't want to be driving such an obvious vehicle after it's reported as being stolen by the Hipster Killer.

I am exhausted, but I have no choice but to move. I throw the bank card out the window as I head for I-80.

It is pushing 4:00 a.m. by the time I get on the highway. I have to stop for gas, which is a bit of a challenge to buy without a credit card. First I have to give the teller $20. Then I have to pump it. Then I load up on lousy gas station coffee and Oreos, which are vegan BTW, and hit the road.

Down to $175. Still, I'm out of the city and moving farther away, and I have more money than I started with this morning.

I feel okay, but exhausted.

I keep my speed just a bit higher than the speed limit. The last thing I need is to have the police stop me. Not only am I wanted, I'm also driving without a license, and I must be above the legal alcohol limit. I creep up behind a slow minivan and let them set the pace, driving through the ugly halogen-lit outskirts of Jersey City.

I'm so tired now that my eyes start to close. I roll down the windows, turn up a hip-hop station, and lean forward but still find myself nodding off.

I remember a trick my dad told me about years ago. I pull over, take off my socks and shoes, and it works. It makes it superhard to fall asleep.

The sun is a red ball rising over the refinery towers by the time I get to Scranton. I drive downtown, find a big parking lot in front of a mall, park the car, crawl into the backseat, and fall asleep.

# 34

Wayne and I shared a cab uptown, which was nice. He confessed he was relieved that the bowhunting client was a dud, admitted the whole subject appalled him.

"The way these guys talk in their web chats is . . . horrible," he said, searching for words. "They're so insensitive to the suffering of these animals."

He asked me about ethical veganism, and I told him how I gave up animal products after watching a documentary on factory farming. He told me that he was still eating meat but found himself increasingly troubled by it.

By the time we got to Central Park, I felt like if I didn't watch myself, I'd find myself snuggling up against him.

We were headed to the Parkview Lounge, a big shiny lounge on the fourth floor of the Time Warner Center. Normally, I would have been excited going there, but thinking about seeing Alvin again, I felt bile in the back of my throat. As we rode the escalator, I sneaked an Ambien and immediately felt calmer just for having taken it.

A stylish woman in a cocktail dress led us in. The place was full of rich media businesspeople, from Time Warner or whatever, and a sprinkling of rich tourists, who were themselves likely media businesspeople. Japanese. French. Italians. Australians. TV people, with good clothes, hair, makeup, and cosmetic surgery. They were swilling expensive cocktails and drinking good wine, showing off, striding over marble floors to stand and look at themselves in the mirrored bar, eyeballing the expensive, beautifully lit bottles of fancy liquor, watching other people come and go.

Alvin and Rebecca were already seated and had a great table, right in front of the window, looking down on Columbus Circle, where there are always yellow cabs and limos going around the Christopher Columbus statue.

Alvin rose from his mauve silk chair to shake my hand first then Wayne's.

"Nice to see you both," he said, smiling.

He was in a beautiful gray suit with a creamy, open-collared white shirt. Rebecca was in a form-fitting black cocktail dress. An ice bucket with a bottle of Moët & Chandon was on the table. Alvin gestured and a waiter soon had all of us holding flutes of champagne.

Alvin held up his glass for a toast. "To success!"

We all joined in, and then he turned to me.

"So you're selling cheese," he said.

"Last time I checked, two hundred and sixty-eight conversions. I sent out the big blast right before leaving the office. I expect to hit a thousand tonight."

"Becca tells me you got your hands on a list," said Alvin.

"I did."

"Where did you get it?"

"I promised I wouldn't tell. It's that kind of deal."

He smiled and nodded and then suddenly his smile was gone.

"No," he said and fixed me with a hard look. "Cut the shit. Where'd you get it?"

That threw me for a loop.

"What do you mean?"

"Where'd you get the fucking list? Did you steal it?"

I looked at him more closely and saw that he was testing me.

I smiled. "I have friends who want to help me."

He was suddenly smiling again.

"Ha!" he said. "No doubt you do. One does. Good. Good. We don't need to know. Fair enough. You promised."

His eyes narrowed.

"You're a funny one," he said. "One night you stomp off because I said 'pussy.' The next day you tweet a tit pic."

"I was hacked. I'm so sorry if it caused any problems for SoSol. I'm doing everything I can to remedy the situation. Believe me, it's been a nightmare."

He snorted.

"I couldn't give a fuck if you tweet pictures of your tits every day. They're your titties. It's a free country. I'm just saying I don't have a read on you yet."

I didn't know what to say. I smiled, frowned, looked away, cleared my throat. Thankfully, he turned to Wayne.

"How are the bows and arrows going?" he asked.

Poor Wayne!

"Terribly," Wayne said. "Every bowhunter already knows Bow hunting.com. I can't find a target market that needs reaching. I'm link-pimping but I don't think it will work."

"So either it's a dud or you are?" said Alvin.

"I suppose so."

Alvin nodded, then clapped his hands.

"Okay," he said, leaning in conspiratorially, drawing us all closer. "I was just telling Becca here that this afternoon I got a signature from my old buddy Jeff, the CEO of WordUp. We have a deal to push them clicks for three months."

He looked around to see if we were getting the import of this. We were.

"We get a piece of the action for three months," he said. "It's all open book. They see everything we do, regular reports and all that happy horseshit. Our job is to pimp it, spam it, SEO, SEM, drive motherfucking clicks, not design it or invent it. We eat a piece of what we kill, but the real prize would be in convincing them to sign up for longer. I want you two on this full-time," he said, nodding at Wayne and me.

"Is there a budget?" I asked.

"If we need one," he said. "Becca and Craig can handle those decisions. We'll get an outline of their social media strategy tomorrow, I hope. I want a plan, within a day or two, for how to proceed. How we going to sell this?"

I cleared my throat.

"I have a list," I said. "Or I can get one. Again, I promised not to say where I got it, but it will make this a lot easier."

I had his attention, and Rebecca's and Wayne's.

In my pocket my phone kept buzzing, a sort of steady repetitive buzz, distracting me as I tried to make the sale.

"What kind of list?" said Alvin.

"Net-savvy book lovers. Millions of them. Their email addresses."

"That would make this a lot fucking easier," said Alvin. "Where'd you get it?"

I didn't answer.

"Let me frack it. Like I did with the cheese."

Rebecca cleared her throat.

"This makes me nervous," she said. "Fishy lists make me nervous."

"There's nothing fishy about it," I said. "Nobody needs to know how I got their emails."

Alvin was nodding, but Rebecca looked unconvinced. Wayne looked like he didn't know what to think.

Alvin stood up.

"Let me think about it," he said. "I'm going for a slash. Be right back."

"Me too," I said.

I needed to check my phone so I followed him toward the bathrooms.

"Yours is that one," he said, pointing, with a smile I didn't like.

# 35

I wake up with a bad kink in my neck in the backseat of the Mustang. FML.

I have to pee and I am so hungry.

I crawl out of the car, make a mental note of its location, and head into the mall, which looks like it's getting murdered by the big box stores.

First thing I need is a new hat. A Devils hat won't help me blend in in Pennsylvania.

I drop the Devils hat in a trash can and wander around looking for one that says DON'T BOTHER LOOKING AT ME, so I go in and out of the crappy stores that gird the loins of Scranton's young and restless. Old Navy, etc.

Ugh. Do I have to look like a Scranton mall rat? Would such a person like NASCAR? Should I get a hat with a country singer's name on it? Like Toby Keith or somebody? Like, really? How do girls dress here?

There are two looks: mall rat and young professional.

I decide to eat a veggie sub, have a coffee, write, and think about my new look.

I went proletarian in Jersey. Now what if I change it up, go upscale? I am kind of freaked out by how much the idea cheers me up. I come up with a plan.

I go to a salon.

"I'm looking for an asymmetrical cut," I tell the gum-chewing lady there, a fashion nightmare with a turkey neck and a port-wine stain on her cheek, someone I would normally never let near my hair.

"Like a bob?" she asks.

"Sort of, but higher on one side than the other."

"Like Jennifer Lawrence had?"

"That's the one. In that movie."

The result is surprisingly good. I look like a striving, wannabe upwardly mobile young person, like a Scranton yuppie.

I need clothes to match. At the clearance racks at Abercrombie & Fitch I find a spaghetti-strap black cotton dress that would pass, on casual inspection, for weekend casual wear. I get a cute little pink ball cap.

I put on my new outfit and go to the drugstore to buy a bottle of blond Clairol.

I feel good about my makeover, although the mall day leaves a dent in my getaway stash. I am down to $124.

Not good.

# 36

I went into the fancy bathroom, then into a stall to pee, and checked my cheese conversions. Eight hundred and twenty-eight! Yes!

Then I checked my messages.

I had a series of one-word text messages from Presumably Declan, almost a hundred of them, delivered every ten seconds for the past fifteen minutes.

Hey.

Hey.

Hey.

Over and over again. Another one landed as I held the phone in my hand. Each time one landed, the phone buzzed.

Hey.

What?

I don't like when you ignore me.

I didn't know what to make of this.

What's up?

I need you to see what you're about to share with the world.

What do you mean?

Then he texted me a photo, which I recognized with horror.

It was a picture of me and JFXBF, or part of him.

Back when we were deeply in love, JFXBF wanted to take sex pictures, so on his birthday last year, I let him take pictures of me while I had my way with him, on the condition that he use my phone, so that only I would have the pictures, which were locked, safely I thought, in my phone's memory.

The light was garish and my makeup was smeared and the whole thing looked like it belonged in the Twitter feed of @amateurhawties. POV BJ. My mascara had run and my face was, uh, wet.

I broke out into an icy sweat.

Don't send it. Please don't send it. Please.

Take off your panties.

Not that again.

Leave them in the bathroom. I want you to
go back to the table without them.

And you won't send the tweet?

I won't.

I needed to regain control of my Twitter account, or failing that, delete it. I also needed to delete each and every nasty picture from my phone. I couldn't do those things now. I could do all that when I got home. For now, I had to stop him from tweeting that picture.

Okay. I'll do what you say.

I know you will. Don't try to trick me. I'll know. Take off your panties and throw them in the trash. Now.

I had to do it so I did it. I took off my underwear, smoothed my skirt, left the stall, tossed my underwear in the trash, and washed my hands.

My phone vibrated again. I pulled it out. WTF? I always have my phone set to no vibration.

Was that so hard?

Why are you doing this?

You have to do what I say. If you fuck with me again, it could be bad for you.

How did you get that picture?

I'm helping your career. In return, you're going to do some things for me. Nothing too bad. But you have to do them.

This is cruel.

Go back to the table. ttyl

Don't tweet that picture.

I checked my Twitter feed. My last tweet had been that afternoon. Whew.

I wanted to break down sobbing but everyone was waiting for me. I pushed my anxiety down and headed back to the table with a fake smile on my face.

"Excuse me," I said, trying to look chipper. "I just checked the cheese account. Eight hundred plus conversions."

Rebecca said, "You go, girl," but Alvin looked irritated. His iPhone was on the table and he glanced at the time.

"All right," he said. "Candy, I want you to give Rebecca a plan, a proposal, for WordUp. A few pages, whatever. Then we can consider next steps."

"Brilliant!" I said. "I'll work on it tomorrow."

Rebecca nodded. We all stood up.

The champagne had apparently already been paid for. I drank the last little bit in my glass.

"Thanks for the champagne," I said.

"My pleasure," said Alvin. "You hustled your ass to sell that fucking loser Cheese of the Month thing. Nice to see it. The hustle, I mean. Not the ass, although it's nice, too."

I was turning away from the table as he said that. I was shocked to feel him give my bottom a squeeze and a slap.

"Whoa," I said, turning to scowl at him. "Mr. Beaconsfield, that's not appropriate."

I could see he knew I was thinking about slapping him. He held up his hands in a gesture of innocence and ducked his head in mock fear.

"I'm going to get myself in trouble again, aren't I?"

Rebecca sighed.

"There's a line, Alvin," she said. "Not everyone gets your jokes."

He frowned, thought about it, and then smiled.

"Quite right, Becca," he said. "When you're right, you're right."

He turned to me.

"My apologies, Ms. Walker," he said and held out his hand. "That was inappropriate. I forgot myself and I'm sorry."

I hesitated before taking his disgusting hand in mine.

"Apology accepted," I said. "Thanks again for the champagne."

"Wow," he said. "When you get mad, you really blush, don't you?"

He turned to Wayne and took his hand.

"Don't worry about the fucking bows and arrows, kid," he said. "That was a shit sheet."

He kissed Rebecca on the cheek and was gone.

"You okay?" Rebecca asked me.

I nodded.

"I'm okay, but I don't want him to touch me again."

She put her fingers to the bridge of her nose and squeezed.

"He won't," she said. "I'll talk to him about it."

"Rebecca, that was so out of line," said Wayne.

She suddenly looked very tired.

"I know," she said. "I didn't sign up for this."

# 37

In my stylish new dress and haircut, I set out to find the Scranton public library, which is, thankfully, a short walk from the mall.

I sit down at one of the computers and learn that the news of the manhunt for the Hipster Killer is not good.

The police found Douchebro, so now this is officially a crime spree. The *Post* is milking it. There was a short wire article that was carried by the *New York Times* and a bunch of other outlets.

But the *Post* story is particularly not good.

Headline: "Cops Hot on Trail of Hipster Killer."

A witness saw me doing shots with Douchebro at the bar. And the reporter found Irena, who was no doubt thrilled to tell her story.

There's a picture of me from the bank machine security camera in my Devils hat, and a picture of Douchebro with his car, in happier times. They even interviewed his mother about what a nice guy he was.

It enrages me. I want to smash the monitor. There's nothing in the article about how Douchebro tried to rape me. I am sure I wasn't the first. Doesn't serial rape count as a crime spree?

And they've used the topless picture of me, with little stars over my nipples, making me look like a sex-crazed lunatic, and, just to make things really terrible, a picture of the Fourteenth Street subway platform.

The scumbag reporter even talked to my poor mom.

"We are praying for Candace. We just want her to come home and get the help she needs."

I close the window and think, *How did I, the victim of a sick campaign of sexual exploitation, end up looking like the villain?*

Everybody reading the *Post* will think I am completely insane.

Good thing I'm staying a step ahead of them.

Take no chances.

I check Linda Wainwright's Facebook. She has a message from Irene!

What a nightmare! I can't believe it. I haven't been able to work at all since I saw the news, which is too bad because the orders are piling up. If even half of what they're saying is true, then Candace is a terrible person. I don't know what to think, either. She was so nice when I talked to her on the phone. Do you know her well?

I sit there for a while, trying to figure out how to reply, and finally settle on this:

Oh, Irene, thanks so much for responding. I wasn't sure I should message you or not, but the whole thing has been bothering me so much. I'm not surprised you find yourself unable to work. I haven't been able to do anything except obsess about it since I read the first story. There sure are some weird things about this, and it doesn't all make sense. I have to wonder if the truth isn't more complicated than the news stories make it sound. I have some facts about the whole thing that I haven't shared with anyone because I don't know if I should get involved. But Candace told me you have recordings of telephone conversations with her and Craig. I think they could contain information that clears her. If I'm wrong, well, nothing ventured, nothing lost.

What do you think? Can I come see you and explain it all? If we can prevent an innocent woman from being imprisoned, I don't think we have any choice but to try!

# 38

After the meeting, Wayne and I went outside together, and my phone rang.

"Have you decided to reveal my secret identity?"

It was Declan. I held my finger up to Wayne to show that I needed a minute, and he waited while I talked.

"Thanks for calling," I said.

"I thought we agreed on ninety days."

"We did. Don't worry. Your secret identity is not, um, top of mind."

"Yeah, listen. I'm just back from Iceland. Reykjavik. I'm at JFK. Just got your message. I'm sorry I haven't had time to email about your project. I had to fly out early yesterday for a meeting."

"What about the texts?"

"Texts?"

I exhaled and did a lot of thinking very quickly.

"I'm sorry," I said. "This must sound weird, but have you texted me?"

"No. Sorry. Haven't had the chance. Airplane. Iceland. Meetings. Vodka. Airplane."

It wasn't him. I believed him. Hearing his voice, I didn't even want to mention anything more about the texts. He was a normal man, from a normal world. He was a successful businessman, jetting around, conferencing, drinking vodka. He didn't have the time or the inclination to cyberstalk a girl he'd just met. He wasn't needy or warped. I felt embarrassed to be dragging him into my weirdness.

"That makes sense," I said.

"What does?"

"Nothing. Sorry to be so weird. Somebody has been sending me weird texts. I thought it was you, since they started the morning after I met you."

"Nope. Wrong guy."

"And you didn't send me any lists?"

"No."

"I don't know what's going on. Someone has been impersonating you. They've been texting me, pretending to be you, and sending me files."

"What?" he said. "Are you sure it's not just a mix-up?"

"Absolutely. It started the morning after we met and I gave you my contact details. You didn't text me that morning?"

"No. I meant to but got tied up at work. Candace, what's this all about?"

"It's a long story."

"Maybe you can tell me over the dinner you promised me?"

"I'd like that. I'd really like that. I've got to run but I'll be in touch."

Wayne was still standing there.

"I shouldn't eavesdrop," he said, "but is everything okay?"

"I don't know," I said, trying to smile. "I'm more confused than ever."

"Does this have to do with your selfie?"

"It might." I could feel tears coming on but blinked them away. "I didn't post it by mistake. I was hacked. That was Declan. I thought I was texting him for the past few days, but he tells me he hasn't texted me at all. That means I know less than I thought I did, and I'm totally confused now. Somebody's been fucking with me and I don't know what to do."

Then I started to sniffle. Wayne took me into his arms, and I was humiliated that it was necessary, and he patted my back in a brotherly way and said, "There, there," and I had to stop myself from bawling.

I pulled myself away and rubbed my hands across my eyes, hoping my mascara wasn't all smeared.

"You're very sweet," I said.

"What's going on, Candace? If you've been hacked, you've got to get to the bottom of it. You should consider going to the police."

"I know," I said. I stepped away and put my hand to my head. "I need to go home and figure everything out."

"Are you sure you're okay?"

"No. But I will be."

I left him standing there and headed for the subway.

# 39

I am so freaked out by the *Post* story. I don't know how far ahead I am of my pursuers.

I walk back to the mall, fretting about my next move. I need to put more space between me and New York.

I'm lost in thought until a tow truck rumbles past me in the parking lot. It makes me aware of my surroundings again, which is good, because I notice there's a police car next to the Mustang.

I freeze and remind myself that I should keep moving, that most people don't just stand around, immobile, on the sidewalk. I head off again, right past the mall, like a normal woman out for a walk.

The tow truck pulls up next to the Mustang. Ugh! I keep going, one foot in front of the other, until I'm behind a Staples, out of sight of the police.

This is not good.

I obviously need to dye my hair, keep my head down, and get out of Scranton.

I wander aimlessly for half an hour, past boarded-up buildings, looking for someplace where I can have a shower.

I walk through the Courthouse Square, where a homeless-looking guy sitting on a bench next to a statue catches sight of me. He's young and high on something, likely Oxy. He has long brown stringy hair and is wearing an orange down vest and no shirt. He gets up off his bench.

"There you are," he says. "Darlene. Wait for me."

"No sale," I say, and he suddenly realizes I'm not Darlene and wanders back to his bench.

Eventually, I find myself in front of the Radisson Lackawanna, a pretty stone building that looks better than anything else in town.

I walk around the block, admiring the handsome hotel, keeping my eyes peeled for police cars. I don't see any, so I stroll in, just like any regular guest, walk through the beautiful lobby, and head downstairs, hoping there's a pool.

You need a key card to get into the changing room, so I skulk in a stairwell until a distracted mother trailing two whining kids passes me. I follow them in. No problem.

I have a long, lovely shower, and I first bleach then dye my hair, which takes forever. While I wait for the goop to set I write in my Moleskine. I think my handwriting is getting better with all the practice.

When my hair is done, I have to say I like it. I've never been blond before. I was smart and got highlight stuff, so it looks pretty good.

With my little black dress and my new haircut, I look like a soon-to-be suburban mom, a young woman at ease in the passenger seat of her boring husband's SUV.

Disguise complete.

I walk into the hotel bar, a surprisingly pleasant place, except for the customers, who all look like bored business travelers.

I take a seat at the bar, order a local craft beer, and feel almost civilized.

I take a long sip of the beer and feel myself relax, but the feeling doesn't last.

I look around. How the fuck am I going to get out of this place?

# 40

I was exhausted after the conversation with Declan. I spent the subway ride trying to figure out who had been harassing me but found it hard to come to any conclusions.

When I got home, I had a glass of wine, popped two Ambiens, and collapsed. When I woke up, I was already late for work. My phone, which I use for my alarm, was dead.

I brushed my teeth, got dressed quickly, and ran to the subway, where I sat trying unsuccessfully to restart my phone.

When I got to my desk, I popped open my laptop, and discovered I had a fresh email from my sister, which was odd.

**From:** Jess Walker
**To:** Candace Walker
**Date:** June 21, 2018
**Subject:** What is that on your Facebook page????

Mom is freaking out. I'm freaking out. What are you doing?

I clicked on Facebook. The Notifications logo showed I had dozens of comments. I clicked on my page and felt like I was going to vomit.

My profile pic, which had been a nice shot of me with a goat, had been replaced by the topless picture.

I emailed my sister: Fuck!!!! I've been hacked again.

I switched back to Facebook and deleted the image.

I thought for a minute and entered a status update: Apologies everyone for the profile pic. My account has been hacked.

My sister emailed me back.

You've been hacked? For real? Someone stole your private photos and keeps posting them? That's illegal. You need this to stop.

I know. I thought I fixed it. I changed my passwords.

Change them again.

I tried to do that, opening the settings and looking for the password page, but it was really hard, because my eyes were filling up with tears. I couldn't help myself. What would everyone think?

I could hear Beatrice say, "Hey, want to see something really funny, guys?"

She turned to look at me and could obviously see I was upset.

"Hey, Candace. Are you okay?"

"I'm fine," I said, my voice cracking. I got up and headed for the bathroom. I didn't want everyone to see me bawling.

In the hallway, I ran into Wayne, on his way into the office.

"Candace?" he said. "Are you okay?"

I didn't say anything, just fled to the bathroom, where I hid in a stall.

My phone vibrated in my pocket.

Fuck! Why wouldn't it stop vibrating? Wait. It was dead.

It was not dead anymore.

I looked at it and saw a text message.

That won't work, silly goose.

It was from Not Declan, whoever was tormenting me.

Did you do that Facebook post?

You tried to block me.

What do you mean?

You changed your passwords.

I took a deep breath, rubbed the tears from my cheeks, and stared down at the phone. There was no way I was going to let Not Declan blackmail me like this.

You're trying to wreck my life.

Take off your panties and go back into the office.

Why are you doing this?

Everybody's checking out your tits. I thought
a whore like you would like that.

Stop. Stop.

Do you want to get raped?

I want you to stop.

Do not defy me. Do as you are told and you will
prosper. Defy me and you will regret it, roastie.

I powered the phone off.

I washed my face, fixed my makeup, and walked into Rebecca's office. She had changed the sticky note emoticon in her window to :-P. She was typing. I waited until she looked up and registered my expression. I definitely had her attention.

"Rebecca, I've got a problem I'd like to talk to you and Craig about."

She frowned. She probably thought I was talking about Alvin grabbing my ass.

"It has to do with my phone. I think it's been hacked again. Someone used my Twitter and Facebook accounts to post that topless picture of me."

The frown was gone. She looked freaked out.

"What? Are you serious?"

I nodded. I was very serious.

"At first I thought that I might have sent that tweet myself by mistake, but this morning the same picture was posted as my Facebook profile pic. I know I didn't do that. I think someone's hacked my accounts and is messing with me. They're sending me the worst messages. They just threated me with rape."

I held up my phone and couldn't speak anymore because I was going to cry. Rebecca looked alarmed.

"We need to get to the bottom of this," she said.

"That would be really great," I managed to say. "Because this sucks."

She took me to Kevin's office.

"Kevin, it looks like Candace's phone's been hacked," she said.

"Not again," he said.

"Can you try to find out who's doing this?" she asked, then left, saying she was going to find Craig.

"Weird," said Kevin. "You changed all your passwords?"

"I did, but it didn't do any good. In the latest message he told me he posted the topless pic to Facebook to punish me for changing my passwords."

He looked like he couldn't believe what I was saying.

"He texted you that?"

"Yes. And he called me a whore and threatened to rape me."

"Can you show me?"

"I powered the phone down. Here."

He took it from me and rebooted it. I stood over his shoulder and waited for the black screen to come to life.

"Candace, just between us, is there any chance that some government agency is doing this to you?"

WTF? The government?

"Um, not that I know of," I said. "I don't think the CIA is interested in me."

He gave me an odd look.

"It's just, this is strange. Someone was able to hack you again, after you changed all your passwords. You did change them, right?"

"I did."

"So it just makes me wonder," he said. "It's not something that a normal hacker could do. I mean phishing you once, that's sort of, not normal, but something that happens. This is more persistent, makes me wonder if you've been targeted by someone with greater capabilities."

Then the Apple logo appeared, and a little white bar below it.

He frowned and shook his head.

"Bad news," he said.

"What?"

"It's being wiped, again. We're not going to get anything from it this time either."

# 41

Most of the business travelers in the Scranton Radisson are drab AF.

There are basically two categories: stressed-looking middle-aged overweight guy in khakis and golf shirt and stressed-looking middle-aged overweight guy in crappy suit.

I have the feeling they're all involved in auto sales, or storage rentals, or HVAC, but some of them could be union reps, or school board employees, or regional retail managers. I don't know and don't care.

So many lives seem unbearably pointless and dreary to me.

Maybe that's why I'm in the fix I'm in. I don't know. I can't bear the idea of leading a life of quiet desperation, of being that formerly hot mom in the SUV, listening to talk radio, cleaning and feeding the kids, watching Netflix, getting excited about the new Mexican place opening in the mall.

Kill me.

Anyway, it's kind of a nice bar, except that it's full of balding drabbies, heart-diseased drudges slurping beer and shooting the shit. The bits of conversation I overhear are as dull as you could imagine. Cars. Traffic. Weather. Sports. Sports. But I notice one guy who looks a bit different. He's sitting down the bar from me, slowly stirring his cocktail—looks like a rum and coke. He's bored with his phone. When I sit down, he looks my way, not staring but checking me out. I scribble in my Moleskine until I'm halfway through my second beer, when I decide to eyefuck him a bit.

I look up from my notebook and turn toward him. He's kind of cute, in a hot dad sort of way. He has salt-and-pepper hair. He seems to be tall. He looks less overweight than most of the guys in here. He is in the suit, rather than khaki, category, which I think suggests he's of a higher social class, although you can't tell as easily these days as you once could.

He notices me looking at him. Oh. Hi.

I hold his gaze for a moment and don't smile or not smile, but he smiles and looks flustered. Holy. He takes off his wedding ring, under the bar. One minute he has it on, the next minute it's gone. Abraca-dabra. He's single.

I guess I'm the best thing going in this Radisson. Obvi.

He's coming over.

# 42

Rebecca found Craig and we went into his office and they asked me about the second selfie.

I told them about the threatening texts while they nodded sympathetically. Craig said he was going to find a way to fix this, but when I asked how he would do that, he was guarded and noncommittal. Then Rebecca asked a series of pointed questions. Had this ever happened before? When did I take the topless picture? Did my ex have a copy of it? Were there more pics? Did he have my password? Who else had my password? Where did I get the list of emails for the Cheese of the Month Club?

Then there was a knock on the door. Rebecca went to open it. It was Jess, looking business-like and upset. Big lawyer sis to the rescue!

I got up and gave her a hug.

"I couldn't get you on your phone, so I jumped in a cab," she said.

She introduced herself to Craig and Rebecca, mentioned her law firm, and sat down without being invited.

"I'm worried about my sister," she said. "I'm concerned that SoSol isn't protecting her privacy."

Rebecca made an Oh-this-is-like-that face.

Before she could say anything, Kevin showed up with my phone. He passed it to me.

"Kevin, any clue what's causing this?" asked Craig.

Kevin shrugged.

"It was wiped. Sorry. It's like it just came out of the box now."

Jessica gave Craig and Rebecca her business card.

"Again, I'm concerned about the situation."

"We all are," said Craig. "We need to figure out what's been happening. Until we know that, we want to do everything we can to make sure this is taken care of."

He turned to me.

"You've changed your Facebook and Twitter passwords?"

I nodded.

"It sounds like you're starting to realize you've got a problem you need to deal with," said Jess. "I'm very concerned that my sister's rights have been violated. She's been the victim of a systematic and devastating campaign of sexual harassment."

As she spoke I realized that was true.

"When you finish your analysis of the phone," Jess said, "we are going to want a copy of everything, to make sure you haven't missed anything."

Craig and Rebecca exchanged glances.

"We'll get back to you about that," Rebecca said.

"I think you would be wise to review SoSol's handling of the whole thing," said Jess. "Until we know who has been doing this to Candace, we can't be sure it wasn't an employee, even a manager. We need to think about calling the police."

Craig and Rebecca looked rattled.

"For now," said Jess, "I think Candace needs to take the rest of the day off."

"Of course," said Rebecca.

"Do you have the capacity to do a decent in-house security review?"

"I think so," said Craig. "But if not, we'll get the capacity. Immediately. Candace has been through the wringer."

My sister stood up, so I stood up. It was time to leave.

"Guys, thanks for looking into this for me," I said. "I'm so disappointed that this has distracted me from my work. I'm so excited about my job here, and I can't wait to get to work on the WordUp campaign."

"Candace, this is just awful," said Craig. "But we're going to get to the bottom of it. If we can't, we should go to the police."

He and Rebecca walked us out.

Jess steered me to the elevator.

When the door closed, I was fighting back tears. She gave me a hug. "Poor Candace."

When the elevator door opened in the lobby, Wayne was standing there, waiting to get in.

I broke off my embrace with Jess and wiped my eyes.

"Candace!" he said. "There you are. Are you okay?"

"No. But we're working on it."

I introduced him to Jess and blew my nose.

I told him I'd been hacked again and he shook his head.

"I can't believe it. Who's doing this to you?"

He reached out and took my hand in his. I could see real sympathy and affection in his eyes and I felt such a powerful feeling of attachment and gratitude I had to look away.

"We're trying to get to the bottom of it," said Jess.

"You know, I might be able to help," he said. "I know a bit about hacking."

"That would be great," I said. "I'm sure you know more than we do."

"Would you be comfortable keeping that to yourself, though?" said Jess. "I'd rather that you not tell SoSol what we're doing. Just in case."

"Of course," he said, nodding. "That makes sense. I can even spy for you."

"That's a good idea," said Jess. "Let's meet at six p.m., at the bar at the Jane. So don't mention it to anyone at work and don't email or text us about it."

He looked surprised at that.

"You think they might be snooping in my emails?"

"They have the legal right to do so," said Jess. "So it's best to assume they are."

# 43

"Are you writing the next great American novel?" he asks.

He's a bold one. He stands right up and walks over, drink in hand, wedding ring in pocket, stands in front of me, all confident and tall and actually surprisingly handsome, with a cocky smile and an air of complete ease.

"No," I say.

I make myself smile.

"Nothing so interesting," I say. "Just a journal."

"And it's not interesting? I find that hard to believe. You look . . . interesting. Mind if I pull up a stool?"

Wow. That was fast. He is next to me, ordering us both a round, before I have time to think about it.

This guy knows what he's doing.

He is Adam, forty-eight, divorced, two kids back in Pittsburgh, who he sees every other weekend, a lot of time on the road.

He's a lawyer, specialized in human resources.

I almost blurt: Just like my sister!

The stylish blond woman that Adam is drinking with is an only child. Amy, twenty-seven, single, from Providence, Rhode Island, two cats at home, retail consultant, brought in by chains to do spot checks on how well their outlets are implementing retail strategies.

"Like a secret shopper!" Adam says.

"Kind of. They don't know I'm coming, but then they know when I get there and tell them."

"That sounds really interesting!"

"No it doesn't. It can't. It's so dull I sometimes think about running away and joining the circus."

He laughs.

"Tell me about it," he says.

He starts to laugh really hard.

"If I have to negotiate another termination agreement with another middle-aged executive who's suddenly surplus to the requirements of Acme Corporation, I will . . . well, actually I'll just do it, because I have child support payments to make."

Oh, you fucking slimeball. Pretending that you're divorced. I think about his wife, looking after the kids at home while he palms his wedding ring and tries to talk himself into the pants of every hottie he meets on the road.

Men are awful. Not all men, I suppose, but a lot of them. Maybe all of them. I don't know. Maybe the ones who aren't awful in this way—the cheating way—are awful in some other way. Maybe they're detestably weak.

That's my new theory. All men are either awful would-be cheaters or simpering weaklings kept in line by fear of women.

I think about my theory while we chat, but manage to keep up a fairly witty level of banter, and find myself enjoying Adam.

He has the bored detachment of the professional traveler and keeps up a pretty good light patter full of jokes that sound like they were lifted from late-night talk shows.

He tells me the mildly interesting history of the hotel, which used to be a railway station. We move to a table to order dinner.

We discover a shared taste for making fun of ridiculous menu language. It isn't much, but it's enough to make us laugh, a couple of strangers trying to snatch a bit of fun at the Scranton Radisson.

"Maybe I should have the lasagna," says Adam. "It's made with artisanal ricotta."

"Is it oven roasted? A lot of the items are oven roasted."

"Nothing roasted in a pit in the woods? Always in the oven, eh? Seems passé."

After the menus are gone, we make fun of the customers and staff.

"That fellow's in a hurry, isn't he?" he says.

"I hope he's hurrying to a haberdasher's."

"That is what is known as a Full Cleveland. Mark it well. You don't see it much anymore."

He keeps topping off my wine and I keep laughing

I have to remind myself, from time to time, to tell him that I never do this kind of thing and, after the wine kicks in, to give him the sudden glazed-eyed look of affection, which he has, no doubt, seen many times before, in other hotel dining rooms.

He waves for the check.

"We should take a walk," he says.

Then he gets up to go to the bathroom.

"I'll be right back," he says.

"I'll be waiting."

As soon as he leaves the dining room, plop!

Roofie time!

# 44

I spent the whole afternoon in a conference room in Jess's office going through everything that happened since I started at SoSol. We had a stainless steel carafe full of coffee and a big pitcher of water. She asked me questions and typed and did web searches and sent emails.

She was in lawyer mode, which was like the bossy big sister of years past, except that I couldn't escape her instructions.

We reconstructed, to the best of my ability, the whole thing. I did what I could to recall the text exchanges with Not Declan and described the horror show at the Guggenheim, the threats delivered when I was in the bathroom at the Parkview, my brief conversation with Declan about the whole thing, and that morning's Facebook post.

I have a really good memory, and I think Jess was impressed by my ability to recall it all in detail. She stopped me with follow-up questions from time to time, drilling down to details that I hadn't put in order. She asked me over and over again about the party at Alvin's, about his challenge to Wayne, and about the moment he grabbed my ass.

"Do you think that all counts as sexual harassment?" I asked.

"It's open-and-shut. It's not time to think about this yet, but we could easily file a claim and he'd probably pay you out as soon as he talked to his lawyer. If he's behaved like this in the past, it likely wouldn't be the first payout."

"Wow."

"I need to talk to Wayne, on his own, ask him to recall the same events, see if your stories match. I also want to know if Alvin was texting while you were in the bathroom at Parkview."

"Oh, God! That would take some balls, wouldn't it, to be taunting and harassing me while sitting at the table with my colleagues?"

"Sounds like Alvin has no shortage of balls," she said. She shook her head. "It's actually kind of amazing that somebody could think that he can behave like this. It's not 1975."

"Do you think he might be behind the whole thing?"

"He's my chief suspect."

"But whoever texted me seemed to know details of my conversation with Declan. I spilled a drink on him."

"Didn't you say that Rebecca was there when you bumped into him?"

"She was. I think so. Yes."

"So maybe she told Alvin. Like, 'Candace was so drunk she spilled Declan's drink.'"

"That's true."

"Your phone came from SoSol. If Alvin wanted to, he could have installed a program to allow him to control it remotely. He could have easily hacked your Twitter and Facebook that way."

I started to wonder if Alvin was playing a fucked-up game, luring me into a sick relationship where I accepted harassment in exchange for cheese sales.

"But we have no proof."

"Not yet," said Jess. She gestured at her pile of notes. "But we're getting started."

"Could it be someone else, though? I mean, Declan denied it, but how can I know? He would have access to the files that someone sent me."

I couldn't believe he would do it, but felt I should see what Jess thought.

"He's the other suspect," she said. "But his story about Iceland does check out."

She turned her laptop so I could see the screen. She had found a story about the Digital Innovation Summit in Iceland. It featured a photo of Declan giving a talk. She flipped to another screen, with the conference schedule.

"He was giving the keynote when you got the first texts," she said. "See? His talk started at noon. Iceland is four hours ahead of New York. You got the texts at about nine thirty, right?"

"Yup. Right. That makes sense. He really doesn't seem to be the type to sexually harass somebody. He wouldn't have to. He's, like, handsome, rich, funny, and nice."

"Hm," said Jess. "Too cute to be a suspect. Okay. You know sexual harassment is about power, right?"

"You're right, I know. But I just don't think he'd do it. I bet I'd know for sure if I saw him again."

"Sounds like a good idea. But don't sleep with him."

I rolled my eyes. "As if."

She smiled at me and shrugged. I could see she was thinking of some ill-considered trysts in my past. I decided to ignore the implication.

"Are there any other suspects we should consider?" she asked.

"Beatrice was asking about JFXBF. But I don't think he would have the energy or ability to pull off this kind of thing."

"I agree," she said, and laughed. "No."

"I know. So it looks like it's Alvin," I said.

"Or Declan," said Jess. "Or someone else."

# 45

When Adam gets back to the table, I figure I should let him know I've had some second thoughts.

"Did you get lost? Trying to remember who your date is tonight?"

He laughs and sits down. Mr. Cool.

"As if," he says. "Believe me, I'm not much for dating. When I get time off, I like hiking. I really like it when I can take the kids, but I go by myself a lot."

Expert moves. Pivots away from my needy affirmation-seeking to manly independence.

"So there's not a woman in every town?"

"No," he says, laughing. "Have you had a look at the women in Scranton? Or Watertown? Syracuse?"

We laugh together and both sip our wine, looking at each other in silence. I smile.

"So, want to go for a walk?"

"Where?" I ask, swirling the dregs of wine in my glass. "Your room?"

"Sure," he says, drains his glass, and stands up.

"Is there wine there?"

"Minibar," he says and cocks an eyebrow.

"Sold."

The rest is easy. I actually decide to let go a little bit, enjoy myself for a few minutes, until the roofie kicks in. Once we're in the room, I kick off my flip-flops, sit cross-legged on the bed, and demand he bring me wine. He does as I bid, and I give him a tiny little kiss on the lips as thanks and push him away. He stares at me with real desire from the armchair. We look at each other over our wine.

"I really like you, Amy," he eventually says.

I let that sit for a while, take a drink of wine, and then get up and walk over to the armchair. We make out for a little while. He is tender. By the time he starts to get druggy he's removed my dress, I've removed his shirt and unbuttoned his pants, and he's on the bed on his back, in a stupor, but his body is obviously still capable of carrying out its role. I am sad when he turns into a roofied automaton and wonder whether I want to carry on with what we had started.

He grunts and reaches for me. I stand in my underwear and look at him.

"I should have waited," I tell him. "You took your medicine too soon."

What to do?

# 46

Jess insisted that we not go over my recollections or our theories with Wayne, since she wanted to make sure that we didn't suggest answers he wouldn't come up with on his own.

He arrived at the bar at the Jane with news.

"Craig is out," he said. "About an hour after you left, Alvin came by for a meeting with Craig and Rebecca. Craig came out of his office. He thanked us all for our hard work, then said that he would always remember his time 'stretching boundaries' at SoSol, but he had chosen to embrace another opportunity."

"Did he look like he was excited to embrace another opportunity?" asked Jess.

"He looked like he had just been fired. I was afraid he was going to cry. It was . . . awful."

"They're circling the wagons," said Jess.

"What do you mean?" I asked.

"If this ends up in court, or mediation, they can say, 'Hey look, we learned that the manager in question had allowed an unhealthy environment to develop, so we took action.'"

"But if the problem came from Alvin . . ."

She held her finger up.

"Which we don't know," she said. "But even if it did, it's sort of a script, a process, a step that indicates seriousness. I've been through quite a few of these in the past few years. There are two ways they go.

Double down and deny any problem or fire the manager and prepare a settlement."

"So this might be a good sign," I said.

"Seems like a really good sign," she said.

"Poor Craig," said Wayne.

We all sat silently for a moment and thought about poor Craig.

"They'll be paying him to go," said Jess. "Don't worry about him too much."

"You're smart," said Wayne, and he looked at Jess admiringly. "How long have you been doing this kind of work?"

I didn't like that. He was my future boyfriend, not Jess's.

Jess touched her hair. She was a little too happy with the compliment.

"Two years," she said. "You start to see the same patterns recurring."

"You must deal with some real dirtbags," said Wayne. "Sexual harassment is so unpleasant."

"That's why it's against the law," she said.

"How do you think Candace's situation will play out?" he said.

"It's too early to say. We don't have all the facts. After we finish these, I want to take you to my office and ask you some questions. Do you mind doing that? It could theoretically have a negative impact on your employment."

Wayne laughed.

"I don't care about this job at all. I have a real job in California starting in September. This is just something to keep me busy during the summer. I could walk away tomorrow. So sure. I'll happily answer your questions. Nobody should be able to get away with treating anyone like they've treated Candace."

He turned to me.

"This is not okay," he said. "It's going to follow you for the rest of your life. No matter what you do, you'll have to live with the fact that every creep in every office where you work will see that picture."

God, he was adorable. I looked at him admiringly. So did Jess.

"I was talking about it last night to my friend Lenora," he said. "She writes for Pandora, a website that runs a lot of stories . . ."

"I love that website," said both Jess and I.

We all laughed.

"Anyway. She's a really good journalist, really nice person, and she thinks that this would be a good story. Young woman, just starting her career, gets hacked."

"That could be a good idea," said Jess. "By telling your own story you at least gain agency, get your version of events out there."

"Instead of being a victim who had something bad happen to her, you could be a strong young woman overcoming an attack," said Wayne.

"And it would likely immediately solve my SEO problem," I said. "It would be the first thing anyone would find out about me when they google me, instead of the crap on Reddit."

"I'll flip you her email," said Wayne, and he fiddled with his phone.

"Okay, fun's over," said Jess, glancing at her watch and our empty glasses. "Time for me to drag you back to my office, Wayne, and submit you to a thorough interrogation."

"Okay," said Wayne. "But I was kind of enjoying my drink."

"I might have some wine in my office," she said.

He gave her a warm smile. Grrr.

They looked at me like I was an afterthought.

# 47

I snuggle up to Adam, who is snoring peacefully, and take stock of my situation.

I decide that I should completely stop thinking about getting a lawyer to clear my name. The more I think about it, the more I realize I would never be able to do that.

I had been planning to get someplace safe for a few days, so that I could consider my options, but I realize now that giving myself up is not one of those options. I could deal with jail, maybe, but not the public humiliation, and I don't want to ever see the video of the station platform.

So that means that I have to turn my back on everybody I have ever known, which will really suck for my mom and Francis and a few other friends, but I don't have any choice.

Good-bye, Mom. Good-bye, Francis.

I have an okay plan. It has two parts: (1) Get Farther from New York, and (2) Continue to Avoid the Police.

I am one step ahead of them. I would like to be two steps ahead of them, then three, then ten. I should be able to do this, but I have to think really clearly and not make any mistakes.

Take no chances.

I make an inventory of my assets:

One jean jacket.

One black dress.

One pair of flip-flops.

One pair of dirty jeans.

Assorted disgusting underwear.

Toiletries.

One chef's knife.

One notebook.

Four roofies.

$524.

Adam, happily for me, has just been to a bank machine. He has twenty twenty-dollar bills in his wallet.

Well, he used to.

I need to get on the highway, get in a vehicle heading north, and, hopefully, get one more step ahead of my pursuers.

I decide that I won't take Adam's car—likely one of the black SUVs in the hotel's parking lot. I could just wander around the lot, beeping the unlock button until it lights up and drive off. It would be great to cruise along in style, but if I steal his car, he will have to report it.

If I just leave him as he is, he won't go to the police. He won't remember what happened, might not even know for sure he's been roofied.

Drank too much. Took girl to room. She's gone.

No need to mention it to the police, or the wife.

# 48

I stewed all evening.

Well, I popped two Ambiens and drank red wine and monitored social media and stewed.

I didn't like the way that Wayne and Jess became such fast friends.

That was all I needed, to have my supersuccessful big sister scoop up my crush. It ate at me.

We'd been tight when we were small, when we used to have our little adventures in the woods, but after she hit puberty, she dropped me for friends her age, which hurt my feelings. And then there was the stuff with Dad.

I think I resented her, and Mom, for not being there for me when I needed someone to protect me. When I eventually realized that what had been happening was wrong, and Miss Busy started acting out, how could it not have been crystal clear to everyone that something was wrong with Candace? Except there wasn't anything wrong with Candace. There was something wrong with Dad.

Now Jess was helping me like she helped me deal with the Gary issue. I was grateful to her then, but it felt like she wanted me to be even more grateful, and I was already getting that feeling again.

And her overfamiliarity with Wayne rankled.

It was not a productive evening. I didn't feel like I was in the right state of mind to tackle the huge image-repair job that I faced, not if I wanted to drink a bottle of cheap red wine, which I felt was a more important priority.

Before too much of the wine was gone, I emailed Francis, promised to catch up soon, and called Mom, which was not easy.

"Oh, honey," she said. "How *are* you?"

"Good, Mom! I'm sorry I haven't called. I've been busy with my new job."

"But Jess told me that you're not going to stay there because of that . . . picture."

"That hasn't been decided yet. Everything is still kind of up in the air."

Are lawyers supposed to share information without permission from their clients? I didn't think so. I had no idea what Jess thought she was doing, except that she was trying to help, by making decisions—like what to tell Mom—that should have been up to me. I understood the impulse—she wanted to help—but it was by no means clear that her judgment was better than mine. I hadn't wanted to tell Mom about this hacking business until it was over. Much less of a worry for her.

"I think it might be better if you get out of that place," Mom said. "I mean, it sounds like a nightmare. My poor Candy."

She started to cry. I could tell she was confused and hurt by the whole topless selfie thing, and I kept having to explain to her that I was hacked, which she didn't really understand, and then she'd cry some more and I'd cry along with her, and she'd ask more questions and get confused again and I sort of got a little mad at her and then she cried and so did I and I really wanted to get off the phone.

My mom is a sweet person, but she was always a homebody, ignoring the world beyond Newtown, busy raising Jess and me, looking after Dad, while he took the train in to fight insurance dragons and bring home the paycheck.

When Dad had a massive heart attack three years ago, she was suddenly his nurse, and she did a great job, although not great enough to stop the second massive heart attack, which killed him a year later. Meat kills.

Since then she's been kind of, I don't know, cut off. Both Jess and I are busy trying to make lives for ourselves in the city and Mom doesn't get what that means, which makes it hard to share much about our lives, which is what she wants.

So the good conversations end up being about her, talking through her days, with her volunteer activities, walks with friends, health worries, house maintenance concerns, and all kinds of other stuff that is basically everything I don't want my life to be about.

Anyway, Mom wanted me to go home and stay with her for a while, until Jess helped me get to the bottom of the whole thing, which was not happening.

"I can't," I said. "I have a job that's actually going really well in a lot of ways. Did I tell you about Cheese of the Month? I'm making sales. I'm good at this and I want to keep doing it."

"But, honey, it sounds like a terrible place to work. I want you to get out of there. Either they're harassing you or . . ."

"Or what?"

"I don't know."

I felt like I was twelve again, when Jess and I were at each other's throats, and everything was so bad. I started to get upset.

"What did Jess tell you?"

"She said you can't figure out yet who has been doing these terrible things to you. I wish you'd come down here for a while, even a few days, until you're feeling yourself."

"I am myself. It's just a thing I have to deal with so that I can move on with my career and my life. Don't worry so much. It's not helping."

I wanted to kill myself.

I actually thought about that seriously for a while after I finally managed to get off the phone. I could just end it all. I would leave a note. I drank more wine and thought about what the note would say.

I could thank Jess and say I hoped she'd be happy with Wayne. I wouldn't mention whether it was ethical for a lawyer steal her client's crush.

I got myself in quite a state. I was absolutely convinced that Jess and Wayne were going to end up kissing on her desk, beginning a romance that would inevitably end in marriage. I couldn't bear the thought of being the scorned little sister.

I even thought about going to Jess's place over in Jersey. I had her spare keys. I could sneak in to see if she was home yet, hide in the bushes out front and watch for her. I didn't do it but I seriously thought about it.

Instead, I opened a second bottle of wine.

# 49

Adam starts to stir at about 4:00 a.m., and I decide I'd better leave before he wakes up.

I collect all my stuff, put on my jean jacket, give Adam a kiss on the cheek, and take the elevator downstairs. I slip past the reception desk and stop in front of the hotel to orient myself. I don't want to go wandering around in the dark looking for the highway, and I can't ask for directions from the desk clerk.

As I stand there, a young black woman comes outside, startling me. She lights her cigarette even before she gets outside. She has dyed blond hair, high heels, short skirt, low-cut top. Sex worker.

"Hey, girl, what's happening?" she says.

"Hey, not much."

"Getting paid?"

I laugh.

"I might be."

"You trapping here, girl?"

I don't know what to say. *Trapping*. Does that mean turning tricks?

"I might be."

"You must know, girl," she says. "I'm trapping and I know it. I'm not one of these hos pretends she's a veterinarian."

I laugh.

"I came up with a guy from the city. Now we're done and I'm headed home."

"Girlfriend experience?" she asks.

"Yeah. I only have a few clients. I'm going to school."

"Only diploma I got is in ho-ology. You could make real money you hit it full-time, girl. Nice-looking white girl. My man is coming to get me. He sort you out. Get you making big dollars, girl."

Suddenly I don't like talking to her.

"That's all right. Thanks, though."

God. I sounded like I was greeting someone at a PTA meeting.

"He fix you up, girl. No problem. You want to get your smoke on? Where's your driver at?"

I am trapped. I have no driver. I have nothing to say. Fuck.

"Actually. I'm going to go back in and wait for him. He'll text when he's here. Nice talking to you."

She stares at me as I go back inside.

Fuck.

I decide to pretend that I'm going back to the room and instead go out another exit. There has to be one. I walk through the lobby and find the back exit, which goes to a parking lot with railroad tracks running along the back. I head for the tracks.

As I cross the lot, I hear a car. A black SUV with tinted windows pulls around the corner and stops in an empty spot between me and the tracks.

When I pass it, the window of the passenger side rolls down.

"Girl!"

I turn. It's the sex worker.

"There you are," she says. "Your driver a no-show? Come on. We give you a ride."

I smile and shake my head.

"I'm great," I say, feeling stupid with my fake smile. I start moving again. "Thanks all the same."

The SUV honks its horn. I stop and turn. The woman has her head and arm out the window. She's beckoning to me.

"Girl, come on," she says. "Don't be foolish. You attracting attention. Trying to give the police a reason to fuck with us?"

I wave at her and turn and walk faster toward the tracks.

She shouts after me.

"Where your driver at, bitch? Ho need a driver."

On the right, the railroad tracks go past a football field and a dark parking lot. On the left, they cross a highway overpass, with a chain-link fence on the sides, likely to stop the local losers from dropping cinder blocks and malt liquor bottles on passing cars. Beyond the bridge, I can see an expressway. I step onto the crunchy oversized gravel of the railbed and head that way, with a purposeful stride, a stride that says, I hope, *Don't fuck with me. I am not a victim.*

# 50

I woke up hungover and feeling emotionally vulnerable.

Jess had emailed me to tell me we had a meeting at 10:00 a.m. at SoSol. She said everything went well with Wayne, which didn't make me feel better. I was now sure she had fucked him, or at least made out with him.

Probably she was smarter than me and waited for a certain number of dates before giving up the goods. She and her friends all read *The Rules* when they were in law school and used to talk about the husband-getting tips it contained.

I was doomed, I was sure, to the lonely life of a resentful lovelorn sister.

Still in bed, I checked my phone. I had several emails from Wayne's friend Lenora, all very keen.

She wanted to talk to me! She couldn't believe what I'd been through! It was totally a cautionary tale that young women should know about! She lived near me in Brooklyn and was having a coffee at the Black Brick. Could I come down now?

I had a quick shower and went to meet her.

I liked her right away. She was like a nicer version of me, except with tattoos and piercings. She even had red hair. I thought the two of us looked funny sipping our lattes side by side, because we look so much alike. Not like you would get us mixed up but that we were obviously both examples of a type. Redhead Brooklyn hipster girl.

She told me about her career, which started with a journalism degree from Columbia, where she did a long feature on rape culture, exposing campus sex assaults and inaction by university administrators. Shitty investigations. Bad trials. Rape kits that never got processed. She freelanced for a year, working on similar stories, before Pandora noticed that she was delivering half their traffic and hired her.

She described how she got sex-assault victims to open up and told me some enraging stories that she couldn't run because the details were impossible to prove to the satisfaction of editors and lawyers.

I realized with a jolt that I'd read some of her stories.

By the time she got around to trying to convince me to give her an interview, it was unnecessary.

"Stop," I said. "I'm ready. I believe you'll do your best to look out for me. Let's just do it."

She smiled and took my hands in hers, promised she would do that, and took out her recorder.

I spun out my story, telling her about the Twitter and Facebook posts and the awful messages. It was easy to talk about the slut-shaming social media reaction, and she seemed pleased with what I had to say about that.

I talked about how I had to figure out how to live with this invasion of privacy, which was profound and damaging, but not fatal. I said that in many ways that meant I was like any number of people in society—women, people of color, LBGTQI—who had to try to remain optimistic and keep moving forward although they faced personal experiences of oppression.

We both thought that was pretty good.

She got me to talk about my reaction to the postings and the texts and then wanted to know the details—dates and times and so on. I told her I couldn't be as sure as I wanted about some stuff because my phone had been wiped. When I lifted it to show her, I noticed that the notification notice said I had 128 text messages waiting for me. Oh oh.

I opened it up.

Oh fuck. I showed the screen to Lenora.

She gasped.

One after another, 128 messages from the same unknown number, all identical.

Hey.

Hey.

Hey.

"Just like the last time," I said.

"That's him?"

"That's him."

I scrolled back. The first message was different from the others.

Hey, roastie. Check your Twitter.

Oh God. I felt like I was going to vomit. Lenora and I looked at each other.

Then the phone rang, startling us both. It was Jess.

"Hi," I said.

"Candace? You need to shut down your Twitter and Facebook accounts right now. Do it right now. K? Then we'll talk."

# 51

As the sun starts coming up, I am running flat out across the highway from the railway tracks to the other side, where there's a garbage-strewn gravel shoulder. I run because when the cars and trucks come around the corner they're moving fast, scaring me, and I don't want to get hit. What the fuck am I doing?

I really want to find a donut shop, have some hash browns, coffee, and orange juice, but there's nothing in front of me but more road. I could easily get hit here. The trucks are so close to me that I feel the air turbulence from them as they pass. The shoulder is narrow and the embankment is steep, so I'm stuck. I walk quickly, scared and cold.

I'm thinking about trying to climb down from the expressway into the scrub woods at the bottom of the hill when a black SUV pulls up in front of me, blocking my path, and the driver's door opens and suddenly a huge black man is standing in front of me, with his arm against the door.

"There you are," he says. "Little hiking ho."

"Hi," I say.

"Hold up," he says. "Let's chat for a minute."

I have no choice.

"You like walking?" he says. "How come you got nobody looking out for you?"

"I'm all right. I don't need any help."

"You trapping in Scranton you might need somebody's help. You not in Vegas here, girl."

He smiles. He has a closely trimmed beard, looks like he's in his forties. He's dark, tall and muscular, wearing a tight, expensive-looking sweater that clings to his chest. His brown eyes are on me.

"I'm not trapping in Scranton. Just passing through."

"Yeah? Where you going?"

I feel like I have to answer him.

"Back to the city," I say. "Back to school."

He looks me up and down. It feels like he's assessing me like a product.

"Maybe you is. Why don't we go sit down, chat about it? Go through the drive-through, get some Mickey D's, go back to my place, have a little chat?"

"Thanks but I'm tired and I just want to get back home."

"How you going to do that? Where's your driver? Where's your phone? I can get you a driver."

He turns to the woman in the car.

"Macy," he says. "What's Larry doing today? Can he drive this lady back to the city this morning?"

She says Larry could.

"All right," he says and opens the backseat door for me. "We got you covered. Get in before you piss me off."

I shake my head.

"No. Thanks but no."

Then, over my shoulder, he sees something.

"Shit," he says. "Po po. You can come with us or you can wait to talk to them."

A police car is turning onto the expressway. If they drive off, the police will surely want to know what I'm doing walking on the expressway. Fuck. I can't have that.

I jump into the SUV.

# 52

I flipped open my work laptop and looked at my Twitter. Lenora stood over my shoulder.

Not good. My account had tweeted the sex picture of me and part of JFXBF with the text "Madskillz." It was ten minutes old and had already been retweeted eighty-eight times. Ninety-five. One hundred twenty-two.

Oh God. I was going viral.

"I have to close my account," I said.

I was icily calm. So was Lenora.

"Go to account settings," she said.

I followed her instructions and within seconds had the satisfaction of seeing the "That User Does Not Exist" message.

Next: Facebook, where my profile pic had also been replaced with the porn shot. I didn't read any of the zillion alarmed comments. I just followed Lenora's calm instructions and shut it down.

When I confirmed that it was done, I picked up the phone.

"I shut them down," I told Jess.

"Good. Are you okay?"

"No. It's pretty bad."

"It is. But on the plus side, it probably increases pressure on SoSol to settle this, put it behind them."

"Should I issue a statement or something?"

"No. Keep your head down until we meet. I'm writing to Twitter, asking them to take down any retweets, although that won't stop the screencaps. I'll have more of a plan by the time we meet. See you at noon at Blossom?"

"Okay."

"You just have to get through this day. You'll make it."

"Thanks."

I hung up and turned to Lenora. I kind of did a little karate chop, like I was severing what just happened, cutting it off. Then I looked at her. She had her phone in front of her. I could see the picture on her phone. I looked up at her face. She was on the verge of tears.

"Fuck," I said.

She started crying and took me into her arms. We embraced and had a sisterly sob. She wiped my cheeks and held my head in her hands.

"You won't believe the story I'm going to write about this," she said. "You think that picture is going viral, just wait for my fucking story."

She let go of my head and we both sat back in our chairs.

"When?" I asked. "When will it go up?"

"Tomorrow. Hang in there. Everything will seem a lot better once the story's up. Believe me."

"Thank you. I can't. I can't. I mean I don't know."

I felt completely lost and distraught. Powerless.

I had to see how bad it was.

I typed in a Twitter search for my handle.

Immediately a column was filled with screencaps of my hacked tweet, with terrible comments.

Some jerk had put the picture side by side with a blog I wrote complaining about slut-shaming and sexism in the mass media with the headline: "Busted! SJW Roastie Guzzles Jizz!"

I could see that it had been retweeted many times.

"What's a roastie?" I asked.

"Huh?"

"A roastie. This guy calls me a roastie. So did the guy who texted me."

"Oh. Gross. It's incel slang for a woman, uh, of ill repute. A slut."

"Incel?"

"Involuntary celibates. An online community of guys who can't get sex and blame women for it."

Who were these men? How could they live with themselves? Didn't they realize they were hurting someone who didn't deserve it?

I wanted to make them suffer. I stupidly tried to delete their comments and the picture, which I obviously couldn't do.

I started punching the screen, which felt really good. The laptop fell off the table onto the café floor. I stood up and stomped on it. The hinge separating the screen from the keyboard gave way and I could hear the insides crunching beneath my feet.

I jumped up and down a half-dozen times, while Lenora looked on. The barista looked scared and a couple of students sitting in the corner looked like they were getting ready to run.

I held up my hands to show that I'd got myself under control and sat down.

"Fuck," I said. "I feel better now."

Lenora stared at me with horror, then we both started to laugh.

"That's the lead," she said.

# 53

Scary Pimp keeps his eyes on the rearview mirror as we pull out into traffic.

"Girl, if they stop us, you tell them I'm your driver, okay?"

"Yes."

"You tell them anything else, they'll think I'm your pimp and I'll go straight to jail."

"You're my driver. You're driving me and Macy home."

"Goddamned right."

But the police don't pull us over, thankfully.

"You didn't want to talk to the po po, did you, girl?" he says, eyeing me in the rearview mirror. "You on the run? Where's your phone? Usually, I talk to a ho she's fiddling with her phone all the time. How come you got no phone? What kind of ho don't have a phone?"

"I'm not on the run. I'm a student. I do GFE every now and then. Craigslist. I don't need a manager or anything. I want to get back to the city. It's really nice of you to give me a lift!"

"Relax, girl. I don't need to strong-arm no hos, do I, Macy?"

Macy turns and looks back at me.

"He never strong-armed me," she says. "I applied for this position. I was the most qualified candidate."

She laughs and the pimp joins in. I find myself laughing with them. Macy is funny. I need to make it clear that I am not going to work for him, though.

"Okay, but I want you to know I'm not looking for a position. If you can take me to the bus station, that would be great."

"You sure?" he says. "I know people would really like a taste of what you got. Let me set you up for a day or two, make some money. Get your smoke on. Have a little fun."

I am not going to go along with his plan.

"I don't do coke. I don't want to start sucking off twenty guys a night in some shitty motel room while you keep the money. Thanks, though. I just want to get home. If you can't drive me to the bus station, maybe you can just drop me off here."

"You think we lowlifes?" he says. "You think we small-time?"

Shit. I've made him angry. He looks back at me. His eyes are moving fast. He shakes his head and turns back to the road.

"We going to take you to the bus station."

He doesn't, though. When we leave the expressway, we drive to a McDonald's drive-through. He orders Egg McMuffins and hash browns and orange juice. He gives Macy the drinks and keeps the bag between his legs.

I want to object, to get out, but I am hungry and exhausted and I stay slumped in the seat, feeling defeated. We drive through some seedy-looking suburban streets to Motor Rest, a terrible-looking one-story concrete motel. The paint is peeling and there's garbage on the broken pavement of the parking lot. Barbecues and cheap-looking bikes are chained outside some of the units. I look at it with despair.

"Come on," he says. "Breakfast time."

I follow him and Macy into a shabby room.

I am so tired.

There's a cheap TV, a minifridge, a horrible carpet, falling-apart furniture, one of those quilted polyester bedspreads with a sun-faded floral pattern. Their suitcases are open and I can see their gaudy clothes. There's a bottle of Smirnoff and some dirty glasses on top of the fridge. It smells like stale sex and old cigarette smoke.

"Let's eat," he says. "Then I'll take you to the bus station."

He and Macy sit down on the bed. I sit down on the single, disgusting chair.

He takes the lids off the cups of orange juice and pours vodka into them. He hands me one. I look at it for a second, exasperated, then I realize that I actually want a drink. I take it. We all toast.

He gives me hash browns and an Egg McMuffin.

"I don't eat meat," I say.

"More for me," he says and takes the Egg McMuffin back.

I gobble my hash browns. I'm still hungry. He gives me his as he eats my Egg McMuffin.

"Thanks."

When we are done, Macy lights a cigarette and the pimp picks up his phone.

"Just one thing," he says. "I'll take you to the bus station, but first you got to do a little favor for me. I got a guy, Bruce, coming here in twenty minutes. I promised him a bj from a white girl. You're going to do it. 'K?"

No.

"No. No. I'm not blowing anybody."

I put down my spiked orange juice and stand up.

"I'm going to leave. I'll go to the motel office and call a cab."

I head for the door, moving quickly, but he's too fast. He's on me. He wraps his hand around my neck and squeezes. I grab at it with both my hands, but his thick wrist is so strong. My air is cut off. I am terrified.

"You need to shut the fuck up," he says. "You are pissing me off."

I feel my face turning red. I nod, enthusiastically. He relaxes his grip.

"Okay. Okay. No problem."

"I don't want you to fuck with me. I'm helping you. You are going to help me."

He squeezes again for a second, then relaxes his hand. It is awful.

"I'm sorry. You're right. I'm sorry."

He takes his hand away and I gasp.

I rub my neck and go to look in the mirror.

"Don't worry," he says. "No marks. I never leave marks."

He and Macy laugh.

"Girl, your eyes got so big," she says. "You were scared shitless."

She mimics me, bugging her eyes out with panic.

"But don't worry," she says. "Chris wouldn't choke you to death. Just needs you to listen to him. You listen to him he won't put a hand on you."

I can't believe this. I hate her. I hate him. I hate my situation.

"I get it. I'm going to listen."

Chris is watching us through hooded eyes.

"We gonna get along fine now that we understand each other," he says.

He finishes his drink and looks at his watch.

"Bruce will be here in fifteen minutes," he says. "Let's have another drink."

I get up.

"I'll mix them," I say.

"There's more juice in the fridge," says Macy.

If I can slip roofies into them, I can avoid the blow job to come, avoid getting choked again, avoid the rapes and beatings that I am sure Chris has in mind for me.

It is a good plan, except that they're sitting on the bed watching me. The roofies are in a pillbox in my little bag. I can't get at them. I try to think of a way to do it. Can I go to the bathroom with my bag? Not before making the drinks.

I mix the drinks, without roofies, and hand them to Macy and Chris. He raises his drink to toast.

"To new friends," he says.

We all drink. I need to roofie them. Fuck.

"I want to fix my makeup," I say.

I pick up my bag and stand up.

"Go ahead," says Chris. "But leave the door open."

The bathroom is disgusting, with stains on the tub and mold on the cracked tiles on the wall. There are towels on the floor. I stand in the doorway and look at myself in the dirty mirror. I look terrible in the bad fluorescent light, tired and scared.

Chris moves to the other side of the bed so he can keep an eye on me. I smile at him.

"I also need to pee," I say and move to close the door.

He laughs.

"Girl, I don't mind if you do. Nothing I ain't seen before. But you gonna leave the door open."

I see that I can't defy him. I dig around in the bag for my lipstick and eyeliner. I manage to find the pill bottle with the roofies. I carefully open the bottle and take two of them into my hand. I see no way to get them into the drinks right now, but I can have them ready.

When I'm done with my makeup, I sit down to pee, preserving my modesty with my dress, while Chris leers at me. I look back at him blankly and pee. He grins at me as I wipe myself. It's humiliating, but I manage to slip the two roofies into the front of my underwear without him noticing.

# 54

I felt strangely calm by the time I got to Chelsea for my lunch with Jess.

I love Blossom, which likely helped calm me down more. It's such a stylish, elegant room. Understated vibe. Gentle music. Vegan deliciousness.

Jess started by outlining all the social media damage control she'd undertaken on my behalf. She'd sent cease-and-desist letters to Twitter, Facebook, and Reddit, demanding that they take down the picture.

"Even if they all take it down, it's still going to be out there forever, though, isn't it?" I said.

"No question. For the rest of your life, it's going to be part of your past. But it will get further in the past as time goes by."

"Really? Seems to me it will also always be with me."

She looked at me blankly, then nodded and shrugged.

"It is what it is."

"So how did it go with Wayne?" I asked. "Did his recollection match my recollection?"

"For the most part, yes. He certainly backed up everything you said about Alvin's behavior, which is totally actionable."

"What about the rest of it?"

"There were minor differences in your stories. Nothing important, I don't think. I'd rather not get into the discrepancies now and I don't think you and he should discuss it until after we've met with SoSol. I don't want any sign of story straightening."

"When will we meet them?"

"They want to meet Monday at ten a.m. at the office. They'll likely offer a settlement."

Hm. So she would get Wayne to herself for the weekend.

My spider senses were tingling again. I felt like when I most needed my sister, she was scooping up the boy I liked. My situation was tense enough without fretting about her and my crush. The only thing I could think was that it was the least of my problems. It didn't feel like it, though. My breathing was shallow and my stomach was knotted and sour. I'd had only two bites of my cashew-cream ravioli.

I was afraid Jess would see that I was freaking out. I needed an Ambien but that would have to wait until after lunch. I made do with two glasses of Chardonnay.

"So I did the Pandora interview this morning," I said. "I was actually doing it when you called to tell me about the latest pic."

"Oh shit."

"What? You thought it was a good idea."

"Yeah, in theory. Shit. You probably signed a nondisclosure when you were hired by SoSol. Do you have a copy of your contract?'

"In my desk at work."

"Can you see if she can leave the name of the company out of it?"

"Sure. I'll email her."

"Okay. When's it come out?"

"Tomorrow."

"That makes it a lot less likely that you'll ever return to work at SoSol. I think you had pretty much decided that anyway, but they don't know that. It means we have to go in with a different strategy."

"What else should I do?"

"Have you talked to Declan yet?"

"No. I'll email him and see if he's free."

"That's good. Best if you approach him, see what his attitude is. If he has helpful stuff to say, I'd meet with him."

"Anything else?"

"How are you? Can you handle this situation?"

"Do I have a choice?" I asked. "What do you mean?"

She looked up at the ceiling, then fixed me with what was meant to be a cool, professional look.

"I mean, if you feel fragile, like it's all too much, you need to tell me," she said. "We can't go in there loaded for bear if you can't keep your cool, or if your story falls apart."

I stared at her. She was thinking, I could see, of teenage Candace, who, like a lot of teenage girls, had her ups and downs. It seems very Jess, more than a little bitchy, to allude to that now.

"I'm fine," I said. "Anything else?"

She gave me a nod, as if she'd checked off a box she had to check, and then smiled.

"Nope," she said. "I think we're good."

Exit Candace, gulping Ambien.

# 55

After I pee, it's time for Macy and me to go next door to wait for Bruce.

It has the same terrible furniture and bad smell as the first room. We sit down in the same spots as in the other room, her on the bed, me on the chair.

"It's easy, girl," she says. "I'll take the money, leave you with Bruce. You just got to be nice to him, get that dick in your mouth, get him off, and you can get your white ass back to the city. Anything goes wrong, bang on the wall."

I just look at her. I am not her friend. I don't want her advice.

"I'm only sucking one dick," I say. "Then I'm going."

"Maybe two," she says. "That's up to Chris."

I look at her and shake my head.

"One," I say.

She shrugs, takes out her phone, and looks at it. I have no phone. I just sit there.

Soon, there's a knock on the door. It's Bruce.

He's in his fifties, a fat, nervous white man, wearing a big pair of Dockers, a cheap golf shirt, and a nylon jacket. He has a ridiculous gray mustache and a NASCAR baseball cap.

"Hi," he says.

"Come on in, honey," says Macy. "This here is Crystal. She's going to show you a good time."

I smile at him. He smiles at me and steps inside.

"Isn't she pretty?" says Macy. "She gonna take care of you."

"Hi, Crystal," he says. "She's right. You are pretty."

He is laughing nervously.

I reach out and shake his hand.

"Hi," I say. "Nice to meet you."

"I'll leave you two alone," says Macy. "I just need the fee."

Bruce gives her some folded bills, which she counts.

"You kids have fun," she says as she leaves. Then she's gone.

Bruce sits down on the bed and grins at me.

"You're just so beautiful," he says.

He spreads his legs and rubs the front of his pants. Oh God. This is not happening. He is smiling at me in anticipation. He is so stupid, I can tell. And poor. His teeth are yellow and he smells of stale cigarettes. I can't do this. No way.

I get up from the chair and look out the window. There's a blue Ford truck sitting there that wasn't there when we came in. It's a semi, the cab of an eighteen-wheeler. He's a trucker. Of course.

I turn to Bruce.

"Pennsylvania ZBC 2977," I say.

He looks back at me.

"That's my license plate," he says.

"That's what I'll tell the cops. And they can use that to find your real name."

He blinks at me blankly, swallows.

"Sorry, Bruce. I don't do this. I'm not a hooker. There's a big pimp in the next room trying to force me to do it. It's human trafficking and it's illegal. I could go to the cops but I don't want to. I just want to get away. So you're going to sit here for fifteen minutes, give me a head start."

He blinks repeatedly. He can't understand what's going on.

"But I paid," he says.

"You can ask them for the money back after I'm gone. I don't care. But I'm not sucking your dick, and if you don't give me fifteen minutes I'm going to the police and telling them to track down the guy who owns a blue Ford, license plate ZBC 2977."

He swallows.

"Bruce, if you like, we could just call the police," I say. "Would you rather we do that?"

He swivels his head around, opens and closes his mouth.

"This is a scam," he says. "You and that black lady are ripping me off. Give me my $30 back."

"Look, Bruce. There's a great big guy in the next room named Chris who was choking me half an hour ago. I am afraid he'll kick the shit out of me. Please help me. Just give me a head start."

I realize I can give him $30. I dig into my purse and find some bills.

"Here," I say. "There's your money back. Just please sit here for a few minutes."

He takes the money and frowns. The situation obviously requires more thinking than he's capable of. He may have some mild handicap.

I stand and go to the door.

"Please, Bruce," I say. "Just give me fifteen minutes. Please."

I open the door and look at him, pleading with my eyes.

"Please."

# 56

After Jess and I finished our lunch, and I finally popped an Ambien, I went uptown, where I sat out in front of her office building. I wanted to see if anyone was going in to meet her there. Wayne, actually. I got a seat outside a café across the street, ordered a glass of wine, and went through the tasks she'd assigned me.

I emailed Lenora, who quickly let me know she hadn't ever planned on including the name of my company.

She also told me she had talked to a friend—Wendy—a producer for CNN, who really wanted to talk to me. Lenora vouched for her. I emailed her. She suggested a drink at four at Bemelmans.

Then I emailed Declan, who, it turned out, would be delighted to meet me for dinner Saturday.

I can't believe what's been going on in your life, he emailed. I hope you're okay.

Not really, I replied. Fair warning.

My wine was done. There was no sign of Wayne. I ordered another glass and kind of blanked out, watching people walk by, letting my mind wander.

I checked my phone when I was getting ready to leave. I had an email.

**From:** Wayne Timmons
**To:** Candace Walker

**Date:** 3:45 p.m., June 22, 2018
**Subject:** Did you like them though?

I don't really understand what you mean, Candace. What's going on?

I realized it was a reply to an email I had sent him.

**From:** Candace Walker
**To:** Wayne Timmons
**Date:** 3:33 p.m., June 22, 2018
**Subject:** Did you like them though?

The pics.

What? What was he talking about?
Oh my God. My phone buzzed in my hand. I had a fresh text.

Ha ha. U dum.

It hadn't occurred to me that someone could hack my email the same way that they'd hacked my social accounts. What must Wayne be thinking? What if he was with Jess? He would show her. This was catastrophic. But I didn't have time to fret about it.

I quickly sent a reply.

**From:** Candace Walker
**To:** Wayne Timmons
**Date:** 3:48 p.m., June 22, 2018
**Subject:** Did you like them though?

I didn't send this. Sorry. My email's been hacked.

I shut down my phone and went to meet Wendy from CNN. I would deal with my email security later.

She was waiting for me at a quiet table under one of the famous murals, wearing a big smile. She was Chinese American, corporate stylish, a bit nerdy, with a Donna Karan handbag but inexpensive walking shoes.

She waved when she saw me, gave me a friendly hug, got the waitress to bring me a glass of wine.

She told me, quickly but carefully, about her career, which seemed to revolve mostly around her ability to convince people to go on television and then make sure they performed as expected and didn't get exploited by the network.

She told several stories about the little ways she looks out for interview subjects, telling her senior producers to back off if necessary. I don't think I have ever met anyone more solicitous or sensitive than Wendy.

Then she got me talking.

She was so easy to talk to. She seemed to know exactly how I felt about everything that happened, empathizing with me, probing me with gentle questions, which spared me having to explain, at painful length, what it was like to have everybody I knew see a picture of me with a penis in my mouth. I found myself opening to her, trusting her.

She gave every impression of being ready and willing to put me on TV.

I was sold. I was also running out of time.

"So do you want to interview me?"

"I think so. If you can handle the exposure. It should be overwhelmingly positive. What happened to you is a huge cautionary tale. It would be great TV."

"Would you show the pictures?"

"Maybe, but blurred versions, to give people the idea of what they were. It's a lot better to show people things than tell them things in the TV business."

"I don't want people to think I'm manipulating this for my benefit."

"They won't think that. That's not what we'll tell them. They'll think, 'Oh that poor girl.' That would be the script."

I looked at her dubiously.

"Seriously. This is what I do. This is who I am. I'm kind of a mess as a person. Single at fifty-two. No kids. No cats. Drink too much. Don't have any real hobbies. Neglect my friends. But I know TV. And I know that what we have here is a simple, classic story. Nice girl gets the shaft."

"Then what happens to the nice girl?"

"That would be your story to write. This would allow you to make your story your own. Right now, it's a story about a girl who might have been hacked or might have posted dirty pictures of herself. Even the Pandora story won't completely change that. A TV story would. It would make you the cute redhead who got hacked."

"Do I want to be that girl? I kind of want to be the cute redhead getting ahead in the exciting world of social media."

Wendy gave me a sad smile.

"I know," she said. "It's terrible. Maybe you can be that girl again someday. But I have to tell you, that's not who you are right now."

I knew she was right.

I told her I'd think about it and then I got on the subway and went home to change my Gmail password. As I did it, I realized that my old password was the same as my old Twitter password. Maybe this would end it, I thought, and then I had a big glass of wine.

# 57

I leave Bruce looking confused and head for the highway. I walk quickly past another terrible-looking motel, past a vacant lot. I can't see I-81 but I can hear the trucks going by. My heart is pounding. I am exhausted and terrified and a little drunk. I need to get away from Scranton.

It isn't going to happen, I realize, when a black SUV pulls up beside me. The passenger-side window rolls down and I can see Chris in the driver's seat. Fuck. He must have been sitting in the parking lot, waiting for me to run.

"Get in," he says. "We need to talk."

I'm walking past a Hyundai dealership. There are woods behind. I could run into them. I can't let Chris get his hands on me again.

I'm turning when he shouts out.

"Candace! You need to stop fucking around right now."

I stop. How does he know my name? I'm fucked. If he calls the police, they'll have me within the hour. I feel like crying.

I give up. I stand there, staring at him. I'm trapped.

"I don't want you to choke me again."

He smiles.

"Don't worry," he says. "I won't. Get in. You're in a lot of trouble and I can get you out of it."

"Promise. No choking."

He smiles, then laughs and for a second he looks almost kind. He leans over and opens the passenger door.

"I promise. No choking. Get your ass in here."

I get in and he drives back to the motel.

"I'm serious about the choking. I can't take it."

"Just wait. We'll talk in the room."

I follow him meekly back to the room. I'm acting like a child.

"Where's Macy?" I ask.

"She's in the other room calming Bruce down, sucking him off," he says, closing the door. "At least I hope so."

"I gave him his thirty dollars back," I say.

I sit down on the chair. He sits on the bed and stares at me.

"I realized while you two were in there," he says. "I remembered the story about the Hipster Killer."

He holds up his phone.

"I don't know why you didn't want to suck a dick, girl," he says. "I know you know how to do it."

He turns the phone to show me the picture of me with JFXBF in my mouth.

# 58

On Saturday morning, I slept late, then met Beatrice at a patio near her place in Flatbush, and we had kimchi tofu tacos and beer and watched people walk by for a while.

She made a big deal of showing me her latest needlepoint.

"Whoa," I said, freaked out. It was the topless picture of me, half rendered in thread or wool or whatever.

"You like it?" she asked.

She looked at me intently, watching for my reaction.

I didn't like it. It was stolen. It represented misery and suffering.

"It . . . I don't know."

"I thought I might use it as the motif for my show. It says so much about how women are exploited by the use of their objectified bodies."

"But it's different from the other pieces. Those women were paid to do what they did. This was stolen."

"I know! That's what makes it perfect. It makes that link to exploitation."

"I don't know. It makes me uneasy."

"Okay," she said, putting it back in her purse. "We'll talk about it again before the show. Do you have any better idea of who did this to you?"

I told her the convoluted story of how my life was continuing to go off the rails, leaving me in a state of perpetual confusion.

"I have a short list of suspects," I said. "Alvin. Declan. Kevin. Maybe you can help me make is shorter. How well do you know Kevin?"

"Pretty well. He used to do tech stuff for the phone sex company Rudy worked for."

"Wow. I didn't know she did phone sex."

"They."

Her face got hard.

"Right. Sorry. They. I guess I was thinking of her as a woman because it was before she transitioned, back when she was Liz."

"Don't deadname them. They were never a woman, not really."

"I know. Sorry. It's hard. I'm used to calling everyone he or she. If I have to start calling some people they or it, I get mixed up."

"It?" said Beatrice. "Tell me you didn't just call Rudy it."

Her upper lip was a thin line. She was angry, struggling to hide it.

"No," I said. "Whatever. A new pronoun. I'm sorry. Bad choice of words."

I changed the subject.

"So could Kevin be the one fucking with me? If he wanted to, he would know how."

"No. Now that I think about it, he's not the type," said Beatrice. She looked as if she wanted to explain, but shrugged.

"He seems like a creeper."

"I don't see him that way," she said. "I like him. He lives around the corner from us and comes by for beers sometimes. He's kind of nerdy but nice. He's never been creepy with me."

I felt kind of hurt that she discounted my experience of Kevin.

"Creepers aren't creepers with everyone all the time," I said.

I thought, but didn't say, *Well, he wouldn't necessarily be creepy with you, Beatrice, because you're kind of a big girl, so you might not be the best one to judge whether he's a creeper or not.*

"He has his own theory," Beatrice said.

"He does? He hasn't shared it with me."

"You went to Sandy Hook, right?"

"Yeah. Why?"

"Did you know Adam Lanza?"

"We were in the same class in elementary, but no. Not really."

"Kevin wondered if this hacking could be linked to Sandy Hook."

That didn't make any sense. I was at NYU when it happened. It was a big awful thing, terrible for Mom, but I wasn't part of it.

"I don't see how it could," I said.

"I don't know either. But Kevin thinks there's some kind of conspiracy. He thinks the shooting didn't happen. Maybe the government's trying to mess with you because of something you know, maybe something you don't know that you know."

I was about to tell her how dumb that was, but she looked at her phone, said, "Oh my God, I'm superlate to meet Rudy," then gave me a perfunctory hug and ran off.

I went home and had a postbrunch nap. I was woken up by a call from Mom. I let her go to voice mail, but she hung up and called again, so I picked up.

She couldn't understand how any of this could have happened. It likely didn't help that Susan Pennyman, a neighbor, had shown the pictures to her mother, who had commiserated with Mom, no doubt reveling in the opportunity to rub her face in it.

Susan is dumb as a post, but somehow managed to marry a doctor and pop out a couple of babies, and I'm sure her mother loves reminding my mother of how smoothly Susan's life is going.

Mom hadn't seen the pictures, thank goodness, and Jess had patiently explained to her several times that someone had somehow stolen them, but she kept asking me how it could happen.

"But these are sex pictures," she said.

"They were stolen from my phone, and the awful part is that I don't know who took them. But Jess and I are hoping to figure it out."

"But how could they get them?" she asked.

"Mom, are you crying?"

"I'm not," she said, but I knew she was.

That made me cry. I felt so frustrated, the two of us silently crying, connected by phone in mutual misery. This was not helping me get my life together.

"I don't see how somebody could steal them," she said. "I mean, how?"

"It's phishing. With a *P-H* instead of an *F*. They got me to click a link and I downloaded a Trojan horse or something and they took over my phone. It's a hacker. It's what they do."

She went silent and started crying again.

"But the picture," she said. "That was on your phone?"

I realized that what she really wanted to know was how I could have taken such photos. She didn't understand, and I couldn't explain. Or she did understand and was upset that I had shamed her. Unlike Jess, who had a career Mom could brag about, or Susan Pennyman, who was raising a doctor's babies, I had brought her embarrassment, humiliation.

"There's nothing I can do about it now," I said. "I'm superupset with myself. It's probably the second-worst thing that has ever happened to me. But it's too late. It's done. I just have to keep on going somehow, get past it."

"But people will see these for the rest of your life. Anybody who wants to can see you . . . I don't know. Jess says I shouldn't look at them but I wonder if I would feel better if I saw them."

"Mom, please, you're not helping. Do not look at them. I promise you it won't help."

"I still think you should come back here for a while. Take a little break, give yourself a breather. I'm worried about you."

"Mom, I can't run away from my problems."

"What are you going to do now? If you lose this job, how will you pay your rent?"

"I'll figure it out somehow. I always have. I'm not going to give up and move home."

"Look, Candace. I haven't told you, and you need to know, that I'm not going to be able to help you financially. I can't. Your father worked hard, and invested, but the market . . ."

"Mom, don't cry. It's not helping. Really not."

I had to sit and listen to her sob.

"I wish your father was here," she said, finally. "He would know what to do."

That shut me up.

It made me wonder if Mom remembered him as he really was or if she had developed an alternative memory, where he was a wonderful, nonabusive father. I didn't want to force her to confront all that, make her acknowledge it, but I wanted to rattle her a bit as she had rattled me.

"Well, he's not," I said. "He's not around to tuck us in at night. We're on our own. And I need to focus on getting my life back on track."

"You need to come down here for a little while. I'm sure everything would look better if you could have a little break. You're under so much pressure. This is all frightening me, Candace."

I had to be firm.

I told her I loved her but I had to go. It was time for dinner. She was still crying when I hung up.

# 59

When Chris shows me the picture, and I see how he has me trapped, I break down. I have nothing left. I am defeated. He pulls me to him. I resist, but I'm crying so hard I can't see, and he's much stronger than me. He holds me in his big powerful arms and I keep sobbing. It makes me think of being in my father's arms when I was a little girl. I think of Miss Busy, who needs to step up, like, right now.

"It's okay, baby," he says. "It's okay. You think I'm a scary man, but I'm going to look after you now."

He kisses the top of my head. I'm gulping in huge breaths.

"I'm sorry for choking you. That's not what I'm like. I've had a bad, bad couple of weeks. I've had some problems in my family. Bad problems. Maybe I was too rough. No. I was too rough. That's not me. I'm sorry. Now I am going to make it up to you. You a scared, lost little girl. You don't have to be alone anymore, running from the police. I'm going to look after you."

He rubs my back. I let my head rest against his chest.

"You can't do it on your own, girl," he says. "The police will catch you and then you going to go to jail for the rest of your life."

He takes my chin in his hand and lifts it up.

"Look at me."

I manage to wipe my tears away and open my eyes.

"You want to go to jail for the rest of your life?" he asks.

I shake my head.

"No, you don't," he says. "Believe me, you don't want to go to jail.

I been to jail and I didn't like it. And I'm a big strong man. You just a little girl. So I'm going to help you. Okay?"

I nod at him.

"Good girl," he says, and kisses me, his big lips pressing against my little mouth.

I see that his eyes are brown and liquid and kind of nice, with little crinkles around them that somehow suggest kindness.

He takes me in his arms and plunks me on the bed.

"Look at you, you all a mess," he says and steps into the bathroom to grab a wad of toilet paper. He comes back, smiling, and sits down next to me on the bed.

"Let's clean you up," he says. He wipes my eyes and nose and then holds the tissue to my nose while I blow into it. "You been through a lot. You need some sleep. You got bags under your pretty eyes."

He kisses me again, on the forehead.

"You get some sleep, then you and I are going to get out of Scranton, okay?"

I nod at him.

"Where will we go?" I ask.

"Miami. I got some friends there can help you. They don't need to know who you are. You're just my friend. But you can get some money, get new ID, a phone, new clothes, get on with your life."

"You want me to turn tricks?"

He looks at me, like he's trying to decide how to handle it. He nods.

"It's an easy way for you to make money. You're a beautiful girl. After you get a few dollars together, get ID and a phone, you can figure out what you want to do, but first you need some money. You worried about it? You afraid of sex?"

I shrug.

"I don't want to give blow jobs in a place like this, to guys like Bruce."

He laughs.

"He was disgusting," I say.

"Don't worry. It won't be like this. You the escort type. We put an ad online, you go on dates with businessmen, they act like little bunnies, meek and mild, so glad to be with a hottie like you. Always use a condom, keep yourself clean, make a thousand bucks in an hour. It's not that bad," he says. "If you like sex. Do you like sex?"

I nod.

"I do," I say.

He puts his hand on my cheek and pulls me to him and kisses me, harder than before. Here it comes.

"I bet you do," he says and kisses me again. He puts his hand on my breast. I kiss him back. His enormous tongue goes into my mouth.

One of his hands is on my breast and the other is on the back of my neck. I feel tiny in his grip. He could break my neck with his hand. Or he could close it around my throat again and cut off my air until I am dead, or until I do whatever he says.

He pulls away and looks at me closely.

"You like that?" he says.

I lick my lips and nod.

"I can always use a condom?" I ask. "Like, now?"

He smiles.

"Yes, girl," he says. "I'm clean, but how you supposed to know that? Nobody ever going to force you to do something you don't want."

He puts his hand on my breast again and squeezes it. I lean forward to kiss him.

He kisses me and slips his hand inside my dress and kneads my breast. Then he stands in front of me, smiling down at me. He undoes his belt.

"I'm going to get a condom," I say, and I stand up. I go behind him, reach into my bag, and find the handle of the chef's knife.

I kiss him on the back of the neck, sucking and biting, and put my hands on him. He moans and arches his back and leans his head so I can stick my tongue in his ear.

Then, without hesitating, I see myself bring the knife up and stab it into the side his throat as hard as I can, thrusting through the skin and gristle, putting all my strength into one desperate cut. Miss Busy wants to kill him fast. She stabs quickly again, before he can react. He twists and lets out a strangled grunt when he feels the cut, trying to grab my arm, but then he puts his hands to his throat, which is open in two places, spouting blood. One more stab.

Is it good enough? I am intent, observing the moment, the slick of dark blood on the blade of the shiny knife, his grimace, the tight knot my fist has made around the handle of the knife. Is he dying, or will he kill me? I scramble away from him but he drops to his knees and I watch, see with relief that blood is spouting from between his fingers, lots of blood, covering his hands, spilling down onto his chest and the dirty motel room carpet.

He looks up at me, shocked, his eyes bugging out. He can't speak. I look back at him and see that he is about to die.

I give him a nice smile to look at as his life ends.

# 60

Declan was waiting at a nice table by the window at Candle 79, my favorite restaurant, a vegan white-tablecloth place that even meat eaters like.

It was my date spot, my place to have dinner with men, although I hadn't had much cause to use it for that purpose. Was I using it that way tonight?

I felt like I was when Declan rose, like a gentleman, to greet me, and then elegantly pulled me to him to exchange cheek kisses like Europeans.

He seemed freshly good-looking in that stubbly way, and surprisingly gallant, pulling out my chair for me and ordering a really nice bottle of California pinot noir.

I was half seduced by the time our wine arrived. I had to remind myself that I was on a fact-finding mission, as directed by Jess.

"You've been through a lot in the days since I've met you," he said.

"FML. You have *no* idea."

"So what happened?"

"You want the whole story?"

"Can you bear it?"

"I can," I said. "It might do me good. We might need more wine, though."

I explained how I got a text the day after I met him from someone who pretended to be him, convincingly, joking about his shirt.

"Creepy," he said. "Deeply creepy."

Then I told him about the cheese list, which I thought was from him, the subsequent threatening texts, the first topless tweet, and the whole sorry saga, concluding with my computer-smashing breakdown when the bj tweet went out.

"Jesus Murphy," he said when I finished. "You've been through the wringer."

"Yes," I said. "I feel like I've been run over by a truck full of social."

"Do you have any idea who's done all this?"

"No," I said, gulping wine. "Well, maybe."

"You thought it was me at first?"

"Well, yeah. But the moment I talked to you, and you told me you'd been in Reykjavik, I kind of, I don't know, it didn't add up."

"I'm not the type."

"You're not the type."

"Alvin could be the type."

"How well do you know him?"

"Not well. Our paths first crossed in a deal that didn't happen, then he invited me for drinks to kick around business ideas. I decided he wasn't the kind of guy I wanted to do business with, but I kept going to his parties."

"Why didn't you want to do business with him?"

"He's not a serious person. I like to do business with rational actors. Like, greedy people, people who want stuff. He's not greedy. He's bored. He is investing in businesses to have fun, and I don't want to depend on someone who might do something irrational because it's fun. And he's got a funny idea of fun."

"How do you mean?"

"He has a cruel side." He suddenly looked uneasy. "I won't be going to any more of his parties."

He wouldn't meet my eyes.

"What is it?" I said.

"What?"

"You look like something's bothering you."

I thought, *Is he afraid of Alvin?*

"I don't know if I should mention it," he said. "Or I think I should but I don't want to."

I didn't like the sound of that.

"Spit it out."

"Well, I may have been hacked, too."

"What?"

"Someone stole my laptop."

I stared at him.

"Please don't mention it to anybody. I shouldn't tell you because there are potentially serious questions about disclosure. There were proprietary databases on it. I wanted to tell you, though, on the off chance there's a link."

"Oh God," I said. "What happened?"

I felt queasy. I needed more Ambien.

He couldn't meet my eyes.

"I don't know for sure," he said. "But I can tell you when it happened."

"When?"

"The night of the party," he said.

"I remember you had your laptop bag hanging on your shoulder when I met you," I blurted, irrationally delighted to be helpful.

"Right. I had it then. I remember putting it down when I went out to the balcony and I believe I picked it up before we left. Do you remember?"

I shook my head and tried to think.

"I was drinking quite a lot," I said.

"Do you remember whether I had it when we got to my place? Or did you see it in the morning?"

I suddenly felt stomach sick.

"Wait," I said. "You don't think I took it, do you? I'm not sure I could handle that right now."

He winced.

"No," he said. "You were asleep beside me, and I didn't wake up when you left, but no, I'm not accusing you."

The night came back to me in a hurry, as he sat there and looked at me quizzically. I had a fuzzy memory of lurching out of a cab and into an elevator with him, kissing him in the elevator, entering his huge condo hand in hand, admiring the view with a big drink of brandy. I had no memory of the laptop but I remembered his hands on me, being on top of him on the bed, his face looking up at me as I rode him. That was where the memory ended, until I hailed a cab on the street in the small hours of the morning. I must have slept in between.

He watched me, could see the confusion on my face. I could tell he thought I was a nutcase.

"Don't believe that I did it. Please. I know it must look that way but . . . just no."

He looked like he wanted to get away from me.

"Are you okay?"

"No," I said. "I'm sorry. I feel like I'm going to be sick."

I couldn't be there anymore.

I got up and ran out of there and vomited on the sidewalk. I looked back and could see him looking at me through the window with an expression of alarm and disgust. He was trying to pay the bill.

I ran down the street and away before he could pay.

So, not a great date.

# 61

Chris is dead. I stand there for a minute to make sure of it. I'm afraid he's going to jump up at me like the villain in a horror movie. Then I can see that's silly. There's something about his inertness that makes it obvious he's dead. He's a thing now, not a person. He is a very bloody thing.

I go to the bathroom, where I vomit. I flush it away and wash the blood off my hands. Macy will come back when she finishes blowing Bruce. I need to hurry. Miss Busy has to look after this. This is a job for her.

I take a big breath and feel myself calm down. I go back into the room. I need to flip Chris over to dig into his pockets. I have to put my back into it because he's so big, but I know that I can do it. His arms flop around and blood gets all over him. I am careful not to get it on me. In one pocket there's a thick wad of bills, which I drop into my bag. In the other pocket he has three little plastic bags full of brown powder. Must be heroin. I leave it.

I find a gun in his jacket pocket, hanging on the back of the chair. I don't know anything about guns, but I take it out and look at it. It's black. It says Smith & Wesson on the side. There's a safety switch, I see. I switch it to off and hold it up, see how it feels. It feels good. Heavy. Powerful. I think if I pull the trigger it will shoot.

I need to get to the highway. Take no chances. While I am standing there, planning, I hear someone coming. Without thinking, I step into the bathroom to hide.

I know it is Macy when I hear her gasp. It's a deep, raw sound.

"Oh my God," she says. "No. No. No. Tell me you're not dead. Tell me you're not dead."

I hear her crying. I'm standing behind the door, with my back pressed against the wall. I see her coming in the bathroom mirror, holding the knife, her face drawn and intent. She sees me. What to do?

I see myself step around the corner and point the gun at her. She keeps coming. Her eyes are narrow and hateful. She wants to cut me, wants to kill me, wants vengeance for her man. I pull the trigger and she stops, a little hole in her chest. She lurches toward me. I pull the trigger again. Another little hole appears in her chest, below the first one. She stops, looks surprised.

"Bitch," she says and drops to her knees next to Chris. The knife falls from her hand. She is not going to cut me. Blood is pouring out of the new holes in her. I am ready to shoot again. She opens her mouth to speak but her voice is strangled and she has blood in her mouth, which she has to spit out. Then she falls back and is still. Blood pools around her.

I wait and watch to see if she moves, but not for long. She is on her back, still. The blood pool is growing. She is now as inert as Chris. They are things. I have to get out of here.

Everything is very still. I feel completely calm. I am thinking, calculating.

I clench my teeth and think again: *Take no chances*.

How to get out of here?

I take the wad of tissue Chris used to wipe my face and I carefully wipe the handle of the gun with it. I put the gun into Chris's hand.

How much time will police spend on this crime scene? Not much, I think.

It depends on whether anyone sees me leave. I go into the bathroom, look into the mirror. I look fucking crazy, wild-eyed and weird, but there is no blood on me. I take five seconds to compose myself, then go out and grab my bag, being careful not to step in the blood pooling around the corpses. Am I leaving anything? I look around. No.

What would I do if I were the sad person, likely a middle-aged Indo-American guy, who runs this motel, and I heard shots? I would call the police. I wouldn't go outside. I pull the curtains aside and peek out. There is nobody there. Okay. Time to go.

I open the door and start walking quickly, toward the highway.

# 62

After vomiting on the sidewalk in front of Candle 79, I ran toward Central Park.

Did someone really steal Declan's computer and download the data files?

If he was responsible for everything I'd been through, that would be a good story to make up. If he put it out there that I had stolen his lists, that would tie up a big loose end and make me look like the kind of crazy girl who would tweet dirty pictures of herself and then play victim.

And how well did I know him, really? My impression of him was based on casual observation at one party and half an hour of drunken sex.

I headed over to the park, walking past all the precious Upper East Side apartments, whose tasteful furnishings and beautiful art seemed to taunt me, reminding me that many people in this city weren't hanging on to their shitty apartments by their fingernails. That part of New York always makes me feel poor and resentful.

I walked toward the running path around the pond, moving fast, my mind spinning. I couldn't figure it out. I considered one alternative, rejected it, then considered another and rejected it. Either Declan was lying, which just didn't seem like his style, or someone stole his laptop and used the files to snare me, which seemed too elaborate. Then I thought about how thoroughly my life had gone off the rails in the past week and felt sorry for myself. It was unproductive.

I sat down by the jogging trail and, full of envy and resentment, watched young moms run by in expensive running clothes, pushing expensive running strollers. I hated them. Why should they have everything and I have nothing?

I needed to text Jess.

> Meeting with Declan inconclusive. Can't be sure about him.

No way I was telling her about the supposed late-night theft of his laptop.

She texted back.

> That's too bad. Don't forget the meeting at 10 a.m.
> Monday. They'll likely offer a settlement.

> Should we meet to discuss it?

> I have too much work to do. Will you be okay?

> I'll be fine.

Hm. Too much work.

Before I could think about it, I emailed Wayne.

**To:** Wayne Timmons
**From:** Candace Walker
**Date:** 8:42 p.m., June 23, 2018

Hey. Sorry about that weird email. I really was hacked. Free for a drink?

He replied almost immediately.

**To:** Candace Walker
**From:** Wayne Timmons
**Date:** 8:44 p.m., June 23, 2018

Don't worry about the email. Someone's messing with you. Unfortunately I have plans tonight. Rain check?

Rain check! I replied. Look forward to catching up.

See you Monday, after the meeting, he emailed.

I was now all but certain that my sister and Wayne were an item.

I had a fresh email from Francis, who I'd been neglecting. I agreed to meet him for Sunday brunch.

Then I took the subway home to my wine and my Ambien.

# 63

Head down. One foot in front of the other. Not too fast. Don't run. Is anybody looking at me? No. There's nobody on foot. That's good. Or is it? That makes me stick out. There's a steady stream of cars going past me as I walk past car dealerships and miniplazas. No police cars. No police cars. No police cars.

I have to keep slowing myself down. My heart is pounding. I can feel it in my ears. I want to run. Walk more slowly. What did I do? I stabbed a man to death, shot a woman. I killed them. There was blood everywhere, and dead bodies. I want to hide. I want to cry. I am crying. Stop crying. I am going to prison. I belong in prison. I can't go to prison. I should kill myself. I start to think about opening my throat like I opened Scary Pimp's throat, picturing it in detail. One quick cut, knife severs the artery, I lie down on my back, eyes open, watch the light fade to dark. Good idea. That's what I will do, what Miss Busy can do.

The new plan snuffs out my anxiety about what has just happened. It is such a relief.

The woods on the left are so nice, a mix of pines and little hardwoods, climbing a hill. Looks like a good, peaceful place to die. I leave the road, walk into the trees, up the hill a little ways, looking around. The ground is springy, covered in leaves and pine needles. I sit down on a dead hardwood in a tiny clearing. I am only twenty or thirty feet from the road, but it is like a different world. The light is pretty, greenish and soft. I can barely hear the cars going by. I like it here.

Miss Busy is in charge. She is going to cut my throat. I am calm. I put my bag between my knees to take out my knife. Oh. It's back in the motel. Right. I need a new plan. I need to get another knife.

I'm headed back to the road when I see the cat. It's a big orange tabby, with a collar, sitting on a stump in the sun, watching me.

"Oh, hi, kitty!"

Kitty meows at me. I want to be friends. I walk over slowly, talking quietly, reach out my hand. She turns as if to jump and run away, then turns back, curious. I step up, making kitten-soothing noises. I reach out my hand, and she pushes her head against it, lets me pet her, closes her eyes and rubs her head against me. This is so nice! She has a tag on her collar with her name.

"Hi, Sadie. You're a pretty cat, aren't you?"

She likes it, rubs her head against my hand. I am crying again.

Will she let me pick her up? She will! I gather her in my arms and sit down on the stump. I rub behind her ears and whisper her name. She snuggles into my lap and purrs! I put my face into her fur and inhale her scent, pulling it deep inside.

Oh no. I get tears on her fur. She doesn't like that and tries to wriggle free. I have to hold her firmly to stop her from running away. Then her claws dig into my arm. I am sad, but I let her go. I'm not the kind of person who would hold someone against her will.

She meows at me and walks away.

"Bye, Sadie."

Her work here is done.

I no longer plan on killing myself. I want to live, to hold kitties, make them purr.

Okay. I need to get out of this shithole town. Back to the road.

I end up having to walk a long way on the gravel shoulder of the road. I don't have much of a plan. I need to get in a car, somehow, and get far from the grisly scene at the motel. I need to find a gas station.

———

I am really tired by the time I get to one, but it's worth the walk. It's better than a normal gas station. It's a big truck stop, in the middle of a huge parking lot full of eighteen-wheelers.

I've never been to a place like this before. It's like a little mall for truckers. There's a deli, a barbershop, a store, a buffet, showers, a TV lounge. The truckers are wandering around, playing with their phones, a bunch of overweight white dudes in sweatpants and ball caps.

The smell of grease hits me and I'm suddenly starving. I will myself to walk slowly, looking like a bored suburban lady, not a hipster killer who has just cut a pimp's throat and shot a sex worker. I buy a banana and a cup of coffee and a muffin at the deli counter and take them outside. There's a busy gas bay, with a steady stream of cars and trucks coming in and parking, filling up, people going in to pee and buy coffee and snacks.

There is an empty picnic table next to a dumpster. I sit down there and eat my banana and muffin and drink my coffee. I count Chris's money. $261. My new total is $755. I'm getting there.

I watch the cars come and go and try to figure out how to get in one of them and get out of here. I go inside to pee and fix my makeup. I look haggard, like I've been up all night, which I have. I do my best to cover that up and go into the store and walk around. There's all kinds of trucker stuff, patriotic T-shirts, leather vests, work gloves. I stop when I get to a display of knives. I need a knife. I pick out a folding combat knife, a nasty-looking black thing called Extreme Ops. It costs $19.99.

I'm nervous, but when I put on the counter, the subdued-looking young guy at the cash register doesn't even look at me.

I sit down at one of the tables by the deli and take the knife out of its plastic casing. I drop it into my bag when a trucker with bristly gray hair and a yellow mustache plops into the seat across from me. He's holding a tray with a disgusting-looking plate of bacon and eggs on it.

"Hey, miss," he says, with a smile that is meant to be rakish. "Mind if I sit here?"

Yes.

"No," I say. There are no empty tables, so it makes sense. I need to get out of here. He is a trucker. He's going someplace. I smile.

He takes a big bite of his disgusting food and gets yolk on his dyed mustache. He wipes it off and gives me a once-over.

"Are you a driver?" he says.

I laugh.

"No. Just passing through."

He smiles.

"I'm just kidding, little lady," he says. "I've never seen a lady trucker as pretty as you."

Ugh.

"Thanks, I think," I say. Forced smile.

He takes a piece of bacon and holds it in front of his mouth.

"No need to thank me," he says. "Just the truth. Most of them, my goodness, I wouldn't touch them with a barge pole. A lot of extrawide loads, if you know what I mean."

"Then it's not much of a compliment," I say.

He laughs, nods, and eats his bacon. His eyes are small and quick, darting up and down, checking me out.

"You're pretty enough," he says. "You are the prettiest thing I've seen in a while."

"Well, thank you, then," I say.

He smiles. One of his front teeth is a different color than the others.

He sticks out his hand. I hesitate, then take it.

"Rick," he says.

"Amy."

He nods at the empty knife package.

"You get yourself some protection?"

Shit. I shrug.

"It was on sale."

He smiles again.

"Good thing for a girl to have," he says. "Especially is she's working. Got to take care of herself. Some of these lot lizards come to a bad end. All kinds of strange hombres in this kind of place."

He thinks I'm a truck stop hooker. This suggests my makeover wasn't as successful as I hoped. His comment makes me more tired. I frown and rub my eyes.

"Hey," he says. "Don't get the wrong idea. I didn't mean to insult you."

I make myself smile again.

"I'm not a lot lizard," I say. "I'm just passing through."

He's watching me closely.

"Look here, missy," he says. "I'm not going to shit in a bowl and tell you it's macaroni. I'm a straight shooter. If you want to come out to my truck with me, I could make it worth your while. I'm not saying you're a working girl. I'm just offering you a little work. Who knows? You might even enjoy yourself."

He winks. I can't even.

"No thanks," I say and stand up. "I think it's time I got going. Have a good day."

When I stand up, I find myself blocking the path of another trucker. He's holding a tray with bacon and eggs. Fuck. It's Bruce. He's as surprised to see me as I am to see him.

"Crystal?" he says.

I look at him and smile, trying to look confused.

"No," I say. "Sorry. I don't know you."

"I thought you said your name was Amy," says Rick.

I don't like any of this. I head for the exit. When I go through the doors, I glance back and see the two men talking together and looking at me.

I need to get out of here in a hurry.

I go back to the picnic table where I ate my breakfast and watch the vehicles come and go. I need to get in one of them.

A dirty-looking redneck pulls up in a clapped-out Ford pickup and parks next to my picnic table. There's a pair of truck balls hanging from his rear bumper. He's unshaven, wearing a sleeveless Kid Rock T-shirt and a Ford hat. He looks like he smells bad.

I come up with a plan. I get up from the table and walk past him, eyeing a little Toyota Prius with Ontario plates. The driver, a middle-aged, bearded guy in a golf shirt and cargo shorts, is putting away the hose. All done.

When Redneck and I pass, I turn and look at him.

"Hey," I say.

He looks at me expectantly, the beginning of a smile at the corner of his ugly mouth. Honestly, dude, you can't think that. Look at yourself.

I stand there looking at him. He looks back at me. Here goes.

"No," I say. "No!"

I shout.

"Leave me alone!"

He stands back, baffled.

"I don't know what you're talking about, crazy bitch," he says.

"Just leave me alone!" I shout again.

People turn to look. I walk quickly to the pumps, to the bearded man standing by his Toyota. I can see his wife sitting in the passenger seat.

"Sir," I say. "Can you help me, please?"

He looks concerned.

"What can I do?" he asks.

"I need to get away from that guy over there," I say, moving close to him, trying to look scared. "I'm afraid he's going to hurt me."

I look over my shoulder. Redneck guy is giving me a dirty look, headed into the station. Bearded guy sees him.

I start to cry.

"He won't leave me alone. I just want to get away from him."

His wife is now out of the car.

"You want us to call the police?" she says.

"No," I say. "I just want to get away. Can you drive me to the next exit, please?"

She looks back at the redneck, who is now standing inside the gas station, angrily looking out at me. I wonder if he's trying to decide if he should come out and tell me off.

"Get in," she says.

I am Amy. I am from Watertown, in upstate New York. I am a Rutgers student. I am in Scranton with college friends. We went to a party that got out of hand, so I left, because I didn't want to be around certain kinds of things. I was walking to the highway, hoping to find a bus for Watertown, when this truck started following me. It was one of the scary guys from the party. He won't leave me alone.

This is what I tell Simon and Karine. They're nervous. Simon keeps checking the rearview mirror and Karine keeps looking over her shoulder.

"He won't follow us," I say. "Guys like that, they look for weak people to exploit. He thought I was one of them. But I'm not."

Eventually they relax, and we start to talk. They tell me they can drive me all the way to Watertown, no problem.

Simon is a pudgy journalism professor from Ottawa. He and Karine are headed back to Ottawa after a journalism conference in Philadelphia.

As we get farther from Scranton they feel better about rescuing me. It's probably the most interesting thing that has ever happened in their dreary lives.

I imagine them with their lumpy colleagues, having celebratory dinners in pretentious, unfashionable restaurants, exchanging bitter stories about who was denied a trip to what conference, who was stealing research, gossiping about gross middle-aged professors preying on nearsighted, plain grad students.

I liked being at college because I got to spend most of my time doing basically whatever I wanted—which often meant getting high with JFXBF and binge-watching TV series—but I never really liked college, like, as a thing.

It's a power structure where the dullest, hardest-working nerds get to run things. To get ahead, you have to suck up to them. I hated that. Simon and Karine remind me of how much I hated that, since I have to suck up to them to get them to drive me to Watertown. I repeatedly praise them for heroically saving me and chat pleasantly about my made-up life.

But I am tired and start to make mistakes, and they are dull but not stupid. I mention casually, while discussing my imaginary academic career (working on an undergrad in psychology) at Rutgers, that I like living in New York City.

They ask me about Watertown, and I don't know anything about it, since I have never been there, and try to change the subject, but Karine persists.

I decide to have a nap before my Amy facade completely collapses.

When I awaken, we're pulling into a roadside Denny's at the Syracuse exit. They're chatting quietly in French.

"We thought we'd stop for some breakfast," says Karine. "Are you hungry?"

"I'm starving."

"Let us buy you breakfast," says Simon.

"You guys are too nice!"

# 64

Francis, sweet Francis wrapped me up in his catty, funny, kind world as he filled me full of drinks during a lazy Sunday afternoon drinking beer in Village dives.

Before I could tell him all my troubles, I insisted that he tell me about himself. *How was Jason? He was cute!*

"Jason dumped me," he said. "I guess he was just using me for sex."

"Francis, no. I liked him."

Francis always kept a happy face for the world, but I saw he wasn't feeling good about this.

"It's fine," he said. "The sex was fun. He was too young for me. I realized that on Saturday, when we went to Langston for a few cocktails. We ran into some of his friends on the dance floor. They wanted to dance and I just couldn't. I suddenly felt soooo old. So I did an Irish exit."

"You need someone more grown-up," I said.

"I know, but if they have abs, that would be okay, though, wouldn't it?"

I laughed and gave him a hug and for a second I thought he was going to cry.

"Anyway," he said. "Forget about my love life. You have real problems. Spill."

I unspooled everything that had happened since our post-Guggenheim dinner, which took hours and many beers. It was just what I needed.

When I finally finished with the story about my vomit-interrupted date with Declan, he gave me another beer and fixed his gaze on me.

"Is there any way you did it?" he said. "Any chance you stole his laptop, and, like, forgot about it? Left it in the cab?"

"No! I was hammered enough that I'd banged a guy I just met. I was way too hammered to steal a computer."

"You were mixing Ambien and booze, right? You sometimes forget things when you do that."

"No way. I wasn't sleep-stealing."

"So he's lying. He's your tormentor."

"Really?"

"Yes, really. Think about it. He had access to the lists. He has the computer skills. He's telling a bullshit story designed to blame you. The only reason you don't think it might be him is because he's charmed you."

"I don't know. His personality . . . he just . . . I can't see why he would do something like this."

"Tell me," said Francis. "Did you tell me that he said you promised him dinner?"

"That's right. He was joking, but yeah."

"When did you promise to buy him dinner?"

A light bulb went off in my head.

"When he sent me the list," I said. "Oh my God. You're right."

"See?" he said, obviously pleased to have spotted a clue I'd missed.

"But that doesn't prove one hundred percent it was him. My memory could be muddled."

"Do you think it is?"

"No."

But Francis, like Jess, also thought Alvin could be behind my troubles. I was going in circles again.

I told him about the Pandora interview and the possibility of doing a CNN interview, which got him excited.

I checked my phone.

"While we've been sitting here talking, in fact, I got an email asking me to clear my schedule for an interview tomorrow at two p.m. with, ahem, Anderson Cooper."

He mouthed *What?* and made such a happy face that I felt good for the first time in a while.

Francis had long lusted after, and actually loved, Anderson Cooper, often asking me if I'd watched his stupid show, which I never had.

We drank more beer and discussed, at length, what I should say. He insisted that we do practice interviews, with him in the role of Cooper, and we were laughing and having fun until, suddenly, he got a booty text from Jason.

He held up the phone to show me the text.

Want a drink?

"Do you think I should?" he said. "I just finished telling you he's too young for me."

"Go. Go enjoy his abs."

"I know, right?"

He kissed me and rushed off, leaving me drunk and suddenly much less cheerful.

My thoughts turned to Wayne and Jess. I imagined them entangled in each other's arms. I kept thinking about their affair while I walked to the subway. At Penn Station, I found myself getting off the subway, without thinking about it much, and making my way to the PATH station, where I boarded a train for Jersey City.

Apparently I was going to pay Jess a visit.

# 65

The only customers in the Denny's are two New York State Police, sitting at a table overlooking the parking lot and the highway beyond. My heart starts to pound when I follow Simon and Karine into the place. Of course, they take a table near the troopers. The guy sitting facing us is an older white guy with a bushy gray moustache. He looks at me closely as we walk in. I'm convinced he's about to stand up and arrest me. I start thinking about how I could run for the door and into the woods, where I might have a chance of getting away. Then he gives me a cocky grin and I realize, with relief and disgust, that he's just ogling me, that he thinks he has a chance with me, which is so ridiculous I feel like laughing. I am a very attractive young blonde. He is a broken-down overweight guy with a droopy mustache. How could he think I'd be attracted to him? I avoid his eyes and slide into the seat with my back to him and his partner.

Simon and Karine both order Denny's All-American Slam, three scrambled eggs, bacon, sausage, hash browns, and toast.

"That sounds good," I say. "I'll have the same."

I have decided that Amy, unlike Candace, is an omnivore, at least for now.

Like a caterpillar turning into a butterfly, I need to transform myself.

It feels so strange to tear into the flesh of a pig. I have to stop myself from thinking that way and focus on the unaccustomed sensation of salty, chewy meat and eggs in my mouth.

With that first bite of sausage, I feel like gagging, and Karine asks, with concern, if I am okay.

I manage to choke it down and give her what I hope is a bright smile.

"It's delicious. Mmm."

"So," says Simon, "are you going home for a little visit, then returning to your studies?"

"Yes," I say. "I want to see Mom and Dad."

They both smile and nod.

I realize I've messed up again. I had told them my dad died.

I suddenly see that they both know I'm lying about everything and are carefully trying not to let me know. They're scared.

Karine tries to cover it up by talking about her school days, in Toronto, talking about how she used to save up her laundry for her mom to do back in Quebec. Ha ha ha.

They're humoring me. They're too weak, too soft, too Canadian, to confront me and tell me they know I'm lying. Instead, they let me continue to humiliate myself.

I fight to prevent my anger from showing on my face, shoveling more disgusting meat and eggs into my mouth. I ask Karine about her school days and pretend to listen. I can feel Simon's piggy little eyes on me, observing me, though, and I'm not surprised when he has some bad news for me.

"Karine and I have decided that we're going to turn here," he says. "We want to go have a look at the Finger Lakes. We'd planned on doing that if we got here early enough."

"Oh," I say, surprised. "Well, of course. I can get the bus from here, I'm sure."

"Will you be all right?" asks Karine.

Now I know what they were talking about in French. How do we get rid of crazy girl? Let's take her for breakfast, then ditch her. I'm like something disgusting they picked up on their shoe. Like dog shit.

*No way,* I think. The police are sitting here. If they leave me here, and get into their car and drive away, Officer Pervert and his partner will see and wonder what happened to the blond hottie. No way.

"I'll be fine," I say, all smiles.

Under the table, I hitch up my dress and slip my hand into my underwear, where, thankfully, and improbably, two roofies are still tucked against my bristly skin. I palm them.

"You guys have been soooo helpful," I say, brightly. "I'll never forget the way you rescued me. That guy was so scary."

"You're sure you can get a bus here?" says Simon.

As if you care.

"Absolutely. I think. I'll ask the waitress."

Then he has to go to the bathroom, and Karine has to get up to let him out of the booth, and, without either of them noticing, plop plop, I roofie their coffees.

# 66

I had the spare keys to Jess's place on my keychain, which I used to get in the front door of her condo building.

A little voice kept telling me I was ill-advised to be popping in on her at 11:00 p.m., unannounced, but a louder voice kept telling me I had to know if she was in Wayne's arms.

The little voice lost out, but it did convince me to send her a text from the lobby.

> Jess, I'm here at your place. Can I come see you?

I sent it and then got on the elevator.

> This isn't a good time.

I got her text in the elevator and pretended that I hadn't. I knocked on her door, first quietly, then louder. I posed, teary-eyed, in front of her peephole.

"Candace, what are you doing?" she said through the door.

"Jess, I'm so upset," I said. "Can I come in?"

"Just a minute."

She came out in her robe, holding her keys in her hands.

I gave her a hug and cried on her shoulder.

If she wouldn't let me in, that meant that I was right. Wayne was in there.

She stroked my hair and consoled me.

"My life is ruined," I said. "For the rest of my life people are going to be looking at those pictures."

She rubbed my back.

"Minnow, you need to go home and go to sleep," she said. "We've got a meeting at ten tomorrow. We might sort all this out then."

"I don't want to go home. Can I sleep on your couch?"

"I think you should go home."

"Why can't I stay here?"

"Minnow, I have somebody here."

It had to be Wayne. I knew it.

"I don't care," I said. "Just let me curl up on your couch."

Then the door opened and Wayne peeked out.

How I despised them both. My life was being destroyed and my sister didn't care. It brought back the worst kind of memories, bad old feelings.

I couldn't show them how I felt.

"Wayne?" I said, acting surprised, not upset. "What are you doing here?"

"Hi. I was talking to Jess about your case."

What bullshit. Why is she in her robe? Is that how lawyers usually meet with witnesses?

Jess let me into her condo then, and the three of us spent five hugely awkward minutes pretending that the two of them had been having a meeting about my situation. I pretended that it didn't bother me at all.

Jess gave me a glass of water and they gave me a little pep talk about how the meeting might clear everything up. Jess was obviously desperate for me to leave. Wayne was, I don't know, like a confused puppy. I started to wonder how smart he was.

I cried and let them comfort me. I told them that I might be on Anderson Cooper's show. They seized on that as a way to cheer me up. I let them pretend that it worked, and, after a little more jollying, apologized tearfully for showing up, and Jess ordered me an Uber.

In the car on the long ride to Brooklyn, I fumed at the injustice and dishonesty of my sister and Wayne. I couldn't believe it.

My stomach hurt. I'd had too much beer and not enough food. As I cruised along, I wrote suicide notes in my head.

# 67

When Simon comes back from the bathroom, Karine stands up as if to leave. Neither of them have had their roofied coffees.

I stand up with her.

"I hope we were able to help you," says Simon.

I smile and thank them again.

Then as they turn to go—leaving their roofied coffees on the table—I start to cry. I sit and put my head down.

They turn, uncertain about whether to go or not. I keep my head down.

"Are you okay?" says Simon.

I look up through my tears.

"I'm fine," I say. "I'm sorry about everything. I'm sorry I lied to you. I'm just so scared."

I can see that Karine wants to get away from me, but I have Simon's attention. He nods at Karine and they sit down.

"I'm sorry," I say.

"What's going on?" says Simon.

I grab a napkin and blow my nose and wipe my eyes.

"It's okay, Amy," says Simon. "Take your time."

I'm thinking, *Drink your coffee!*

"I'm not Amy," I say. I bite my lip and wipe my eyes.

"I'm sorry. You two have been so kind to me and I feel bad because almost everything I told you is a lie."

Simon takes a little sip of his cold coffee. Yay!

"I shouldn't have lied," I say, "but I was afraid of what you would think of me if I told the truth."

Karine isn't buying it, but Simon is paying attention.

"I just don't want you to leave here thinking that I manipulated you. I'm sorry. The truth is my name isn't Amy. It's Monica. And I'm not a student. Not anymore. I'm an escort."

Then I bow my head and sit, hunched and shaking, until Karine comes around the table to comfort me. I take her hand in mine and look up at her, my eyes brimming with tears.

"I'm so sorry I lied."

"It's fine," she says.

The waitress comes by and, through my tears, I ask for a splash of hot coffee. So does Simon, and then Karine.

They sip their coffees—yes!—while I tell them my story, speaking quietly so the police don't hear.

I had been a psychology student, at NYU, not Rutgers, but I found New York so expensive that I started working as an escort, just once every couple of weeks, to make ends meet.

I wasn't doing well at school, though, and the money working as an escort was really good, so soon I started doing more tricks and stopped going to classes. The work freaked me out, though, and I found that cocaine made it easier for me to get through the experience, and soon I was blowing all my money on coke. I had no friends, only clients. I've never had a good relationship with my family, and now I'm isolated and depressed, high all the time.

They buy my story, and my tears, and they sit, rapt, sipping their coffee.

# 68

As my Uber took me across Brooklyn Bridge, I got tired of thinking about dramatic ways of ending my own life and decided to distract myself with my phone.

It had been a while since I'd facecreeped JFXBF, and I realized I had no idea how he was reacting to his starring role in my hacked sex pic. It rattled me to realize how little thought I'd given him lately, which was good in a way, since for weeks after we split up it was all I could do to keep myself from physically stalking him.

I checked out his Twitter and Instagram, but they still featured nothing but his old picture of a disgusting beer.

I clicked through his list of Instagram followers and found the account of JFXBFNGF and had a look. The newest post was from twenty minutes ago. It showed a plate I recognized. Breadfruit tacos @ Chimmi's! Can't wait! #vegandeliciousness

Fuck. She was at Chimmi's, a funky vegan Mexican place where I used to go with him for birthday dinners and dates. Now she was there with him, stuffing her ugly face.

I realized I needed talk to him, so I told the driver we had a new destination.

I schemed about ways to handle the confrontation, hunched in the back of the car, all the way to the restaurant, but as soon as I got inside, my plans seemed silly. Of course, they were sitting at the table where he and I often sat. He had his back to me, but she saw me come in and looked at me with an expression of surprise and hostility. She said something to him and he turned and his face fell.

I walked up smiling.

"Hi, guys," I said. "How were the tacos?"

"Hi, Candace," said JFXBF. He looked scared. Scared of her, I imagined.

"What do you want?" she said.

She was not fucking around. She looked like she wanted to hit me. I don't know when anyone has been so openly hostile to me. Her ugly face was all scrunched up. I looked down at the table and could see the remnants of churros with coconut milk ice cream, the dessert that JFXBF and I always got. Seeing that pushed me over the edge.

I gave her a cold smile.

"I'm not here to talk to you, sweetie," I said.

I turned to JFXBF.

"I'm here to talk to you," I said. "I need to know why you posted those pictures."

I didn't think for a minute that he had the computer skill or motivation to do that to me, but I could feel the moment sliding away from me and I wanted to see what he would say.

"What the fuck are you talking about, you crazy bitch?" said JFXBFNGF. "You need to leave us alone."

"I'm not talking to you," I said. God, she really was ugly. Her hook nose and pointy chin looked like they were reaching for each other. It offended me that my ex could go from someone like me to someone so homely. It made me wonder if he'd actually been up to my standards.

I turned back to JFXBF, who looked like he wanted to die.

"You were the only other person with copies of those pictures," I said. "I need to know what you did with them. You hacked my social media accounts and posted them and I need to know why. This is going to follow me around for the rest of my life."

JFXBFNGF interrupted me.

"This is not our issue," she said. "You need to learn about bound-aries."

I ignored her and turned to him. I wanted to spit on him, the cow-ard, for failing to speak to me.

"Why did you do it?" I asked. "Why did you put those sex pictures on my social? How could you do that? Was it *her* idea?"

People at other tables were watching us openly now. I could see a server—Miki, who I knew well from previous visits—start to head over to the table. It was official. I had made a scene.

I looked down at Jeff. He looked high. Ill-equipped to deal with this. He was stammering.

"Dude," he said. "Candace. No. Just no. It's not like that. Like I would do that? Like Tanya would want me to do that? You are just, no."

Tanya spoke up again. She was the spokesperson, obviously. How had I spent three years with somebody too pathetic to speak for him-self?

"People told me you were crazy but this is too much." Tanya hissed at me. "This is bullshit. They keep wiping the phone and it keeps hap-pening. You weren't hacked. You are wackadoodle. And. You. Need. To. Stop. Fucking. With. Us."

Her voice rose as she spoke, changing from a hiss to a bark.

She pushed her chair back and spoke again, this time to the room.

"Help us, please! This person needs to leave us alone."

People at nearby tables were now openly staring. A big guy started to get up from his seat, looking at me carefully.

Miki arrived.

"Hey!" she said, trying to turn me toward her, away from the table. "Hey! Candace. Can I talk to you over here for a minute."

I looked down at Jeff.

"You didn't do it?" I said.

Miki now had her hand on my arm.

"You don't know who did it?" I said. "My life has been destroyed. Tell me if you know anything."

He looked at Tanya and then at me. Tanya was shaking her head at him.

"No, Candy," he said. "No. Ask Beatrice. I have nothing to do with it. You know that!"

Aha. Beatrice.

The pieces came together. Mission accomplished.

Miki's fingernails were digging into my arm. I let her pull me away.

All the hipsters were watching me. I must have looked deranged. I felt hollowed out, betrayed, at the end of my rope.

Beatrice had been filling in Jeff, pumping me for information and telling him that I was wackadoodle.

Miki was telling me how Chimmi's was a safe space, and I was making people feel unsafe, and asked if I was all right as she marched me out. I shrugged her off and walked across Bedford Avenue and plunked myself on the curb and looked at my phone.

I looked at Tanya's Instagram, which I had not creeped in a while. I looked at her list of followers. There was Beatrice's stupid profile pic, which was, of course, a picture of her fat tattooed arm.

I checked her followers, and there was Tanya. Beatrice hadn't been dishing to Jeff. She'd been dishing to Hooknose.

I had been such a supportive friend to Beatrice that it came as a terrible blow. I'd gone to her stupid art shows, made small talk with her unsuccessful chef boyfriend/girlfriend and their loser friends, introduced her to cool people, encouraged her to aim higher in life. We were friends! Like, really good friends. Then I got the job she wanted and she turned on me.

It was jealousy, something you deal with a lot when you're the prettiest girl, someone smart and fun that other people want to be with. You think you have friends and then you realize, No. What I had was a user, a leech, someone who didn't care about me at all, who just wanted to be in my reflected glow right up until the moment that she could put the knife in me.

I closed my phone and got up from the curb.

I should have felt shattered, or been thinking about getting some kind of revenge on Beatrice and Hooknose, but instead I felt cleansed, grateful even. I knew that I had to rely on myself. Better no friends than false friends.

# 69

I tell Simon and Karine that I came up to Scranton to meet a regular client, but things went wrong during our date. He roughed me up and forced me to do things I didn't want to do. He made me have sex with this skeezy guy who works for him.

I start crying again. I need time for the roofies to kick in.

Simon leans forward and speaks quietly.

"I think you should speak to those guys," he says.

Who?

He nods toward the police, who are behind us.

Karine agrees.

"They can help you," she says.

That can't happen. No.

"Please, no," I say, looking back and forth at them, trying to show them how they're worrying me. "What will I tell them? I'm an escort. He's a local big shot. Who are they going to believe? And I would have to testify. My family would find out what I've been doing."

I tell them I fled the hotel on foot after his assault on me, only to find myself being pursued by his friend, the scary redneck they saw.

I thank them yet again for rescuing me, apologize for lying, cry some more and tell them I am headed to Watertown, where I'd never been, to see my sister.

"I need to stop turning tricks," I say. "I need to stop doing cocaine. I need to start over."

By the end, they're taking turns consoling me, and promising to drive me to my sister's house, basically begging me to stop crying.

# 70

The Pandora story was really good.

It went online at midnight, just after I got back to my apartment after my disastrous visit to Chimmi's. It immediately buoyed me.

Lenora opened with the description of my meltdown in the café. If she wasn't such a good writer, I might have come across as unhinged, but she did such a great job of describing how I'd been victimized that I came across as entirely sympathetic.

I curled up in bed, clutching my phone, and read it over and over again.

She didn't name SoSol but she did write about how the hack was going to make it hard for me to work in social media, and she included some stories about other women whose employers had fired them after this kind of thing.

The reaction on social was even more heartening. The story went viral as I watched. I could see the number of shares go up each time I refreshed.

People I didn't know, all across the country, were posting it and commenting on it. It started with New York feminists, but quickly spread. There were shares from guys in small towns, sports reporters, all kinds of people way outside my normal world.

The comments were almost universally sympathetic.

Can't believe what this girl went through.
READ THIS.
This is why we need the death penalty.

I started to think I could get past this, try to find a new job in a more sympathetic environment. I knew I had the skills. The story could become, in a funny way, an asset. I was becoming a symbol of all victims of social misconduct. I started to think about trying to do some kind of online activism about legal protections for women online.

I emailed Lenora to tell her how much I liked the story.

She responded with a thumbs-up emoji and sent me a link to one share, from Wendy, the CNN reporter.

She emailed me again a few minutes later, though.

Have you had any contact from SoSol?

I've just had a nasty email from a lawyer. They want the story pulled down. But don't worry. We lawyered this, asked them for comment. Just thought I should let you know they're pissed off.

Wendy also emailed me, to let me know that Anderson was impressed, both by the story and its virality. He was excited about the interview.

It kind of stung that I'd had to shut down my social accounts, so I couldn't interact with my supporters and thank them, let them know that their messages meant a lot to me. I decided to use Linda Wainwright's Twitter account to send a few messages of support.

I retweeted the story with the comment:

LOVE THIS! My friend Candace is made of tough stuff!

I threw in some heart emojis.

Linda's followers immediately started to retweet it and a couple of them sent me bland messages of encouragement and for a few minutes, for the first time in days, I started to feel hopeful. Nothing could ever make the picture go away, but it felt empowering to think of all the good wishes, to know that many people wouldn't blame me or shame me.

Then there was a reply from @BlackPillForever, who had tweeted mean things about me after the topless pic went up:

Candace. U dum. Ready to do what you're told?

Who knew that Linda was my sock puppet? Someone who hacked me, I guess.

@BlackPillForever tweeted again:

I warned you and you didn't listen. Now you will pay. #RAPE #AQUESTIONOFWHEN #FUN

He then tweeted my address. I felt like I'd been punched in the gut. I screencapped the image, blocked him, and opened an incognito browser to try to figure out who he was.

His tweets were so awful, full of weird MRA jargon I didn't know and didn't want to know. I didn't need to get the finer points to get the message. He hated women, especially attractive young women. One tweet jumped out at me. On June 19 he tweeted two words: Target acquired.

I did some quick counting. That was the day I downloaded the list from Presumably Declan. Someone had planned this whole scheme. I felt thoroughly chilled. I double-checked the deadbolt on my door, got my biggest knife out of the kitchen, and put it beside my bed. As I lay there, not sleeping, I decided that whatever happened in the big meeting with SoSol, it was time to go to the police.

# 71

I wait ten minutes after we're back in the car, cruising up the highway, before I ask Simon to pull over.

"I'm going to be sick!" I say.

It's true. My vegan stomach can't handle the disgusting Denny's breakfast.

Simon pulls over by the side of the road and I climb out and promptly vomit into the long grass.

I drop to my knees and wait, retching and heaving.

Karine comes and puts her hand on my shoulder. She gives me a bottle of water.

"Are you okay?"

"I'm so sorry. I'll just be another minute. I don't want to make a mess in your car."

I make myself retch again and gag up some saliva and mucus.

I look up at her. Am I wrong or is she starting to look drugged? Fingers crossed!

She wanders back toward the car.

I drink some water and pray that the roofies do their stuff. I make fake retching noises and wait.

When I get back to the car, Simon is sitting in the driver's seat, staring ahead with a funny, dazed look on his face. Karine is in the passenger seat, one leg splayed out the door. The car is beeping.

A pickup truck whizzes past and startles me, but it doesn't slow down.

Karine turns and gives me a drugged-looking smile.

"Feeling better?" she says.

"A little. I wonder if it was something in the breakfast. Are you okay? You don't look well."

"No," she says. "I feel weird."

"Come here. I think you're going to be sick."

She takes my hand and lets me lead her to the side of the road. I walk her into the trees and help her sit down on a log.

I go back for Simon.

He is in a stupor. I don't even speak to him. I just open the driver's door, take him by the arm and lead him, stumble-footed, to the tree line, to join his wife, who is now lying on the mossy forest floor. I plunk him beside her.

"I'll be right back," I say.

# 72

I felt terrible as the meeting started, so hungover that I was afraid it was obvious to everyone in the room. Maybe they would look at my blanched face and assume that I was just upset, which I was.

Anyway, I wouldn't have to speak. Jess had told me on the way up that I had to let her do all the talking. If I wanted to say anything, I should whisper in her ear.

She gave me an encouraging smile as we sat down on one side of the table.

On the other side of the table were Rebecca, Alvin, and two men I didn't know: one middle-aged guy in an expensive suit, and a young, Mediterranean-looking guy in khakis and a golf shirt. The older man had a beautiful watch, diamond cuff links, and a pampered, pale face. The younger man had a ratlike face, with one of those permanent five o'clock shadows. He wore an expensive-looking diving watch.

Rebecca introduced them.

"This is Clive Gillespie," she said, pointing to the older guy. "Of Gillespie, Reynolds, and Cohen."

Jess's face was calm but I could see her shoulders tense and she started to tap her foot. That had to be bad.

"And this is Uri Deleon," Rebecca said. "Uri does computer forensics."

"Nice to see you again, Candace," said Alvin, and he gave me an unfriendly smile.

I ignored him. I didn't feel good about any of this.

"Are we ready?" said Rebecca. "Can I get anybody anything?"

Nobody needed anything.

Gillespie started the meeting by sliding a letter across the table to Jess.

"This is to notify you that as of this morning, your client is no longer an employee of SoSol," he said.

He gave Jess and me each a cold smile, frowning between the smiles to show that they were unfriendly.

"See, please, that we are also requesting the return of company property—one laptop and one phone—or, failing that, financial compensation for said items in the amount of $3,782."

Jess was staring at him with a blank face.

"We have reason to believe that the laptop is not going to be returned to us," he said. "Given what we read this morning in Pandora. So perhaps we can make arrangements now for payment."

Jess smiled back at Gillespie, just as quickly as he had smiled at her.

"Have you contemplated the terms of the separation?" she said. "As you are aware, my client has been severely damaged with a series of online attacks as a result of her employment at SoSol."

Gillespie looked as though that confused him.

"Our payroll department tells us that we owe your sister $894," he said. "Given the uncertainty about company property, we will withhold that until the matter of the phone and the laptop are settled. We don't accept that what you call 'attacks' on your sister have anything to do with SoSol."

Alvin was grinning at me across the table, waggling his eyebrows. I tried not to look at him.

"Uri," he said. "Tell her, Uri."

Gillespie cleared his throat.

"Mr. Deleon here is a former IT security analyst for two different Fortune 500 companies. He is a telecommunications security adviser to Shin Bet, the Israeli security agency. He has testified as an expert witness on five occasions in the United States. Mr. Deleon has, at our request, reviewed the electronic record downloaded from the phone that SoSol provided to your client. He is prepared to outline the findings to you."

"Thank you, Mr. Gillespie," Uri said. He looked down as he spoke, referring to notes on his laptop.

"I was hired on June 21 to review records associated with four alleged incidents of hacking in relation to social media accounts of Ms. Walker. I found no evidence of hacking. Electronic records show that all four incidents were traced to SocialBeast, an app authorized and controlled by Ms. Walker and operated from her personal phone. I conducted a review to ascertain whether any SoSol employees were involved. I was able to conclude, decisively, that none were involved, beyond Ms. Walker."

I didn't think this was going well. Neither, from the expression on her face, did Jess. I wanted to shout: *This is crazy. I don't have a personal phone.*

"I see what you're proposing," she said. "Can we discuss this on a without-prejudice basis?"

"Fine with me," said Gillespie. "Uri and Rebecca, would you mind stepping outside for a moment?"

As soon as they left, Gillespie started talking again.

"Look, before you get started, I should tell you that Uri is very good at what he does, and he has found nothing that backs up your client's story," he said. "We traced all the so-called harassing texts with Verizon, the provider. We have records of all texts sent and received by your client's phone, and we can state with 100 percent certainty that SoSol is not responsible."

I couldn't believe what he was saying. I felt like curling up into the fetal position and sobbing. To make matters worse, Alvin kept grinning at me.

"Nobody at SoSol had anything to do with posting those pictures," Gillespie continued. "If you intend to allege anyone did, I hope that you will provide evidence of that to us, and the sooner the better. I should point out that your client's interview with Pandora is a clear breach of her employment contract, so you're starting out on shaky ground."

I turned to look at Jess, who had hardly said anything since we entered the room. I needed her to speak up. She gave me a reassuring look and cleared her throat.

"Mr. Gillespie, you have made a number of unsupported assertions," she said. "Setting those aside for the moment, there's also the matter of the workplace environment, in which my client was subjected to a surprisingly wide variety of inappropriate sexual harassment, considering the short time she was employed here. In front of witnesses, Mr. Beaconsfield on two occasions used incredibly crude sexual language, and at one time actually groped my client.

"Given this behavior, which is shockingly out of step with workplace norms, it's difficult for my client to take it on faith that nobody here had anything to do with the hacking of her personal photos and their posting on social media, which are bound to have a long-term impact on her career and personal life."

Gillespie held up one manicured finger and smiled. This smile seemed actually sincere. Kind. Jess paused.

"Just so you know, Ms. Walker, we have information that makes us very confident about the source of the social media posts in question."

He stared at her.

"Mr. Beaconsfield and Uri are resourceful. We have evidence that we aren't at liberty to discuss, but I want you to understand how confident we are regarding these social media posts. I'm not exaggerating when I say that if you pursue this line any further it could be seen as evidence of mental illness. Do you understand me? The facts are on our side. They are assuredly not on your client's side."

Jess was shaking her head.

"If we take your word for it," she said.

"Have you asked your client about her other phone?" he asked. "You don't have to take my word for it, and you won't be taking our word for it if we get to discovery."

"That's the way you're headed," said Jess. "You're not going to bluff us out."

Alvin started laughing then, opening his enormous mouth and baying with delight.

"I'm sorry," he said, putting his finger to his lip. "Sorry. Bad boy. Sorry."

He kept giggling, though.

"Look," said Gillespie. "We would like to close the door on this. Firmly. We all have better things to do."

He took a document from his briefcase and slid it across to Jess.

"We're prepared to make a payment, to make this, and your client, go away. You have twenty-four hours to consider it. Any public discussion of the matter and we will withdraw the offer. Okay?"

Jess looked down at it and frowned. She reluctantly picked it up.

"This meeting is over. We'll get back to you."

She turned to me and nodded. It was time for us to go. I had to stand up.

Gillespie stood up as we did.

"One thing," he said. "We need the phone. Now. It belongs to SoSol."

Jess glanced at me. I felt weak. She turned to Gillespie.

"I said we'll get back to you. We're done for now."

I could hear Alvin giggling as we walked out.

# 73

It feels great to be behind the wheel, moving farther from the city and my past and toward my hopefully brighter future.

It is about an hour to Watertown from Syracuse. There is no traffic, just me and the sun, the empty road and miles and miles of scraggly-looking softwoods.

It gives me lots of time to work on my new identity, which, the experience with Simon and Karine has taught me, needs to be a lot tighter.

I am going to be reborn. The new woman will share as little as possible with the woman I am leaving behind.

If I want to stay out of court—and I want nothing as badly as that—I have to be brutal with my old self. Eating the disgusting Denny's breakfast was a good start. I am not vegan anymore. Give me meat.

I was a redhead. Now I am a blonde. I was snarky and judgmental about music and movies. Now I am open to everything.

I have to watch my drinking, watch what I say, be slower to speak, listen more. Most people are so consumed with what others think about them that they don't really doubt what people tell them.

I have to bank on that, focus on presenting a smooth wall to the world, an identity that nobody would doubt.

It will be a lot of work, but my future is worth it. Someone has tried to destroy me. The best response, the only response, really, is to make my life a success.

In a way, I am looking forward to it. In the past, I often felt constrained by others' expectations of me, by my own expectations of myself. This crisis gives me an opportunity to re-create myself, to be exactly who I choose to be.

I will write the story of my own past. I will become a character of my own creation. Most people go through their lives buffeted this way and that by their environments, their families, their friends, their economic and social circumstances.

I was like that. Now I will be different.


I finally stop the car at the Watertown Walmart and go inside.

I will make sure my future is not like the lives of the people here. Everybody looks as though they could benefit from some dentistry and a makeover.

That would be a good reality show. *White Trash Makeover.*

It's weird. All my life I've associated poverty with black people and other minorities. Here in Watertown, everyone is white and they have the same horizon-dimmed matter-of-fact fatalism that I associate with poor minorities. Like, their lives are awful enough that they can't afford to care too much what some fool like me thinks of them. They look at me, if at all, with undisguised longing. I am obviously a creature from another strata, a pretty blonde in nice clothes. They want to be me, to have what I have, and don't even have the self-respect to resent me.

Everyone's skin is pasty. Nobody has nice clothes. All the vehicles need replacing. I don't know what happened here, but it looks like the town's industry shut down and everybody who could got out.

Before I do my shopping, I decide to have my first Big Mac in three years. I'm standing in line in front of an awful family. The mother is haggard, with stringy bleached hair. She's wearing sweatpants and a sports bra, so that everybody can enjoy looking at her flabby gray belly. Her waist-high son is bent over a tablet, playing some game that produces explosion noises. His little sister is hanging off her mom. Mom is looking at her phone.

When I get my horrible lunch, I grab a table and sink my teeth into the delicious, disgusting Big Mac. The gross family sits next to me. The noise from the kid's tablet is intensely irritating to me. He can barely look up from his screen to stuff his face with chicken nuggets. Mom ignores him and looks at her phone while she stuffs a burger into her mouth. The daughter, who for some reason doesn't have a tablet, starts to whine when she takes the first bite of her burger.

"They put ketchup on it," she whines. "I can't eat it."

The mother ignores her at first, her head bent over her phone. When the kid keeps whining, she pays her no mind. Then the little girl, a homely little thing, tugs at her mother's sleeve and her mother smacks her, without looking at her. The girl starts to quietly cry. The mother doesn't comfort her, just keeps jamming her burger into her face.

I feel like crying just watching and start thinking about the girl's grim prospects. Her mother's horrible man will abuse her as soon as she hits puberty. Mom will pretend she doesn't know it's happening because she needs the guy around. The kid will resent her mother for denying the truth of what's happening and take off with the first local mouth breather who offers her a way out. I can see her life stretched out in front of her, and it kills my appetite. I decide to dump half my disgusting lunch and finish my shopping.

If I had energy to spare for political feelings, which I don't, this kind of place would make me a socialist. If that little girl is going to go be abused and neglected, why does she have to have bad teeth and a shitty Walmart wardrobe, instead of growing up like I did, with nice cars and clothes and dentistry and soccer and music lessons and sailing camp?

But anytime I think about that kind of political question long enough I realize that I just don't care enough to be a socialist. The fact is that I don't like the little brats whining and mewling behind their white trash mothers at the Watertown Walmart, and I can understand why nobody who isn't related to them by blood could be bothered to do anything for them. Let them vote for Trump and commit acts of incest in their trailers. I don't care.

Anyway, I find what I need: a black bikini, a pair of denim shorts, a little tool kit, a compass, and a GPS.

My getaway stash is now $580. Not bad.

Then I drive around the outskirts of Watertown for an hour or so, which is depressing.

I'm looking for a big, sad-looking used car lot. I find one. Jason's Used Cars and Trucks. It's in the woods. I drive to the back of the lot. I sit there for a while, keeping my eyes on the crappy little trailer with the sign on it where the salesmen must wait for impoverished customers to rip off. Nobody comes out. They must be gone for the day.

Eventually, I get out with my little tool kit and crouch behind the Ford Focus next to me. I use the little wrench to take off its license plate, then scoot around to the front and take that one off, too. I am out of sight of the office so long as I stay low.

Next, I go to a Hyundai parked a few spots away and remove its plates. I replace them with the plates from the Ford, put the Hyundai plates on my Canadian Volvo and put the Ontario plates in the trunk.

Then I crawl into the backseat and collapse and sleep until dawn.

# 74

"Ten thousand dollars," said Jess in the elevator. "They want to give you ten thousand dollars. That's nothing."

"Fuck," I said. "That's not good, is it?"

"That's what an intern gets if the boss hurts her feelings. And, of course, it includes an NDA."

"Which means I can't talk about my experience."

"That's right," she said.

"It doesn't sound like you think I should take it."

The elevator door opened and she marched out.

"I think you have to take it."

I stopped in the lobby.

"What do you mean? It's a terrible deal."

She stared at me.

"Terrible compared to what? Compared to getting nothing? Leaving them free to say whatever they want about you in court documents?"

She checked her phone.

"Where's Wayne?" she said. "He is supposed to meet us now. He's sort of our inside man."

She tapped on her phone.

"I'm going to get him to meet us on the subway," she said. "I have to get uptown for a meeting."

I followed her to the corner and down into the subway. We descended, went through the turnstile, descended again, and found him, sitting on a wooden bench on the platform.

He rose and kissed Jess on the cheek. Ouch. Ouch. Ouch.

He gave me a hug. I sat down next to him. Jess stood in front of us.

"So," said Jess. "Anything to report?"

"I am no longer employed by SoSol," he said. "They must know I'm your spy. I went in this morning, then Beatrice came in and said Rebecca wanted to see me. She said thanks for my work for SoSol but they were reorganizing. There was a security guard there."

"Shit," said Jess. "I don't suppose you've learned anything?"

"I saw Kevin in the lobby. He seemed upset and was kind of venting. He didn't know I'd been let go. He told me that he heard Alvin blamed Craig for the Pandora article and, well, hiring you. Apparently Rebecca wanted to hire Beatrice. Craig pushed for you. Rebecca thought you were trouble and Craig kept sticking up for you."

I stared at him, dumbfounded. He shrugged, as if to say, *I did what I could.*

"BT dubs, great article in Pandora," he said.

"Thanks," I said.

"Are they going to put it back up?" he asked.

"What?" I said.

"They just pulled it down a few minutes ago."

I checked my phone. There was an email from Lenora. Lawyers' orders. Story was down, at least for now. She had follow-up questions about my SocialBeast account. SoSol was saying they could show login records connected with all the posts. She said Pandora's lawyers were considering posting a retraction and apology. It was really important to get back to her.

I felt sick to my stomach.

"They made a settlement offer," Jess told Wayne. "They say they can prove that nobody at SoSol had anything to do with posting the pictures. Their lawyer was so confident."

"Wow," said Wayne. "That's not how you hoped it would go."

Jess turned to me.

"Look," she said. "Is there anything you haven't told me? What happened to your old phone?"

"I only have one phone," I said. "I don't know what they are talking about."

"What's SocialBeast? That threw me for a loop."

"SocialBeast is a social media management app. I use it to send out scheduled tweets and Instagram and Facebook postings."

Jess turned to Wayne.

"They had some kind of high-tech guy there. He went through the phone, discovered that all the nasty pictures were posted by Candace's own SocialBeast account."

"Hm," said Wayne.

"The clear implication was that Candace basically did it herself," said Jess. "From her other phone."

"Which I don't have."

I couldn't believe what Jess was saying, or how she was saying it. A terrible old feeling came back to me.

"You don't believe that," I said.

She looked away.

"It doesn't matter what I believe," she said.

"It matters to me. You're my sister."

# 75

I wake up, confused and cramped in the back of the Volvo at dawn.

I pee behind the car, have a drink of water, and change into my new black bikini, denim shorts, and one of Jess's T-shirts and head to Clayton, north of Watertown, on the shores of the Saint Lawrence River.

It's pretty, a faded resort town with big clapboard houses on tree-lined streets.

There obviously is no money now, but there once was, likely before people could get on airplanes and go to far-off places on their vacations, and the best they could do was sit in some cabin on a riverbank. Whatever. Back when they had money they built nice buildings and are obviously trying their best to maintain them.

It gives the place a rough charm. There are a lot of flags and red, white, and blue bunting on many of the houses. It's like a forgotten small town America left over from the days when Jimmy Stewart was a movie star.

I find the library and spend a few minutes looking at maps, plotting my escape.

Then I go online and check for news on the hunt for the Hipster Killer. The *New York Post* has a short item about Douchebro's car being found in Scranton, and there's a story in the Scranton paper, but otherwise there is nothing. There won't be until someone finds Chris and Macy, or Simon and Karine, but I hope to be far away by then.

I sign into Linda Wainwright's Facebook account.

Yes! Irene has replied.

She blathers on about how upsetting the whole thing is before getting to the point.

> My goodness, Linda, I can't imagine that I would have any information
> that could help with this but I'd be happy to meet with you. I listened to
> the recordings again and they don't seem to have any clues, but I'll play
> them for you if you like.

I actually laugh out loud with delight in the library and leave with a spring in my step.

I walk down to the riverfront, where there are marinas and restaurants. It's cheerful, with gulls making their gull noises and the sun sparkling on the Saint Lawrence.

I get a coffee and walk down to the Antique Boat Museum and watch some kids out sailing little Optimist dinghies, the same kind of boat I used to sail at summer camp.

It seems like a good omen. I feel pretty good. Ready for the end.

# 76

When Jess wouldn't say whether she believed me or not, I suddenly realized that I was in danger of being seen forever, by everyone, as a whorish attention-seeking freak.

She wouldn't even make eye contact with me. She was looking at her phone, and at the tracks, watching for her train.

"Fuck," she said. "I'm going to be in trouble if I miss this meeting."

I stood up from the bench and said her name.

"Jess. Jess."

She finally looked at me.

"Jess, you have to believe me. Somebody has done this to me. I don't know how they did it, but they did. And it's destroying my life."

I raised my voice over the low rumble of an oncoming train.

"It *is* going to destroy my life! You have to believe me."

Wayne stood and went to Jess's side. He looked rattled.

"I do believe you," said Jess. "I believe you have been completely honest with me, but I think we have to consider whether you're right about everything. It's possible that you're confused or mistaken about some things. You need to take a time-out."

Her face changed.

"I got an email this morning from a lawyer, Reginald Parker. He's representing Jeff. Says that you caused a scene at Chimmi's last night, after you left my place. They want a restraining order."

"That's total bullshit," I said. "That's not what happened."

"Minnow, I checked the Uber. You went there after you left my place."

I took a step back. I couldn't believe this.

"You think I'm crazy," I said. "Oh God."

"I think you should likely get a different lawyer," she said. "This is not ideal. I can find someone else for you."

"I have to decide today whether to take the offer. I don't have time to get a new lawyer."

She closed her eyes, took a deep breath, and looked at me the way someone looks at a not-very-intelligent child.

"Minnow, you have to take it," she said. "You have to take the money and go home and stay with Mom for a little while and see a doctor. I think you need help. If I'm wrong, the doctor will figure that out. If I'm right, it's really important that you get help."

Wayne was standing there nodding, agreeing with every brilliant word out of her mouth.

"No!" I shouted at her. "No way!"

My rage was incandescent.

I had to shout over the sound of the approaching train. Its imminent arrival and Jess's imminent departure made my message more urgent.

"I'm not crazy!" I shouted. "I've been sexually harassed! I'm going to go on CNN! I'm not going to let them get away with this."

Wayne looked at me like I was nuts. "I'm not sure that's a good idea."

Jess shook her head.

"You're not going to do that," she said. "You'll look crazy. That producer, Wendy, emailed me today. I told her that the interview might no longer be helpful to you."

Jess was sabotaging me. She was working against me. It was clear. I had always been prettier than her, not as good at school and a career, because I didn't work like a drudge, but people always liked me better. I could see how it ate at her, constantly, for years, and when I was having a crisis, she was conspiring with the people trying to bring me low. I stood there, assessing her, seeing her clearly for the first time, and it was breaking my heart. I was greatly reduced and she was okay with that.

She looked up the track and then at Wayne. I could see that she was just thinking about ditching me and moving on with her awesome, much more functional life.

The sound of the train was getting louder. It wasn't slowing down. It was going express. It wasn't going to stop.

Jess turned to give me a condescending smile. She shook her head.

"Oh, Minnow," she said. "It's going to be okay. You just need some help."

She reached out to put her hand on my shoulder, to give me the kind of reassuring pat that you give a toddler.

It was too much. I angrily swept my arm up to push her hand off my shoulder.

I swung too hard, though, it knocked her off balance, and she took a step backward. She was suddenly teetering on the edge of the platform, arms outstretched, her beady eyes bugged out. Wayne and I both stepped forward to grab her, we bumped into each other, and the train was suddenly there and they were falling in front of it. I reached for them, tried to pull them back, but it was too late, they fell, and the train swept them from my view.

# 77

I take off my T-shirt on the way to Irene's house on the outskirts of Clayton.

It feels great to drive along with the window down, feeling the sun on my body. I look great in a bikini top.

Irene's house is set back from the road behind a lovely row of old maples and a big, well-kept yard. She has a Trump sign on her front lawn.

It's a white clapboard two-story with green trim, and the front seems to be the back, which must mean it was built long ago, when houses faced the river, not the road.

There's a garage next to the house. An old Volvo station wagon is parked there, which ought to mean she's home.

She must have heard the car in the driveway, because she comes to the door, a gray-haired woman in jeans, running shoes, and a faded cotton blouse, looking sort of fretful behind the screen.

Here goes nothing.

I get out of the car and give her a big smile and wave.

"Hi!" I say. "Irene?"

"Yes?" she says, trying to place me.

She looks older and more befuddled than I expected.

"Hi!" I step away from the car. "It's Linda, your friend from Facebook."

For a moment I think she isn't going to buy it, but then she smiles.

"Of course," she says.

"Did you get my message? I just sent it this morning. I was driving up to Boston and thought I'd stop in."

"I didn't," she says. "But that doesn't matter. Why don't you come in?"

I let out a huge sigh of relief.

My plan works. She knows a young blonde in a bikini on the internet. I don't really look very much like Linda Wainwright, but I am a young blonde in a bikini and Irene assumes I am who I say I am.

Her kitchen is homey and kind of sad, spick-and-span and faded. It smells like honey and ginger.

"Would you like to see my little business?" she asks.

Would I ever!

The world headquarters of Cheese of the Month Club is in a little room that must have once been a den. There's a big fridge containing many different packages of carefully labeled cheeses, a shelf covered in special shipping envelopes, and a desk with a computer.

She cheerfully explains it all to me while I enthuse, which takes some doing, since I hate her stupid business and her.

"I've put a lot of time and money into it," she says. "Thank goodness your friend was able to boost my sales. Otherwise, I would have lost money on the whole thing, and on a teacher's pension, you really can't afford to lose money."

That lets me segue to poor Candace.

She offers me—thank goodness—a cup of tea, and as she puts the kettle on in the kitchen, I sit down and start to explain my misgivings. She looks confused as I lay out the case for the defense.

I tell her I believe Candace was set up by her boss, Alvin Beaconsfield, who sexually exploited her and then framed her when he realized he was going to be caught. What happened at the subway was a terrible accident.

Irene listens patiently to all this as she pours our tea and sits down across from me at the kitchen table, but it doesn't mean anything to her.

"I only know what I read in the news," she says. "You said in your message on Facebook that I might be able to help clear it up."

"It's possible," I say, sipping my tea. "Let me explain. It's just a bit complicated. Do you think I could have a glass of water?"

Of course I can. She gets up and goes to the sink.

Roofie time.

# 78

A body hitting the front of a moving train makes a big noise, a terrible thump, even above the racket of the steel wheels on the track.

The train was going so fast that, thankfully, there was little gore to stick in my mind, but for an instant I could see the impact, when Jess and Wayne stopped moving backward and started moving sideways and sort of flattening, molding themselves to the train.

They must have been dead within seconds, which is a comfort to me. I don't like to see anyone suffer.

We all must die. It isn't unjust to die before your time, since, as of the moment of death, you no longer exist. How can someone who doesn't exist press a claim on the living? They can't.

This is an error at the heart of our social order, our justice system, the so-called crime of murder.

Life is for the living. The dead have no interests. They are gone. That's why we make wills. The dead can't own anything. I've been thinking about this a lot in the past few days, as I made my desperate calculations, and I am at peace with the deaths that I caused.

I was not in peace at the moment it happened. I'd sat, in a terrible daze, on the platform, for a few seconds. Then the fight-or-flight instinct kicked in and, without thinking about it, I scrambled to my feet and headed up the stairs, up to daylight.

Few people saw what happened and nobody reacted as quickly as I did. An older woman cried out as I started for the stairs.

"Stop her!" she shouted, pointing at me. "She pushed them."

Most people didn't see it happen, though, and nobody grabbed me, and the old bitch was too fat to give chase.

So I made it up the stairs and out into the street and sunshine and I quickly lost myself in the crowds. I think I wandered aimlessly for an hour, because there's a blank spot in my memory.

When I came to my senses, I was walking by the Hudson. I'd decided I wanted to escape. I realized that I had to get rid of my phone, which was surely tracking my movements more closely than I had been for the past hours.

I swore that I wouldn't let myself be trapped, either by whoever it was who drove me to my current desperate situation or by whoever might falsely blame me for the death of my sister and her lover.

According to the half-literate hacks at the *Post* (can you imagine what a horrible bunch of mediocrities must work there?), security video from the subway shows me pushing Jess and Wayne into the path of the train.

That's one reason why I can never turn myself in. I knew as soon as I read that that I couldn't. There would be no justice for me, not with the *Post* calling me the Hipster Killer. And I never want to watch the video. They would make me watch it, in court, and I won't. Period. I'd rather die. And I'd rather kill than die.

I was friendless, reviled, smeared, reduced to hiding in a storage closet and peeing in a bowl. Who could blame me for doing whatever it took to stay free? And if someone blames me, tell me, why should I care?

# 79

Irene, who isn't that smart, can't figure out how she might shed light on poor Candace's legal troubles no matter how I try to explain it to her.

I have twenty minutes to kill while I wait for the roofie to kick in. I tell her she has the key to proving Candace's innocence.

"But I only know her through a few phone calls," she says. "I don't see how I fit into this."

"Let's listen to the messages, and we'll see if I'm right."

She goes to her office to get the recorder and plunks it on the kitchen table.

"What do you think is on this?" she says. "I listened to them after you messaged me and I don't see how our conversations could be connected at all with what happened."

I smile and try to look like a kindly young woman trying to explain a new technology to her grannie.

"Look at it this way," I say. "If it hadn't been for her work for you, she wouldn't have gotten herself into trouble."

"I'm not sure I agree."

"Well," I say, letting a little annoyance creep into my voice, "the police say she got into trouble over a list she used for your business. So you profited from her trouble. How much revenue did you get from all those conversions? It must be, what, five thousand dollars?"

She laughs nervously, but I see she's not stupid enough to tell me how much she made.

"I don't know if it was that much," she says. "And I had no idea there was any mischief involved."

"I suppose not," I say, smiling again, lest I frighten her. "How would you know?"

"And the cheese business had nothing to do with what she did to that boy in New Jersey," she says. "I found that very disturbing, what she did to him."

"Some people think that what he got is too good for rapists," I say. "Maybe you don't think so? You think it's okay for disgusting men like him to rape young women?"

There's a slowly dawning realization, a rising tide of dread in her old eyes. She suddenly sees that she had made a mistake letting Linda into her house.

Unfortunately for her, I have timed it right, and she's showing the early signs of the effects of the Rohypnol in her bloodstream.

"He wanted to rape Candace," I say. "He put a roofie in her drink. Do you know what that is? It's a drug, a powerful sedative. He was going to take her home and fuck her while she was drugged. Would you like it if somebody did that to you?"

She stares at me dully, her eyes flickering nervously.

She disgusts me. She doesn't care about rape. She would do nothing if her husband abused her daughter. She would likely pretend she didn't know about it, even if the signs were everywhere, even if her daughter came to her, confused and hurt, and explained it.

She is making me angry.

"Nobody would want to rape you, of course, but Douchebro wanted to rape Candace," I say. "She outsmarted him, and switched their drinks, and I'd say he got what he deserved. And Candace got what she deserved, or some of it anyway. She cleaned out his bank account."

"I want you to leave," she says after a moment. "I'm sorry but I'm tired. Tired."

I smile and stand up.

"Sure," I say. "Of course. No problem. I'll be on my way. Just one thing first. I need the money that you made off Candace. It should be about five thousand dollars. She needs to start a new life and she needs that money."

She stares at me. She doesn't understand.

I go to the counter and pick up her purse and rifle through it. She has one bank card and $130 in cash.

"You need to tell me your PIN," I say. "Then I'll leave you alone."

I am glad that she tells me the number without too much trouble. I don't want to use the knife on her like that. She is an old bitch and deserves what she gets but she doesn't deserve to suffer like Douchebro did.

I feel comfortable with her death, and with the deaths of Simon and Karine. They didn't suffer. I don't think they felt anything more than a brief twinge when I opened the ulnar artery, carefully slicing a straight line from the forearm down to the wrist.

Neither Karine nor Simon even knew what was even happening to them.

Maybe Simon did, because he was so overweight that he metabolized the drug more slowly, and I didn't like seeing his futile struggle to stanch the wound as his blood leaked out onto the mossy forest floor, but into every life a little rain must fall.

# 80

I'm writing this in a charmingly dowdy English pub on the waterfront of Kingston, Ontario.

It was Canada Day yesterday, so everything is covered in flags, even me. I bought a cheap Maple Leafs T-shirt, the better to blend in.

It's nice here: boring but clean and much more prosperous than Clayton. There are a lot of college kids, and they are pleasantly exuberant, like puppies, bouncing around and chattering and getting drunk, not like the too-cool-for-school Brooklyn kids. I like being around them. I know I am more woke than any of them, unlike in Brooklyn, where I lived in fear of using the wrong pronoun or failing to be sufficiently outraged by whatever trendy cause was supposed to outrage us that week.

I am in an excellent mood. For the first time since the subway accident, I feel that I am finally a sufficient number of steps ahead of the people pursuing me.

I have a new lease on life. I feel good, even great. I find myself smiling for no reason, except that I am free to order a pint of beer and a shepherd's pie and read the boring newspaper that somebody left at the bar.

I even flirt with the bartender. I might let him take me to his place. He's big and handsome and has the kind of dim-witted Canadian earnestness that nobody could fake. I like his forearms. And he is shy with me, flustered, which, yes, I think, *Why not?* Also, I need a place to sleep tonight.

I have been trying to get to this place, with the police far behind me and no immediate prospect of unjust incarceration, and now I am here, and it feels good. The sense of loss that I had feared would become more acute—the saying good-bye to my past—actually has faded.

I will miss Francis, and Mom, but Francis will cope, and Mom, well, she wasn't there for me when I needed her, so it's hard for me to worry about her feelings too much.

Mostly, I feel like I deserve to relax a bit. I have been very careful, learning as I went, and I took a lot of calculated risks, but they all worked out and I am free and liquid and ready for my new life.

What am I talking about? I'm already enjoying my new life.

# 81

After I got the PIN from Irene, I put on one of her old lady hats, drove to an ATM, and cleaned out her account: $3,080, which brought my escape fund up to $3,790.

I ditched the Volvo in downtown Clayton, with the keys in the ignition and the door unlocked. I hope by now some local loser has stolen it.

Then I made my way to the river, where the sun was setting over the water. I went to a waterfront tourist restaurant, had a Caesar salad, and watched the boats come and go on the river.

When it got dark, I walked down to the boat museum dock, where the kids had left their dinghies tied up. I tossed my bag into one of them, untied it, and pushed off.

I had been nervous about sailing again. I hadn't been in a boat since my father's second heart attack.

We had just sailed from the yacht club in his Shark out to the mouth of New Haven Harbor into Long Island Sound, where the wind was so strong that some of the waves were crested with whitecaps. He was full of beer, as usual, sitting on the high side gunwale, while I steered.

We were kind of arguing, and then he shook his head, rejecting my point of view without even saying anything. He leaned way back out over the water. Then I think he must have had the heart attack because suddenly I was alone in the boat. It was a nightmare getting back to the yacht club by myself, not knowing what had become of Dad, but I usually can keep my cool even when terrible things happen.

I hadn't been in a sailboat since that difficult day, but I had no choice now, so I raised the little mast and dropped the centerboard and the boat started to move out into the river in the light evening breeze.

That was when I was most vulnerable, as I sailed away from the dock, but nobody noticed me, and I was able to sail out of the little harbor and into the broad river, where the wind was stronger, blowing from the west, making choppy little waves that slapped at the boat.

The wind was scary, but it made the boat go fast, and I had the GPS and compass to guide me, and I wasn't going that far. It was a straight run north to Gananoque, an Ontario resort town.

It was colder than I expected and I hadn't thought to bring gloves, so I was shivering when I finally managed to nose the boat into the muddy Canadian riverbank.

I climbed into the long marshy grass and looked around. My hands were cramped but I was otherwise fine. In the distance I could see the headlights on the highway that runs between Kingston and Gananoque.

When I was sure that I could walk to my new life from there, I let go of the rope on the bow and watched the boat drift slowly out into the current in the middle of the river.

*Please*, I thought. *Please. Let this be a new start. Let all of my pain, all of my mistakes, all my sadness, my old life, let it stay in the boat. Let it float slowly but surely away from me, leaving me clean, innocent, and deserving of happiness.*

# 82

I walked, exhausted, into Gananoque as the sun came up, gaping red-eyed at a perfect blanket of mist sitting still on the gray water of the river. I found an empty Tim Hortons coffee shop, and sat in the back corner, waiting for the library to open, drinking green tea and holding Irene's recorder to my ear.

The first recordings were intensely boring: two conversations with a lawyer concerning the disputed will of Irene's aunt. There were also half a dozen conversations with a pension management company call center and a few calls with utilities. I skipped through them all before I got to the good stuff: Craig pitching her on SoSol, talking fast about the explosive growth potential of unexploited niches, the market you can unlock with laser-guided social media targeting. He gave her his bullshit and then tried to get her to say yes and get off the phone. She asked repeatedly if there was any way she would have to pay. He kept saying no. Then she finally agreed and he signed her up.

I sat up and gulped the last bitter dregs of my huge cardboard cup of tea when the next call started. It was Candace, in happier times, two weeks and a lifetime ago, calling Irene to say hi. I impatiently listened to the strained conversation, which was boring the first time, with chipper Candace trying to suck up to overbearing Irene.

Then Irene asked whether she might get stiffed and Candace passed the phone to Rebecca.

As Rebecca soothed her, in the background, the recording captured a faint but clear conversation about phones. I listened closely, rewinding and replaying it. New phone okay? Did I transfer everything over? Am I done with the old phone?

Yes. Yes. Yes.

Then I could hear him ask me, quite clearly: "Can I get the old one back from you?"

"Here you go," Candace replied.

I stopped the recording and looked around the coffee shop. I closed my eyes, inhaled deeply and exhaled.

I knew, at last, who did this to me. It was like waking up from a nightmare and realizing that it was Christmas morning.

It came back to me. I gave my old phone to Kevin. He had it. He had the phone that was used to schedule the social media postings that destroyed my life.

If I hadn't been so busy knifing pimps, roofieing losers, and avoiding the police, I could have figured it out sooner. Of course. It was him. It was Kevin.

He took the phone, unlocked my life, and played with me.

I put it all together.

When he gave me the new phone, he had installed snooping software that allowed him to track my movements, read my messages, and eavesdrop on my every utterance, including all my conversations about him.

He stole Declan's laptop at Alvin's party, downloaded the data files, baited me with them, pretending to be Declan, playing me like a fish on a hook. He posted my pictures, sexually harassed me, fucked with me six ways from Sunday.

Every time I gave him my phone, he pretended to wipe it but gave it back to me, still compromised. I kept changing passwords and he kept seeing me change them. And I never thought to check the apps I had authorized, so he was able to use SocialBeast to post to my accounts. It would have been easy for him to convince the company that I did it all from my second phone, which he had with him all along.

It's amazing to think he did all this because he wanted to creep on me. Mission accomplished, loser. You creeped on me so thoroughly that you basically destroyed my life.

If he is @BlackPillForever, and I am sure he is, then his motive is spelled out clearly in his disgusting tweets. He can't get laid and so he hates the women who reject him, including me.

How ridiculous. I was brought low by a thirsty freak, a perverted misfit who couldn't accept his pathetic lot in life.

The thought of it makes me so angry. Someone like that, someone *so marginal*, shouldn't be able to even inconvenience someone like me, but he had. He separated me from my social media life, stripped me of my networked self, which is like a kind of death sentence. What kind of a life is a life without social, where we can't share, can't connect? Because of Kevin, I had suffered a social amputation, and I am every day living with the phantom pain.

He had driven me to low, desperate places. He would pay for that.

I have learned a lot since he phished me, though. I have gone through hell, but I have resurfaced, and I feel like I am fully myself in a way I hadn't been before. I know my capabilities, and they are . . . well, he will see soon enough.

I suppose, if I am to be honest, I would also have to admit that I've learned some things about myself that are less than flattering, but how many people, under the kind of pressure that I've endured, would have handled themselves as well?

And I am still learning and growing, making new rules for myself. For example: no more Ambiens for Candace. I need to keep a clear head, make sure that my memories are accurate. Telling the truth is easy. When you lie all the time—and thanks to Kevin I have no choice about that—you have to remember all your lies. I need to be super-careful. But I can be.

I was exhausted but happy when I finally left the coffee shop and set out through the sunny streets, plotting my next move.

At the library, at one of the computers, I set up a VPN to hide my IP, then signed in to iCloud. I waited while it processed my password, then breathed a sigh of relief when I was in. I clicked on Find My Phone and asked the server to locate my old iPhone 6. Within a minute, a green dot appeared on the screen over a map of Flatbush. I laughed, quietly, because I didn't want to attract the attention of the librarian.

Hi, Kevin.

CNNarticle.pdf

# CNN BREAKING NEWS

## FBI seeks 'hipster killer' in Sandy Hook swatting death

UPDATED 3:13 PM ET, THUR JULY 12, 2018

(CNN) The FBI is looking for a missing New York woman after hoax messages led agents to fatally shoot a man at Sandy Hook Elementary School, site of the tragic 2012 mass shooting in Newtown, Connecticut.

The New Haven field office of the FBI is seeking the public's help in finding 26-year-old Candace Walker after the apparent "swatting" death of her former coworker, Kevin Reisenger.

Walker, who tabloids dubbed the "Hipster Killer," has been on the run since last month, when she is alleged to have pushed her sister, Jessica Walker, and coworker Wayne Hooper in front of a subway train in New York City, causing their deaths. She is also wanted in the knife slaying of New Jersey man James DeSouza.

Reisenger was shot by an FBI sniper this morning at Sandy Hook Elementary School, apparently after hoax social media posts convinced agents that he was about to fire on the school. Police sources say Candace Walker is believed to have authored those posts, which were posted on a Sandy Hook "truther" website.

Sandy Hook "truthers" believe a government conspiracy is suppressing the real story of the massacre at Sandy Hook, where Adam Lanza killed 20 children and six adults in 2012.

This is the latest example of swatting, in which pranksters make false reports to induce SWAT teams to target their victims. The practice has been blamed for numerous deaths at the hands of municipal police forces across the United States. This is the first swatting carried out by the FBI.

Police sources say investigators believe Walker used Facebook to lure Reisenger to the school.

"This shows every sign of being a carefully calculated act of deception, which had a tragic outcome," said Chris Samuels, the special agent in charge of the New Haven field office of the FBI.

Walker first made headlines last month when nude images of her were shared through her social media accounts, which she blamed on a hacker.

Samuels says Walker, who was last seen in Scranton, Pennsylvania, on June 30, is believed to have changed her appearance. They urge anyone who spots her not to confront her but to report her to the police.

"She is considered to be armed and dangerous," he said. "We are pursuing multiple leads and hope to apprehend her in the near future."

Liste.pdf

**List of items in daypack found at Montreal Airport Marriott on July 12, 2018**

- One black Moleskine notebook
- One folding steel Extreme Ops brand combat knife
- Five pairs of women's undergarments
- One pair of flip-flops
- One Old Navy bra, blue in color, size 34B
- One black Abercrombie & Fitch cotton dress
- Three T-shirts, one black, one yellow, and one blue
- One Old Navy cotton dress
- One pair of blue jeans from Banana Republic
- One iPhone charger
- One hardcover copy of *The Portable Dorothy Parker*, 1973 edition, with markings inside showing it is from the Albright Memorial Library in Scranton, Pa.
- One plastic pencil case containing:
    - A worn toothbrush and travel-size toothpaste
    - Five Trojan condoms
    - One tube of mascara
    - One lipstick
    - One eyeliner pencil
    - One eyeshadow palette
    - Nine Ambiens in an unlabeled pill box
    - A blister pack of 30 Rohypnol tablets with eight pills missing

**To:** Csamuels@fbi.gov
**From:** GBonaventure@svpm.ca
**Date:** July 12, 2018, 4:44 p.m.
**Subject:** Notebook scan as requested

Dear Special Agent Samuels,

Please find enclosed, as discussed in our phone call of earlier this afternoon, three attachments:

1) Walkercahier.pdf: An electronic scan of a notebook an officer obtained this afternoon.
2) CNNArticle.pdf: The CNN story that was on the computer Walker was using when last seen.
3) Liste.pdf: A list of the items in a daypack that Walker left behind with the notebook.

   It is the hope of the Service de Police de la Ville de Montréal that this will help you in your investigation into the death this morning of Kevin Reisenger in Newtown, Connecticut.

   The notebook is a cardboard-covered Moleskine Ruled Pocket Notebook, black in colour, measuring nine by fourteen centimeters, with a glued-in elastic band.

   It was found just before 3 p.m. on July 12, by Constable Augustine LaTendresse, in the business centre at the Montreal Airport Marriott.

   I tasked Constable LaTendresse with visiting the hotel after your ViCAP colleague, Special Agent Ron Smith, contacted me this morning to request our help in locating Candace Walker. He informed me that the IP address of the hotel's business centre was used to send hoax messages that led to the officer-involved shooting that killed Reisenger.

As requested, Constable LaTendresse showed hotel staff a picture of Walker. The business centre manager, Gaeten Ouellette, recognized her as a customer who had just left in a hurry after spending much of the day using a computer there.

Constable LaTendresse discovered the bag containing her notebook in the kiosk she had been using. Constable LaTendresse suspects that she fled when she saw him crossing the hotel's lobby.

Ouellette told Constable LaTendresse that Walker now has short black hair. She was wearing a dark blue dress.

We should be able to provide you with video from the hotel security system later today.

I hope this report will help with your investigation and I ask that you let me know at your earliest convenience if you will be seeking a warrant for Walker. We have already put her on a watchlist for Canada Border Services Agents at the Pierre Elliott Trudeau International Airport.

I have outlined the facts of the case to Chief Inspector Raymond Boucher, who is considering what to do to ensure the safety of Montrealers. He is ready to discuss next steps with your team at your earliest convenience, as am I.

Yours truly,
Detective Sergeant Jean-Frederick Lapointe

# ACKNOWLEDGMENTS

Many people helped me with this novel.

I want to thank my indefatigable agent, Amy Moore-Benson, of Meridian Artists, for her wise counsel, good humor, and sharp eye, and Laurie Grassi, my editor at Simon & Schuster, for patiently working with me to improve the manuscript. It occurred to me during the editing process that most readers don't realize how much editors are responsible for the finished books they read.

I want to thank retired FBI agent Kenneth Gray, RCMP Sgt. Pete Merrifield, and private investigator Derrick Snowdy for helping me with law enforcement questions.

I want to thank the Martin Wise Goodman Trust and Harvard University's Nieman Foundation for a fellowship that gave me the chance to explore new ways of writing and thinking. I'd like to thank Anne Bernays, whose fiction class helped me think about writing in useful new ways, and Professor Mark Jude Poirier and my classmates in Advanced Screenwriting, who helped me fix early problems with this story.

I'd also to thank Preston Browning Jr. and the Wellspring House, a writer's retreat in Ashfield, Massachusetts, a marvelously quiet place to work.

Many friends read the manuscript and offered encouragement and helpful suggestions: Chris Borelli, Carrie Croft, Luanne Gauvreau, Camille Labchuk, Veronique Laffargue, Rena Langley,

Kady O'Malley, Julianne MacLean, Kelly Maher, Andrew Mayeda, Selena Ross, Mike Rudderham, Leslie Stojsic, Wonbo Woo, and Bei-san Zubi.

I am lucky to have such good friends. Thanks, you guys!

# ABOUT THE AUTHOR

Photograph by Tim Krochak

**S. J. MAHER** is an award-winning journalist who has uncovered scandals, reported from remote outports, jails, warships, hospitals, parliamentary chambers, Afghanistan, and Haiti. His second novel, *Salvage*, was shortlisted for awards by the Crime Writers of Canada and the International Thriller Writers. He writes his books at anchor on his old sailboat, *Free Spirit*. Visit him at **sjmaher.ca** or follow him on Twitter **@stphnmaher**.